ARE LOVERS LOSERS?

Hildy and Ann came into the room and saw Niki on the bed. Niki made her announcement. "I am a woman."

Oh, no, Ann thought. Here it comes.

Hildy did not speak.

"I agree with you both," Niki sat up. "It's not worth discussing. I had hoped, I must admit, for more. The earth to turn, transcendental experiences, two becoming one, lightning bolts. Something. But it's another cheat, sex."

"What then did you expect from it?"

"I expected something great. Something to take me out of myself. Or overwhelm me." She shook her head. "The more fool I, right?"

"You cannot separate the body and soul," said Hildy softly. "You make love not with only the flesh."

But Niki still didn't understand . . .

Tell Me if the Lovers are Losers

Cynthia Voigt

FAWCETT JUNIPER · NEW YORK

A Fawcett Juniper Book
Published by Ballantine Books

Library of Congress Catalog Card Number: 81-8079

ISBN 0-449-70060-7

This edition published by arrangement with Atheneum

Manufactured in the United States of America

First Ballantine Books Edition: July 1983

for my mother,
my good friend

I am a part of all that I have met;
Yet all experience is an arch wherethrough
Gleams that untraveled world whose margin fades
For ever and for ever when I move.

TENNYSON, *Ulysses*

Take any streetful of people buying clothes and groceries, cheering a hero or throwing confetti and blowing tin horns . . . tell me if the lovers are losers . . . tell me if any get more than the lovers . . . in the dust . . . in the cool tombs.

SANDBURG, *Cool Tombs*

chapter
1

In 1961, the first hopeful year of John F. Kennedy's presidency, Stanton College opened its doors to the forty-first freshman class. It opened doors not only symbolic, but actual: traditionally, the oaken doors of O'Rourke Hall opened to admit the new freshmen in a welcoming assembly and not again until four years later for the recessional parade of graduated seniors. *Ave atque vale,* hail and farewell. On this September morning, the doors swung wide and the freshmen entered, nearly four hundred girls. They scattered themselves noisily, nervously, on hard wooden seats.

Ann Gardner looked with distaste upon the stranger sitting next to her, here roommate, Niki. The girl had a long face, a jabbing nose and chin, a narrow mouth. Her eyes, like small black marbles, glittered, glared. Her dark hair hung straight and long to thighs that showed round muscles beneath faded blue jeans. Niki hunched forward in her seat, forefinger in her mouth so she could chew on the nail, exuding restless energy. Her eyes roved the audience, her right foot twitched rhythmically.

Ann, sitting straight, sitting back, pulled her skirt down over her knees then refolded her hands in her lap. She tried to dissociate herself from Niki and looked for familiar faces in the audience, faces she had known from her years at the Otis Hall School. She felt awkward, more than usual, seated next to this new roommate with the gypsy face, who looked capable of cruelty. Ann crossed her legs at the knees, neatly, without altering her posture.

"Relax." The dark girl, Niki, turned to her.

"I am relaxed."

Niki shrugged and turned away.

"What's your last name?" Ann asked.

"Jones."

Ann looked to her left, at another stranger. Everybody had clean hair; the assembly hall gleamed as with many candles. Niki threw her body back in the seat. "You play tennis?"

"Some." Ann was cautious. "I'm not very good." Was she being asked to do something?

"You don't look like much of an athlete," Niki said.

Ann stared at her, unable to frame a reply.

"I mean—oh hell, you know what I mean. Do you ride?"

"A little."

"Ski?"

"A couple of times."

"Swim?"

"Of course."

"Hike?"

"No, I never did. Do you do all those?"

Unconcerned, seeming to have lost interest, Niki nodded.

"What sport are you taking?" Ann asked.

Niki shrugged. Ann felt reproached.

The babble in the room mounted briefly then abruptly fell as a diminutive woman, dressed in a baggy gabardine suit, loped across the stage to the lectern. This woman was not young—her face was covered with wrinkles both fine and deep, her hair was entirely gray. It looked as if she had cut it herself and did not care for or about the results. She seemed an odd little figure to be an emblem for knowledge, academic stature, the wisdom and joy of scholarship, for insight, inspiration, excellence. An odd little figure for any purpose. She peered over the top of the lectern, then glanced at a sheet of paper. Her hands were visible and the top of her face; no more.

"It's a dwarf," Niki whispered to Ann. Ann ignored this. Courtesy, to Ann, required silence during a lecture or address. "One of Santa's little helpers," Niki went on. Her whisper was dramatically low and, like any good actress's, audible. "This —assembly—is—being—led—by—a—MUNCHKIN."

A ripple of giggles spread around them. Ann flushed. Yet, unwillingly, the corners of her mouth twitched.

"Good morning." The Munchkin spoke. Her voice was high-pitched and nasal, matter-of-fact. She looked steadily at her audience. The noon sunlight glinted off her heavy-framed glasses. "I am Natalie Dennis. I will be dean of your class. Do *not* confuse dean with den mother.

"First, let me explain something. It is not a pleasure to be dean, though it is perhaps an honor. It *is* a duty. As dean of a freshman class, I can teach only one course. For the remaining three years, I can teach only two. Your class will take up the rest of my time. I am responsible for you. Not to you. You are responsible to me.

"Some of you will learn precisely what this difference means in my Philosophy One course. For now, I will put it as concisely as possible: I do not, nor does the college, stand *in loco parentis*. You are on your own."

"All *right*, Munchkin," cheered Niki in a murmuring undercurrent.

"Stanton College expects no geniuses," the little woman continued. "Statistically, this is only sensible of us. Instead, the College looks for students of high intellectual caliber and distinct individuality. The kind of girl who will be able to set more than one goal for herself, more than two or three goals— and meet them all. A woman who, like Elizabeth Cady Stanton herself, can be a good wife, good mother, good thinker, good leader—and a good friend.

"If you have not heard of Mrs. Stanton, inform yourselves. You will be the better for it.

"We encourage honesty and ambition here. You will work hard, most of you. Some of you will be quite happy in this. A few will leave. On the whole, you will find the next four no more easy or difficult than any other arbitrarily selected quartet of years."

Her eyes searched the audience. "What can you expect from me? Disinterested counsel. Maturity. These are my resources. I have my own work, my proper work: I am a scholar, a philosopher. I do not wish to be distracted from this work for problems or questions that do not lie within my province. Upon those problems and questions that are my proper concern, I will act. So much for me.

"You may remember—and this is the end of my talk—that at the time of your application you were asked to submit some sort of original work. Those pieces have been gathered together and printed up in a small magazine. You will find copies of that magazine in your dormitories. Stanton College does not have a freshman directory; only the magazine.

"You may leave now. Good morning. Welcome." She crossed the stage with her loping stride and exited at the rear, without a backward glance.

Silence lasted for a few seconds before the babble recommenced.

"I guess I'd better get back to the dorm," Ann said.

Niki slouched in the seat, her knees raised against the seat in front, her head level with the back of her own. She removed the finger from her mouth. "I can't tell about her. What do you think?"

"Odd," Ann said.

Niki paid full attention. "Yes, of course, but is that bad or good, to be odd?"

"Neither, not necessarily," Ann answered. "Look, my parents are still here. Can I get out? OK?"

"Sure, sorry. I'll come with you."

Ann shrugged, to say *That's up to you and I couldn't care less.* She wasn't sure how her parents would feel about this roommate.

Niki walked with compact energy. Ann, scuffling beside her along the sun-dappled path, felt the contrast between them.

"How's the room?" she asked.

"OK, I guess," Niki said.

They walked on.

"Where are you from?" Ann asked.

"California."

"Really?" Ann's voice sounded brittle, even to her. "I've never been to California. What's it like?"

Niki stopped abruptly. They were at the gravel path that led up to the front porch of the dormitory. "Why don't we just admit we're in a pigface position and cut the crap. I can't *do* all that small-talk stuff," she explained to Ann's surprised face.

Feeling assaulted, Ann stepped back. In fact, she was surprised by Niki's vehemence, not her observation. She felt the same way, inept at conversation with strangers. But you were supposed to try to make a good first impression when you met people. Ann had known a California girl at the Hall who claimed that all of the state was endangered by earthquake, something to do with something called the San Andreas fault. "I knew a girl from California at school—"

Niki slapped the heel of a hand against her forehead. "Lord defend and spare me. Look," she said, conversationally, "are you comfortable with all this social garbage?"

"No," Ann hung her head down, feeling increasingly uncomfortable with everything, feeling fat and fifteen, disliking herself, awkward, self-pitying. "Why?"

Niki pointed to a third floor window. "That's our room. Is that your mother?"

Mrs. Gardner waved down.

"Is she waiting for you?" Niki asked.

Ann nodded and waved back. She felt Niki's glance.

"What's she doing up there?" asked Niki as they went up the steps.

"I don't know. Why?"

"Because we weren't there to let her in."

"She's my *mother,*" Ann protested.

"Oh, I see," Niki did not conceal the sarcasm. She led the way up a carpeted staircase from the first to the second floor, then up a wooden staircase, its steps protected by linoleum pads, to the third.

"I like, her," Ann continued, to Niki's shoulders.

"Glad to hear it," Niki said.

She won't even try, Ann thought. She doesn't like me and won't try.

Because they were freshmen, they were assigned three to a room; because they were three to a room, they were assigned a big corner room with windows on two walls, with a view over a small valley and back up wooded hillsides. Mrs. Gardner had her back to the window when she greeted them: "You have a western exposure. Isn't that nice?"

Ann introduced Niki and then sat back to observe the encounter. This was the pose she preferred, resting her back against something firm, legs flexed, observing.

"There isn't any closet space to speak of," Mrs. Gardner continued. "I was thinking of taking Ann's winter things back home. You could pick them up over Thanksgiving or we could bring them to you." She looked at Niki as if the girl had asked a question. "We live only a couple of hours from here. Philadelphia. So Ann is quite near home." She was sending out a cautious warmth toward Niki, preparing to become affectionate.

"Lucky Ann," Niki said.

"Yes." Mrs. Gardner switched to a brisker voice and lifted her chin.

"Where is your family from?"

"California."

"You must have flown over." Niki did not answer. "Did your family come with you?"

"Of course not."

"I see." Mrs. Gardner contemplated this creature. She decided, apparently, to side-step. "I don't know how you'll all fit in when the third girl gets here."

"I don't have any dresses," Niki said, "so I don't take any closet space."

Mrs. Gardner, in pink and green tweeds at the center of the room, continued: "Each of you gets bed, bureau, desk and bookcase. The bookcases are small, Ann, you might want to get another. Ann," she explained to Niki, "collects books like other girls collect beaux. She's the bookworm in our family. But there are no full-length mirrors."

"In the can," Niki said.

Mrs. Gardner's smooth face wrinkled in puzzlement.

"The head? The john? The powder room?"

"Oh." She turned to Ann. "Your father's gone to fill the car with gas and make reservations for lunch. I thought the Inn, is that all right with you? Lizzie says they have delicious lunches, although the dinners aren't much. Lizzie is my sister," she told Niki, "who graduated from here—years ago. I don't like to think how long ago. How was your meeting?"

"All right. The Dean spoke," Ann said.

"Who is she? Maybe Lizzie knows her."

"Dennis, wasn't it?" Ann pulled Niki back into the conversation.

"Who, the Munchkin? Yeah. Natalie Dennis. Teaches philosophy."

"I don't think Lizzie would have taken *that*. But why do you—" Mrs. Gardner decided to ignore it, after all.

"I am," Ann reminded her mother.

"Are you?" Niki asked, with interest.

"Philosophy One, that's her course."

"Why?"

"It sounded interesting."

"I wouldn't mind taking a class with the Munchkin."

Again Mrs. Gardner made an effort to establish rapport with Niki. "The third girl—Hildegarde the housemother said her name was—won't be here until after supper. Something to do with a bus." She sat down on the edge of the bed and crossed her legs. "You come from California," she remarked.

"Yes."

"Did you go to school out there?"

"Yes."

"I see. A high school?"

"Yes."

"I understand the California school system is a very good one. The Pennsylvania one isn't, I'm afraid."

Niki looked at her.

"Do you find the East very different?"

"I've only been here half a day," Niki pointed out.

"Yes, of course. Well, I'm sure you'll enjoy it here. You have such an unusual name. Niki."

Ann wanted to say, *She knows her name, Mother,* but tried to help instead. "Is it short for something? Nicole?"

"Nicholas."

Mrs. Gardner laughed, in a short burst. "You're teasing us."

"No, I'm not," Niki said. "My mother wanted a boy. She was sure I was one, *in utero.* But I wasn't."

"Is Nicholas your legal name?" Mrs. Gardner asked.

"No, Niki."

"Did your mother have her boy, later?"

"I'm an only child."

"Oh."

"They're divorced."

"Oh." Intoned with an unspoken *I'm sorry.*

"It started with me. The man determines the sex, you know. My mother genuinely didn't want me to be a girl. My father said just what you did, 'Why not Nicole?' But my mother said she didn't want to be a hypocrite and pretend she was satisfied when she wasn't. She blamed my father."

"I see," Mrs. Gardner said.

"She said it would be dishonest not to say just what she felt."

This time it was clear that Mrs. Gardner actually did see: "Painfully honest," she observed.

"Painful for other people," Niki qualified it. Their eyes met, as equals, and Mrs. Gardner nodded. She relaxed her spine.

"You live with your mother then, out in California."

"No, with my father."

"Oh." The back straightened up again. "And what does your father do?"

"He's an entrepreneur. What does your father do?"

Anger followed surprise over Mrs. Gardner's features. Ann giggled. Then, to Niki's surprise but not to Ann's, Mrs. Gardner chuckled. It was a warm, human sound. "I am sorry. I've been rude. You have every right to be offended." She chuckled again.

Ann was smiling. "My father's a lawyer. Does that make us even?"

"I guess so." Niki grinned at her.

"I wonder what she'll do about books, the other girl," Ann said. "We're supposed to get our books today, for Monday classes. The bookstore is being opened specially."

"Oh, I know that," Mrs. Gardner said. "The Dean's office called and asked you two to pick them up for her. Hildegarde— you can remember that name. Everything has been arranged— the books will be waiting and the charge slips have been verified—but you two are supposed to bring the books here for her. The housemother told me."

"Oh *shit*," Niki said. Mrs. Gardner overlooked that: a visible, conscious effort, carefully overlooking it.

"Mother, what if I hadn't reminded you?"

"I'd have remembered. I always do, don't I?"

Ann raised doubtful eyebrows.

"Niki, would you have lunch with us? I'm sure Mr. Gardner would like a chance to get to know you."

"I can't. Thanks anyway." Niki thought for a brief space. "I have to unpack. It'll take all afternoon to get the books."

"Well, all right, if you're sure," Mrs. Gardner said. "I guess Ann will find you here before she goes to the bookstore."

Ann rather hoped not.

"Probably." Niki shrugged.

Ann's father entered the room, heartily. He was tall and distinguished, dressed in a three-piece suit. He bent to speak a word to his wife, who shook her head. Ann heard Niki singing softly, from "Sumemertime": ". . . yer paw is rich, 'n' yer maw is good looking. . . ." Ann smiled at the dark girl across the room, but Niki ignored her and went to the window. Mr. Gardner shook hands with Niki, then demanded his lunch without further delay and herded his family out of the room and down the stairs.

Outside, standing in warm sunlight, Mrs. Gardner looked worried. "I don't know how you'll get along with her. Maybe you ought to request a change?"

Ann had retreated into a lumpish silence and only looked back, up at the window of her room. She could see Niki standing there, looking down. She thought it must be obvious from the conspiratorial angle of her mother's head what it was she was suggesting. The figure at the window gave her no clue as to how to answer.

The roommates did go to the bookstore together. They had to, in order to bring back the third girl's books along with their own. There would be twelve of them, including notebooks and lab manuals, the housemother said. Ann and Niki returned, arms feeling stringy and stretched. Two armloads of books bounced onto two beds. "Wow," Niki said. "I don't know if I can keep up with this."

Ann—whom Niki had ushered impatiently through the stacks of books—looked at her with troubled eyes. "I know. I'm trying not to think about it. But, you know? I did feel this way my first few days at the Hall, and that turned out all right."

Niki shrugged. "I meant—"

Ann waited for her to continue, then asked, "Meant what?"

"They act as if it was important, the courses and all. Like opening the bookstore especially for freshmen. As if they really didn't know."

"Didn't know what?"

"That it's not real, and not important. The academic life. Ye olde ivory tower. You don't think it is, do you?"

But Ann did think learning was important, real—and exhilarating. Privately, she liked being intelligent and was proud of it. In books, and when you were writing papers, you could think about what was true. You didn't have to worry about being a nice person, or a popular person, or successful. You could look for the truth of things. You didn't have to pretend that something wasn't important because it wasn't tactful, or because whoever was sitting next to you might have his feelings hurt, or might think you were an egghead. And the people who wrote books, great books, used words the way architects used stones, exactly and carefully, aware of weight and balance. Ann knew this put her out of step with a lot of people. But when she could take a sonnet apart and study the imagery and discover the idea and then put it back together and hear how the poem still rang—the language levels deep—then she knew she had her hands on something real, and she couldn't help the happiness of it. She could imagine, however, what Niki would say about this. This was too personal to trot out for a stranger to attack. So she changed the subject: "She's taking two lab courses, did you notice?"

"Who?"

"Hildegarde. Astronomy and Biology."

"You're one of those people that like school, aren't you," Niki demanded. Ann didn't answer. "Why, because it's safe? I bet—you're good at it and it's always been easy."

What was wrong with that? Ann wondered.

"And why don't you have the freshman English text?" Niki asked.

"I got advanced placement so I'm taking Shakespeare." Ann stoically endured the beady glance for half a minute, then defended herself: "I'm terrible in math and science and only fair in history. I've got a gift for languages, literature, that kind of stuff. The really useless stuff," she concluded, as she often had when accused of being smart.

"Oh," that seemed to satisfy Niki. "I'm a well-rounded student myself. Did you want to come here? I mean, was Stanton your first choice?"

Ann thought about that. "It's the only school I applied to. The headmistress and my parents agreed that it was the best place for me. Otis Hall prefers to have you apply to only one college. Unless, of course, you're taking a chance."

"You're kidding," Niki said.

"I kind of liked it. The Hall has a sort of reputation, you see. So the colleges will usually accept a candidate, if the school feels she can do the work. It almost never happens that somebody doesn't get in."

"So they told you where to go?"

"No, not at all. They gave me a list of places, and we went visiting—you know, that visiting trip everybody makes with her parents? I liked Stanton best. So did my family. My aunt went here. There's a good classics department." Her voice dwindled as she realized that she was apologizing again.

"I didn't want to come here," Niki said. "Still don't, but what the hell—I figure if I get decent grades they'll accept me as a transfer student at Berkeley."

"You didn't get in at Berkeley?" Ann asked. Eastern colleges had higher standards than western, everybody knew that.

"I didn't even apply. It would have been a waste of time. They have to take the top three per cent first, and there are enough of them to fill both Stanford and Berkeley. I'm only top seven per cent. My advisor said he thought this might be a way to get there, to do well in an eastern school."

"What do your parents say?"

"What's it got to do with them?"

"I guess nothing."

"Dad pays the bills. He won't buy anything that's not worth its price, so I figure Stanton has a good-enough reputation. He doesn't care, here or Berkeley, as long as he gets his money's worth."

"So you'll only be here for a year."

"I hope so. I don't think I could stick it for longer."

"Why not?"

"You're kidding," Niki said. "You're not," she concluded glumly. "There are too goddamned many circle pins and round collars and—life isn't that plump."

Ann said nothing. It was not that she didn't want to, but that she couldn't think of how to say what she wanted to say.

"I think I'll pick up my copy of that magazine. Want me to get yours?" she asked.

"No—let's *do* something instead. You've got a racquet. Wanna play tennis?"

"I don't know," Ann said, wanting to refuse.

"C'mon. I go crazy if I don't get enough exercise, and I haven't done anything today. By the time I find somebody else, it'll be too dark. Or what? Are you afraid to play me?"

Ann's eyebrows arched. She had been well-trained, she knew that, and had played with the varsity at the Hall. Goaded into it, she agreed.

"What's so special about two lab courses?" Niki asked. They were changing into tennis clothes, and Ann moved slowly, not wanting to take out the tennis dress she usually wore, knowing it would cause comment. But Niki ignored it, pulled on cut-off jeans and a T-shirt.

"Each one takes six hours a week, two labs and two lectures. And science courses are more difficult, in any case. The catalogue said they were arduous. She needed special permission to take two."

"How do you know?"

"In the catalogue."

"I'm taking Biology. What about you?"

"Co-ordinated Sciences. It's for the nonmathematical student."

"Easier?"

"I hope so," Ann said, and was rewarded with a smile.

"Maybe I should take it."

"Why?"

"For the grade."

"If you wanted to, you should have signed up for it in the first place. Why didn't you?"

"I couldn't read the damned catalogue."

"Didn't your father help?"

"I'm old enough to make my own decisions. Besides, he couldn't be bothered."

"They're strict here about switching courses, especially freshmen. Unless you think you'll flunk Biology."

"Oh no."

"How do you know?"

"You heard the Munchkin: high caliber of intelligence."

Ann envied any confidence. When she thought about it, she was not sure that she would do passably well, in anything. And yet, Ann knew her own abilities. She was just scholar enough to assemble the details of a work into something living. So that when King Lear raged against himself for not sharing those miseries the poorest of his subjects suffered, "I have ta'en too little care of this," she felt a quivering within herself that might have been a ripple of recognition along the blood. And she wondered automatically about the nature of kingship, wondered if a man—to be a king—must be a king of beggars as well, and always. It seemed to her, she wanted to be such a king—which was ridiculous, she knew, and also very true. Her mind skittered so—she hoped profoundly that she would not discover at Stanton that she wasn't as intelligent as she had been told she was.

"What did you do for that magazine?" she asked Niki.

"Photographs."

"Really? Are you a photographer?"

"Not on a bet. It's just easy to take pictures. I took a couple of arty ones. You know, ski trails, sand dunes." Ann did not know. "Ready?"

"Do you know where the courts are?"

"I found them this morning. They're clay."

"Of course."

"I haven't played on clay."

"What did you play on? Grass courts?"

"You're kidding," Niki said again.

The six tennis courts were cut out of the woods behind the gym. Trees surrounded them, enclosed them. After the girls had batted the ball back and forth a few times, Niki announced that she was ready.

Ann lost the first three games before she understood what was happening. Niki's form was bad, she swung choppily, her backswing was minimal, she was forever getting to the ball at the last minute. Ann, who played a stylish game, felt confident of her long, smooth ground strokes and her good preparation for shots. Yet Ann lost almost every point. Niki raced around, charged the net to slash at an overhead, hurled herself at lines and corners and won the points.

Ann had played a few tournaments, at school, and she knew how to steady herself down. She did and managed to hold her serve during three hard points before Niki seized control again. Each serve that Ann stroked smoothly across the net was jabbed back at her, and she felt herself being worn down. For the last games, she did not even expect to win a single point. She didn't.

At the end of the set, Ann was hot and tired. Niki was flushed and triumphant. "That's more like it," she said. "Another?"

"I can't," Ann said.

"Rest a minute, then see."

"It's getting dark," Ann said lamely.

"There's half an hour still. We could get some games in, maybe even a set."

Ann shook her head.

"You don't play to win," Niki said.

Ann shrugged.

"You look good, but you don't win."

Ann stared blankly at her.

"You don't fight."

Ann snapped the press closed around her racquet.

"What sport are you taking?" Niki asked.

"I haven't decided. Are you going to take tennis?"

"I might. Or basketball. There's no track team."

"I've been thinking of field hockey. We played that at school."

"What's it like?"

"It's a team sport, with lots of running. It takes some skill too. Basically, it's a passing game, like soccer, not very exciting but . . ."

They walked back toward the dormitory. It was too early in September for leaves to have turned and fallen, but Ann knew how it would be when fall had really come. She loved fall. But she did not think she would ever feel at home at Stanton. She did not think she would ever feel at ease with Niki.

"They don't have much of a sports program here," Niki remarked. She swung her racquet at a bushy mountain laurel. "Almost no competition. I don't know how much fun that'll be."

"You're competitive," Ann observed.

"That, Annie child, is an understatement. You've got to let people know you're worth fearing. You've got to get to the head of things. People call you Annie?"

Ann shook her head, no.

"I kind of like it. It's cute."

Ann didn't, but she didn't say so.

"I wonder how we'd do at doubles. You don't charge the net, but you've got good ground strokes. Maybe we could play doubles sometime. We might be a perfect team."

"Maybe," Ann said. She hoped not.

"I'd have liked a second set." The exercise, instead of deploying Niki's energy, had apparently increased it.

"I couldn't see well in this light," Ann said.

"Play by sound—sonar tennis," Niki answered. "What's your language?"

"Greek," Ann said.

"You're kidding. Why?"

"I took Latin for a long time. Greek shouldn't be too much harder."

"What are you, a Classics major?"

"I'd like to be."

"You don't look it."

"What do you mean?"

"You look like an English major, or History, maybe Sociology. You look too ordinary for anything else. Your type—"

"And what's that?"

"Don't kid yourself. You are a type."

"And you aren't?" Annie was growing tired of denigration.

"No, ma'am. Not me. There are lots of you around, with tans and square jaws and that wavy hair. You all move the same way, muscular but not strong, somebody's idea of femininity. It's a prep-school type."

Ann quickened her step. All she wanted was to lie in a tub with a book and forget where she was.

"And that clear-sighted, luminous glance you all have. And those Topsiders too." Ann glanced at her feet. "Topsiders and loafers, that's what preppies wear." Niki had on a pair of boys' sneakers. Which looked terrible, Ann thought, which made her calves appear springy. Ann was no beauty, but she looked better than that. Why should she feel defensive? she demanded of herself. Didn't she believe in what she knew? Couldn't she trust her own eyes?

Back in the room, with an hour before supper, Ann picked out the *Odyssey*, dog-eared and well-beloved, and announced her intention of taking a long, hot bath. Niki said she would have a shower. Ann said she thought there wouldn't be any in the dorm, because it was so old; just in the gym. Niki declared her disbelief and her inability to take the time for a bath. Ann suggested she then go back to the gym and shower, which, to her surprise, Niki did. Leaving Ann alone.

She opened the window, first. Trees, hillsides, glimpses of sky among, behind, shadows. The smell of pin and sunshine and deciduous growings and rottings: a woods, a forest, beautiful. Their room, empty, was a peaceful, quiet place. She turned, her back to the window, and looked. Without seeing, without wanting to see. A puddle of late afternoon sunlight lay on the wooden floor. Spartan, the beds and accoutrements. Ann regretted the lack of privacy in dormitory living, even resented it. At the Hall she had acquired some tricks to isolate herself: late night studying, quick breakfasts; long afternoon naps. But would these help here? She immersed herself in the emptiness of the room, until her reverie was broken into by sounds from down the hallway. Sounds of unfamiliar voices, unfamiliar plumbing, unfamiliar doors, unfamiliar feet on unfamiliar linoleum hall floors.

Ann decided to delay the bath; she lay down on her bed.

In a strange place, she thought, you are more vulnerable than at any other time. Everything conspires to keep you mentally off balance, ready to alarm. Your face is stiff, expressionless, keeping ready to smile, concealing. You feel, like prying fingers, the glances of strangers sliding over you, seeing the faulty details friends never notice. As if—Ann lay on the bed studying the ceiling and the patterns possible in the cracks there—you had found yourself in lands under the earth . . . an elevator that kept going down, or a cavern you followed too far, or a simple crack in the surface of the earth, through which you would stumble and fall. . . . However you got there, there you were, standing, half-blind in half darkness, surrounded by short creatures with outsized heads. Their long-fingered brown hands, covered with fur like the rest of their bodies, reached out to touch you. Because they had lost sight so many generations back that they could not remember the lamps of their eyes going dim, now they used spatulated fingertips for knowing. And those fingertips reached out at you, touched you to learn what you were. Ann imagined this, vivid for a second, and her mind shuddered. That was what it felt like, being in a new place like this.

Ann got up, made herself undress and prepare for her bath. She opened the door to an empty hall and was smiling when she closed the door of the bathing cubicle behind her. When she was settled back in a steaming tub, Ann picked up the book. It opened to the scene in the Cyclop's cave. Ann read, savoring the words, the picture and the character of Odysseus. She could even work up some ambiguous sympathy for the Cyclops. After all, to have your one eye put out by a sharpened piece of burning wood, worked into your eyeball—like a brace-and-bit, Homer said. Ann could almost feel that. There was something pitiful in the image Homer made: "He pulled the timber out of his eye, and it blubbered with plenty of blood. . . ." She wondered, reading over the scene, why she should relish the language of violence. Adjusting the hot water with an outstretched toe, she remembered the way she had covered her face with her coat during the murder scene in the movie *Psycho;* the way she had felt nauseated and terrified for days afterwards at the memory. Maybe books were easier to take; you could close a book and put it away, so they weren't as real. At least, she thought Niki would say that. It sounded like the kind of thing Niki would say, to show that you were inferior.

When Niki returned, her tennis clothes in a bundle wrapped around with a towel, it was suppertime. Niki burst through the closed door and Ann—lying on the bed reading—was startled into a quick, involuntary leap of the muscles.

"Oh," Ann said.

"Get dressed," Niki said. "There's a line of people down there."

"A line?"

"Well, a gaggle." She brushed her hair at the bureau. Ann watched. Niki's hands knew what they were about, twisting, smoothing, pulling the rope of hair up to make a knot at the back of her head.

"I wish I could grow long hair," Ann said. She pulled a cotton dress out of the closet.

"Why can't you?"

"Mine's too thin."

"What difference does that make? Aren't you ready?"

"Just a belt and my shoes—you can't wear jeans to dinner. Don't you remember that?"

"You're kidding. Why not?"

"There's a dress code."

"So what?" Niki stood still, considering. "There are things to be done about a dress code. We used to have one at my high school. I've got a skirt in here somewhere." She rummaged about in the bottom drawer, to pull out a denim skirt as faded as her jeans. She still wore the high sneakers. Ann did not want to go down to dinner with this girl. She did not want to stand with her, waiting for the dining room doors to open. She did not want to sit with her.

"Let's go, c'mon!" Niki said. They raced down three flights of stairs, but even so were late into the dining room. The housemother, Mrs. Smythe, smiled at them and indicated two seats at her table. "Oh hell," murmured Niki. "Next time don't dawdle, OK?" "OK," Ann said. The room bloomed with some thirty or so strange faces, each one turned to them. Entering just as grace was to be said, they could not have been more awkward. Ann slipped into the seat beside Niki and ducked her head. She stared at her hands. Why had she come to dinner? She had no appetite. She wished she had arranged at least to be in the same dormitory as one of the other Hall girls, even if she didn't want to room with any of them. Just now she wanted, unexpectedly and shamefully, to go home.

Ann's eyes slid over to Niki's hands, which rested on the table, brown and muscular and unkempt. The nails were ragged.

Niki, she saw, did not bow her head for grace. The dark eyes glanced restlessly around the dining room, touching on bowed heads as if trying to attract attention, as if to awaken a sleeper with a push at the forehead. "Why, she looks dangerous," Ann said to herself and was interested in her roommate then in a way she had not been before. The housemother said *Amen* and the room echoed her.

At dinner Ann learned that they expected the other girl, Hildegarde, "sometime tonight and did you girls get her books and notebooks?"

"Did we have any choice?" Niki asked, and Ann quickly

joined in to say "It was no trouble, no trouble at all, we were happy to do it." Niki grinned at her.

After dinner there was a brief meeting to inform the freshmen of the house rules, and after that Ann and Niki went back up to their third floor room. They had really met no one at the meal. Ann had half-planned to visit some of her Hall classmates—thinking it might be a good way to pass the first uncomfortable evening—but decided not to, because she didn't know how to exclude Niki from such a walk. She sat at her desk, accustoming herself to the placement of it, to the quality of light, to the sounds, writing her name and dormitory on the covers of spiral-backed notebooks. Niki stared at her for a few minutes, then left. Ten minutes later she returned: "There's a volleyball game next door. Do you want to come play?"

"A what?"

"Volleyball."

"I've never played it."

"We play it on the beaches. It's easy. Why not?"

"Why not?" Ann rose. "I'll find you. I've got to change if we're going to be doing a sport."

"Good." Niki left. Ann hung her dress in the closet, folded her slip into a drawer, and pulled out a pair of shorts and a matching blouse. Both were freshly ironed. She wished she owned a T-shirt. She wondered if she should wear one of her men's shirts. She got down on her hands and knees to find the sneakers she had kicked off near her bed. From that undignified position, she heard company arrive.

"Did you know Ann was such a meticulous housekeeper?" "What did she do this summer to cause the miraculous change?" "Hi, Ann, how was your summer?" "We're going around sort of collecting everyone from the Hall." "Come with us?" "You won't believe what my roommate wants to major in." "How come you're in this dumpy old dorm?" "How did you get into one of the old houses? I tried but they gave me a modern one." "Are you coming? This is just the third house we've been to and there are lots more of us." "Are you coming?"

"You bet," Ann said. She tied her sneakers and picked out a sweater, glad that she had one to match the shorts. There were four of them as they passed the lighted outdoor volleyball court. Ann saw Niki leap up to punch down at the ball, her teeth biting her lip and her eyes glittering. Niki did not see her, she thought. The pack from the Hall ran on and she was there in the middle of it, among familiar faces, familiar voices.

It was late when Ann returned, just before weekend curfew. The room lay in moonlighted darkness and had that unreliable clarity moonlight seems to give. Ann let her clothes fall in a pile by her bed and rummaged blindly in a drawer until she recognized the fabric of her red nightgown. She dropped it over her head and turned to see if the third girl had arrived.

Only Niki was in the room. Ann thought she was asleep, but could not be sure. If she was asleep then she slept more quietly than she did anything else. Her dark hair spread over the pillow behind her, her eyelashes lay darkly on moon-whitened cheeks, her mouth was slightly open. Her naked shoulder, her naked arm, curved gently. She looked like a statue, Ann thought. A statue of what? Some mythological creature, half-goat, half-woman. She liked Niki better asleep than awake, Ann decided.

Ann carefully folded back the top sheet of her bed and slipped in. She could never sleep in the nude, she thought. The night sky was dark outside the window. (Why hadn't Niki pulled the shades down? They would need curtains.) The empty third bed held a rectangle of moonlight. Ann closed her eyes and slept.

She woke early the next morning. She never slept well her first few nights in a new place, never deeply, never late. The other bed had someone in it; then Hildegarde had arrived in the middle of the night, after twelve certainly.

It was as if the girl had materialized out of that rectangle of moonlight. From what Ann could see—white-blonde, curly hair covering the back of her head, the crescent edge of face beyond the hair, a tanned forearm extending from cotton pajamas—Hildegarde had the moon's colors. Curled in the privacy of sleep, she seemed also to have the moon's qualities, some untarnished mystery removed from the human sphere. Ann was surprised not to have awakened when the other entered the room. On the best of nights she slept lightly.

The sleeper rolled over, enabling Ann to study her face. Round and moonlike, broad cheeks, broad forehead, light eyebrows, a fine, narrow, straight nose. Her jawline was clear, strict. Her full lips were straight and stern, bearing not the lightest trace of lipstick. The hand she could see looked large, long, strong, like the shape of the body under the covers.

Blue eyes opened wide, round blue eyes that moved without hesitation from sleep to awake and—in doing that—reorganized the face around them. It was a face framed for happy surprises, and the eyes beamed expectation. It was not a beautiful face, but it shone bright. Ann opened her mouth to apologize for staring. At the same time the girl put a silencing finger across her lips. she sat up and indicated that they might meet outside the doorway. Ann nodded agreement. Hildegarde got out of the door with an economy of movement Ann could not match. She had to find her robe and slippers, fish her toothbrush and soap out of the top drawer.

"Hildegarde Koenig," the girl said, holding out her hand. She looked at Ann with a puzzled, squinting expression which Ann soon learned was her ordinary way when meeting strangers.

"Ann Gardner. I've got to brush my teeth, first thing. I can't stand it until I do that. I was always that way. I don't know why. What time is it?"

"After six. Can we go downstairs?"

"You'll need something on your feet."

Hildegarde bent down to two suitcases in the hallway. "I didn't want to wake you up when I came in. I'll dress in the bathroom."

They sat on the front steps and watched the sky pinken into blue. They watched the Sunday morning world become illuminated, suffused with light.

Ann tucked her hands into the heavy wool sweater Hildegarde had given her. "What time did you get here?" Ann asked.

"Two, I think. It was beautiful, that drive up from Philadelphia. In Dakota the land is flat. At least, so it is where I live."

"Where *do* you live?"

"In North Dakota, in the central part of the state. You wouldn't know the name of the town."

"Why were you so late? Was there an accident?"

The girl shook her head. "Oh no. I missed the bus."

"In Philadelphia?" Ann knew how poor the service was into the Northeast Section from Philadelphia.

"Oh no. There would have been little harm in that, only a few hours' delay. I missed the bus at Mitchell where there is only one bus a day. Once I got to Chicago, however, I could make up much of the time. So I was only delayed by half a day, at the end."

"You took a bus here? All the way?"

"Of course. It is too expensive to fly, and the trains are inconvenient until you reach Chicago. At that time, I could have switched to a train, but my bus ticket had a special discount because I was traveling such distances."

"How long did it take?"

"Two days. The buses can travel at night, while you sleep. If you care to sleep."

"Didn't you?"

"Not the first night. I am interested in the stars."

"I know. You're taking Astronomy. And Biology."

"How would you know that?"

"Classes start tomorrow, you remember?" Hildegarde nodded. "Well, the Dean's office called to ask Niki—she's our other roommate—and me to pick up your books yesterday at the bookstore. So you'd have them on Monday, for the classes."

"I thank you," Hildegarde said.

"We got everything we thought you'd need," Ann continued. "Notebooks, a few pencils, and I have extra pens if you use those. We got everything they had on the list for you, and a couple of extras. Niki said you might want graph paper and a compass."

"I thank you," the girl said again. Her attention turned to the morning before them. Ann looked at her face for a minute before turning her own attention to the sky. She thought she would like this roommate, strange as she might prove to all of Ann's experience. She liked the stiff way Hildegarde talked, as if she weighed every word before she spoke it. Ann yawned comfortably. The girl's eyes squinted toward the chapel across the street, at the houses lining the road, and down to the small village that lay at the end of the college road; then she looked up toward the distant hills. Hildegarde rubbed her eyes with her large hands, with her strong fingers. "In the cities," she said, "you can't see the stars at night. Did you know that?"

"I live in Philadelphia," Ann said. "When we go to the

shore in the summer, that's one of the things that surprises me every year. The stars.''

"The seashore?"

"Yes. Does your family call you Hildegarde?" to change the subject.

"It is my name." The first car of the morning traveled down the road before the dormitory. Ann watched it. Hildegarde cocked an ear at it but did not move her eyes from Ann's face. "Do you mean a nickname?"

Ann nodded.

"Hildy."

Ann turned and smiled, "I like that."

Hildegarde—Hildy, did not smile back. That was a curious moment: Ann was accustomed to having her smile returned. Hildy's face did not respond; her blue eyes were friendly still, her expression was open and eager, she simply did not return the smile, as if she could not see it.

"It is a good name for a cow," Hildy said. Then she did smile, to show large, even teeth. "And so for me, as you see." Ann took in her deep-breasted, strong-limbed body, in a cotton dress and heavy sweater. "As for all women."

"What?"

"For nursing our babies," Hildy explained.

"Oh," Ann said, unable to comprehend, not from ignorance but from something deeper, inexperience perhaps. "The babies I've met take bottles."

"Not mine." Hildy's voice was proud.

"You certainly plan ahead."

"It isn't so long," Hildy said. "In older times, we would already be mothers, more than once, at our age."

"That would be terrible," Ann said.

"You don't want babies?"

"I don't know. I haven't thought about it. I'm too young to think about that yet. Why"—in a burst of honesty—"I haven't even met a man I want to sleep with."

"Ah well then," Hildy said. "I can understand."

Ann did not ask the questions that were in her mind. Instead she remarked, "The Egyptians thought of the world as flat, and the sky above was represented as a cow with her"—what was the proper word to use here?—"udders hanging down over the earth."

There was a moment of silence broken by the low, mellow notes of the chapel bells, calling. Hildy spoke again. "Do you go to church this morning?"

"No," Ann said.

"You can smell the trees in the air here, and the water."

"The water? We're miles from the ocean."

"No, the moisture in the air. It is less so where I live, because there are so few trees I think."

"Will you go to church?"

"Yes. It is convenient here. At home, we must drive an hour. Often it is impossible to take the time to go."

"You live in the country?"

Hildy laughed, a sound as round and golden as the bells' ringing. "Yes, yes. My father has a farm where he grows wheat and alfalfa. All around us are farms and ranches. Many many acres. And the reservation, which lies between our farm and the town. I live very much in the country."

"Then how did you come here? to Stanton I mean."

"Oh, that was good fortune. I learned of Stanton at my school. There was a woman at my school, a friend, who taught us P.E., who told me I might like it and had recommended books to read. She was a good friend, so I took her advice. I didn't know how I would like the mountains, but now I am here I think they too will be good."

Ann's experience of coaches had taught her to disregard their opinions about anything other than sports. "Your coach told you about Stanton? And recommended books? What books?"

"Histories, novels, scientists—Maeterlinck, Jane Austen, Herodotus."

"You've read Herodotus?"

"Only in translation. I thought of taking Greek as one of my courses, but there was no time to do it."

"I'm taking it," Ann said.

"Then you can teach me some? A little?"

"I don't know how I'll do, but sure, that would be fun," Ann said. "I've taken Latin for years."

"I also."

"That's terrific," Ann said, and meant it. "How far did you get? Who have you translated?" Any school where the P.E. teacher recommended Herodotus must have one whale of a set of academic standards.

"We had begun Caesar."

"How many years did you take it?"

"All four."

"And only got as far as Caesar?" Ann apologized: "I'm sorry if I'm being rude. Am I being rude?"

Hildy shook her head, no. "Our school is poor. Our students are poor."

"But the coach, the P.E. woman—"

"I see what is confusing you. She is an Indian. She would not be hired to teach an academic subject, not to white children. It was fortunate that she had also studied physical education."

"Why?"

"She has three children to support, and her man."

"Her husband doesn't work?"

"She is not married. Two of the children are her own, one is of her younger sister."

Ann put all that into her own frame of reference, "A common-law wife."

"No, no. She does not want to be a wife. Not to the man who will marry her."

"I don't understand," Ann said. "What about the children? They have to have a father."

"Of course. The father is this man who lives with her. If she were to marry him, he would gain rights over her and over the children. So she will not marry him, for her own sake. And for the sake of the children. She has the chance to make them free if she does not marry. She educates them. If he interferes, she drives him out. When he drinks too much, or threatens to beat them, or take them back to the reservation, she sends him away."

"And he doesn't work." Ann assimilated this piece of information. "Then why does she keep on with him?"

"A woman needs a man," Hildy said. She peered into Ann's face. "It must be strange to you."

"Very strange." Ann thought about it. "Sad. Our roommate, Niki, comes from California."

Hildy's face lit up. "I am glad," she said.

A more distant bell tolled. Hildy looked up at the sound. "I must go now. If I go to a seven-thirty service, I can be back in time for breakfast."

"Are you Catholic?" Ann asked. "Or Protestant." There was a pretty little Episcopal Church near the Inn. She had noticed it yesterday.

"Neither," Hildy said. "I am nothing. I just worship." She stood and dusted off the back of her skirt. "Will you be at breakfast? Will Niki be there too? I am eager to meet her. To meet everyone. I am eager to begin this year, aren't you?"

Ann smiled and, once again, the smile was not returned. "See you," Ann said. Hildy raised a hand and turned to walk down the hill to the village. She walked easily, her legs loose and her back straight, as if she could walk miles without tiring. Ann watched her progress, her mind drifting over their conversation. Curiouser and curiouser. The most curious thing was Ann's own reaction to her. She had met the girl without self-consciousness. As you meet a tree, Ann thought, that stands tall and strong, that roots deep into the earth. As you meet something that is entirely itself, and deeply is. An oak or a white birch or a sycamore.

Wondering what to do until breakfast, Ann recalled the magazine that the Munchkin had mentioned. She had yet to look at it, although she'd seen copies of it in some of the rooms she'd visited the night before. Gathering the skirt of her robe tight around her hips, she went back inside.

The living room of the dormitory had a sense of spaciousness, a large, open room, with sofas and wing chairs. Lamps stood on the floor; tables were set before two sofas. The curtains had a rosy-red color, splotched with yellow flowers. From one coffee table, Ann took a copy of the yellow-covered magazine that was titled simply "Stanton College: 1965." The date gave her temporary pause, until she realized that it was their graduation date, the name of their class, too far away to consider real.

Ann pulled back one of the long curtains and curled her legs under her in an armchair. Sunlight fell across the pages of the magazine.

It was not in alphabetical order, but in some other order, the design of which she could not perceive. She flipped pages. The entries appeared to divide about equally between word and picture. Poems and graphic art were most common. Her eye was caught by a photograph that had a page to itself.

Photographed in black and white was a lunch counter. Six

people, four men and two women, sat eating. A waitress had her back to the camera. The cook looked at the photographer. The diners, two blacks, four whites, were all hunched over their plates, as if to protect their meals. Their faces, two young, three middle-aged, one old, were closed off, eyes fixed on food or fork. Mouths were open to receive food; hands gripped utensils. There may have been hunger; there was no pleasure. The waitress, large and black, stood on one leg, her shoulders heavy, her uniform tight over fat hips, her neck angled as if in a last exhausted effort to withstand blows. The cook wielded a spatula, his smooth Oriental face placid except for dark, almond-shaped eyes. Of them all, only he suggested movement, the possibility of change, despite the stained white apron strapped around his slight frame. His eyes, the center of the photograph, were deep and dark in his face. Holding the capacity to dream? Or to hate? He stared out of the picture.

It was a deeply human photograph. Real.

It was Niki's photograph. The one Niki had dismissed as arty. On the page facing it, Ann saw her own name beneath one of the translations of Catullus she had sent in:

> She says that she will love
> No one but me,
> Not even if god Jupiter besought her.
> She says this, but the words
> Of woman wishing love
> Must be wind-written on the waving water.

Not an entirely scholarly translation, but she liked it. She wondered if she liked it because it was her own work, or for any virtue it actually possessed. Nobody had ever commented on her translations, more than to say—as they always said to one another, supporting—*I like it.*

Under her translation occurred three sentences, a short paragraph, as if excerpted from a longer work:

> Sun, stars, silence, solitude, suckle. These are the strongest words. Loveliest and loneliest.

Hildy's name was beneath this odd entry.

Ah. The magazine was organized by roommates. She read

Hildy's words again, trying to understand their formlessness. Then Ann recognized them as possible answers to one of the questions on the application form, "What are the best words you know?"

Ann wanted to know what Niki had put down for that question. If she went upstairs to dress—and she realized, remembered, with alarm, that there was a rule about appearing in the public parts of the dorm in nightwear—she might wake Niki and would be able to ask her what her words had been. And get her down to breakfast, so Hildy could meet her.

chapter
2

Niki awoke slowly, reluctantly.

At first, Ann hoped the noise of drawers and doors would rouse her. But she stayed stubbornly asleep, mouth sagging a little. If there were more light, if the room faced east, Ann thought, as she stood undecided in the middle of the room. The room was lightened, but murkily so, as if she stood in some underground grotto. Not enough light. "Niki?" Ann asked softly. After all, it was almost time for breakfast. If Niki wanted to skip breakfast, how was Ann to know? "Niki?"

Niki rolled over, then back; her eyes opened, unseeing, then closed.

"It's time for breakfast."

A fist pounded on the mattress.

"Are you awake?" Fist still clenched. Breathing regular. "Niki?" a little louder. "Are you awake?"

Niki groaned.

"Oh good," Ann said cheerfully. "You better get up for breakfast. Besides—Niki? Niki!"

"Oh hell. What time is it?"

"Quarter to eight."

Niki clenched her eyes shut. Her voice was soggy. "Don't you go to church or anything?"

"No. Niki?"

"What is it?" exasperated.

"Are you awake? I want to ask you something."

"Not before breakfast," protesting. "Did you hear those bells? I just got back to sleep. Why do they have bells?"

"They're not that bad."

"I thought they'd never stop. Pissing bells. I'm gonna need ear plugs for God's sake."

"I want to ask you a question. Are you awake?"

"Ask."

"I can't see you." Niki rolled over, brushed hair from her face, scowled. "Remember that question on the application form?"

"Don't be indirect. Not at this hour. Not in the morning."

"The one about the most important words. What did you put."

Niki's eyes were baleful. "People," she recited, "environment, music, together." She thought. "I don't know why. Why do you want to know?"

"I wondered. Remember the magazine the Munchkin talked about?" Ann waved it in front of Niki's nose. She started to sit down on Niki's bed, then changed her mind. "Your picture—the photograph? It's terrific." No, that was inadequate. "It's good, really good. But Hildy's entry—"

"Who's Hildy?"

"Our roommate. She got here late last night."

Niki turned her eyes to the other bed. "Oh. Hot damn."

Ann took a breath to buoy up her feelings. "Look. Doesn't that sound like an answer to the word question?"

Niki looked at the page. "Catullus. Who's he?"

"A Latin poet." Ann had forgotten her poem was on that page. She reached out to take the magazine back. Niki held it tightly.

"You gave it to me." She read silently. "Sweet," she said, dismissing it.

Ann opened her mouth; closed it. Niki read on.

"Yes," Niki said, no more.

"Yes what?"

"Yes, an answer to the word question. So what?"

Ann collapsed. "I just thought—I don't know."

"I didn't expect them to put that picture in," Niki said. She sat up in bed, her nakedness exposed. Ann looked away. "I just submitted it for the hell of it. I thought they'd go for sand dunes."

"You underestimate them." *Us*, Ann thought.

Niki shrugged. "Maybe. Do you think she didn't send in any original work? And that's why they put in her word question?"

"They told us at the Hall that Stanton wouldn't even consider you if you didn't have something original to show.

They said it could be almost anything—even the outline of a paper—but it had to be original."

"Me too," Niki agreed. "What's she like? Hildegarde."

"Hildy," Ann corrected. "She's nice. She wants to meet you at breakfast."

"Nice, hunh? Doesn't sound like much. I mean, *you're* nice. How long have I got?"

"Five minutes, maybe ten."

Niki leaped out of bed. Ann turned to the window, so as not to seem to be staring. "Makes you nervous, nakedness," Niki observed. Ann didn't answer. She was watching Hildy stride up the road. Hildy did not take the path to the dorm. Instead she walked across the lawn, to approach through a stand of trees. Her face looked up, but when Ann waved she did not respond.

Breakfast was served buffet style. Flanked by two bowls of eggs, a hotplate held a pan of bubbling water. Further down the sideboard stood boxes of cereal, two pitchers of milk, one of canned orange juice, and a mound of discouraged-looking toast on a china platter. Jam, butter and water were at each plate. Hildy had taken a plate and was eating alone. When they had cooked their eggs and selected toast, Ann led Niki over.

Hildy peered at Ann and smiled. Her face turned to Niki. "Hello. You're Niki."

"Hi," Niki answered. "Don't talk to me until I've finished breakfast, OK? Where the hell's the coffee?"

Ann pointed to a side table. She sat next to Hildy and cracked her eggs open. "How was church?" she asked.

"Oh well, it was fine," Hildy answered.

Hildy did not use that word, *fine,* the way others did, Ann decided. If Ann said something was fine, that meant it was only OK, unexceptionable. Hildy said church was fine in the same way people remarked that it was a fine morning.

Niki sat down and hunched over her plate, eating silently. "Which church did you go to?"

"I don't know. It was white and small." Hildy chewed. "The preacher spoke about the fall of the year and the fall of man. It was not clever, although he wanted to be thought clever. But there was much time for silent prayer, and the choir sang beautifully. I am going to get myself coffee. May I get you a cup?"

"No thanks, I don't drink it."

"She went to church?" Niki asked, in her dramatic whisper.

"Yes," Ann said. Defensive.

Niki returned to her coffee.

Ann, whose spirits were lifting, asked, "What are you going to do today?"

Niki shook her head, whether to decline conversation or to deny plans, Ann could not tell.

Hildy sat down. She looked toward Niki, then spoke to Ann. "You have gotten all my books?"

"They're all upstairs, on your desk. Why are you taking two sciences?"

"I want to. We had a correspondence about it, and the Dean decided that I could try it. She would have liked to refuse, I think. But I explained that at my school there was little in the way of equipment, microscopes and slides, so I know much less than I should. Here, they have good equipment. And the observatory is close enough to use as part of the astronomy course. I didn't want to miss such an opportunity."

Niki left to refill her coffee cup.

"Are you good at science?" Ann asked.

"No. But I am very interested."

"Two sciences will be awfully hard, unless you've got a real aptitude."

"So the Dean said. Miss Dennis. Have you met her?"

"She spoke at the assembly yesterday," Ann said.

"You're talking about the Munchkin." Niki's voice interrupted their quiet talk. "I'm awake now. Hello, Hildy."

"Hello, Niki." Hildy held out her hand. Niki took it.

"The Munchkin is OK in my book," Niki announced.

"I don't understand," Hildy said. "Who is the Munchkin?"

"Miss Dennis is, because she's small, miniature," Ann explained. The question did not disappear from Hildy's face. "It's in *The Wizard of Oz*," Ann said, "the Land of the Munchkins, a sort of merry midget race."

"In her letters she seemed a rather large person," Hildy said.

"She would," Niki pronounced. "I saw you go by last night," she remarked to Ann. Ann flushed. "Some of your prep school friends?"

"Yes. Why?"

"No reason."

"How was the game?"

"OK. We won, fifteen-three, fifteen-twelve."

"Volleyball?" Hildy asked.

"Yeah," Niki said. "Do you play?"

"It was my sport, in high school. I plan to take it here this fall."

"Good God, why do that? It's not a real sport."

"It isn't?"

"Of course not. Tennis is. Basketball is. Swimming."

"And field hockey," Ann added.

"I'll take your word for that," Niki said. "But volleyball—that's just for horsing around."

"Why should you think that?" asked Hildy.

"It's true, for one thing," Niki answered. "And then, there's no skill and not much exercise, except for the spiker."

"If you think that, then you know little of the game," Hildy remarked.

"I know something," Niki said, challenge in her voice. "Want to play a game this afternoon?"

"Is there time for that? There is nothing else we must do?"

"There's a tea at four. A get-acquainted tea." Ann thought further. "Nothing else."

"Can we find enough people to play?" Hildy asked Niki.

"Sure. Easy." Niki was pleased. "Where are you from that you played volleyball as a sport?"

"Nowhere," Hildy said.

"Is that really the name of the town?" Ann asked.

"Yes. Peculiar, isn't it? But the high school was not there. It was fifty miles away, at Huger Ford."

"Did you have interscholastic matches?" Niki asked.

"No. There were no teams nearby. Only the basketball team competed with other teams, the boys. They had to travel many hours to play a game. And they seldom won."

Niki sipped her coffee, studying Hildy's face. "What do you think of winning?"

Ann giggled: "Preferable to losing."

"Butt out. You hear?" Niki glared at her.

"Are you angry at Ann?" Hildy asked. Niki shook her head. "Oh. I thought you were, to hear you speak that way."

"Morning isn't my best time," Niki mumbled. Ann thought

that might be an apology, but didn't know whether it was directed toward her or toward Hildy.

"When is your best time?" Hildy inquired.

"I don't have one," Niki answered.

Ann sputtered with laughter. Niki turned to her, glaring, the nose thrust forward, the mouth stiff with anger.

Ann said quickly, "Come on, that's funny."

Niki grunted, subsided.

"How many people do you need for a volleyball game?" Ann asked.

"Any number," Niki said.

"That's not so," Hildy protested. "You must have six on each side, no more."

"What the hell," Niki said. "If you say so."

"Can you find twelve people to play?" Ann asked quickly.

"We've got three right here," Niki said.

"Not me," Ann shook her head. "I don't know how to play volleyball. I'll cheerlead but I won't play. I'll time, how's that? How much time to a half?"

"No time. You just play until somebody gets to fifteen, with a margin of two points."

"That isn't the way," Hildy said, leaning forward. "You must limit yourself to eight minutes a game for two out of three games. If at the end of eight minutes neither team leads by two points, you play on in sudden death."

"Judas Priest, Hildy," Niki said, "if you crap up the game with all these rules it won't be any fun. Where'd you get them?"

"The woman who coached me had had a chance to coach an Olympic team," Hildy answered.

"Why didn't she take it?" Niki was impressed.

"She had family obligations."

Niki spoke sagely: "Families aren't worth a pot to pee in."

"That isn't right," Hildy declared. Niki stared at her, silent for a moment, then said, "Since when do they play volleyball at the Olympics?"

"Since the next games," Hildy answered. "It is something new."

"So these are international rules you know," Niki said.

"National, International, the rules are the same I think,"

Hildy said. "Although, I am not sure about the time limit. That may not apply."

"We're going to have to figure out what rules we play under," Niki said, "before we start. I wonder if I can find ten people."

"Nine. Ann."

"Ann isn't playing," Niki said.

Hildy's blue eyes studied Ann. "Why don't you want to?"

"I don't know how," Ann answered. "I'll watch, I'd like to watch. You'll need an audience. Every sport needs an audience."

"I can think of one that doesn't," Niki said, smirking.

Ann, her face held bright in a smile, blushed and was furious with herself.

"Volleyball's easy. You can learn while you play," Niki explained. "It's sort of like tennis. You must have *some* athletic ability. You play tennis all right."

Ann refused stubbornly. She never played a game well unless she had been playing for a while. She didn't want to go out and make a fool of herself.

"OK then. How *do* you feel about winning, Hildegarde?" Niki returned to her original topic.

Hildy considered. "I like it," she decided.

"What about losing?" Niki asked.

"That doesn't matter," Hildy said.

Niki pounced: "But winning does."

"I didn't say that. Neither is important, not really. I like to win. But—" She apparently had no words for further discussion of the point. "I like to play," she explained. "If you play well you win, usually. If you play well and lose, then it will still be a good game."

It was clear that Niki didn't believe her. "I'll go see who I can find. To play. What do you think, two o'clock?"

"There is a net already set up?"

"There's an outdoor court and lots of indoor ones. Volleyball seems to be popular around here. Lots of pick-up games. There's some kind of inter-class tournament, in all the sports, each season. Some people last night were talking about it. Freshmen never win of course. Anyway, there are volleyball teams, as well as the rest. It's a friendly game," she concluded, looking at Ann. Ann, in whose memory was clear the image of

Niki's arm upraised, fist clenched to hammer down on the ball, smiled.

Niki had Hildy and Ann down on the lawn beside the volleyball net by one forty-five. She had found two volleyballs. She went to the side and did deep knee bends, while Hildy tried to show Ann how to hit the ball.

"I'm not going to play," Ann said.

"I know. Wouldn't you like to see how it's done though?"

Ann learned to hold her hands so that the heels would contact the ball. She stood across the net from Hildy and returned a few soft shots. It wasn't all that difficult. But it wasn't as easy as it looked. Ann could be sure of getting the ball up over the high net; however, she had no idea of how to put it where she wanted it to go. Hildy had no trouble returning her shots, no matter how wildly they flew. Hildy didn't always make contact with the heels of her hands, as she had told Ann: sometimes—if the ball was low—she would dig at it with her fists; a couple of times—when it flew high—she brought it down with her forearms. Every shot she sent back to Ann was easily within reach.

Other girls came to join them, and Ann stopped playing. "You're good, aren't you?" she asked Hildy as she walked over to return the ball. Ann had played enough tennis to know how good you had to be to return the ball well to a beginner.

"Yes," Hildy said.

People were warming up, going to one side or another as they arrived. Niki still stood apart, now leaping up and bringing her fist down on an imaginary ball. Ann watched. Niki sprang high, stroked, and landed with knees flexed, ready. She reminded Ann of a panther or mountain lion. "What are you doing?" she asked.

"It's called spiking," Niki said, and leaped again. "It's the way you win points," she grunted as she landed. "Like a smash."

"Is this like tennis without a racquet?"

Niki shook her head and leaped. "This is a team sport. You have to win serve, too. And you can hit it twice on one side of the net, before you pass it over. You'll see."

Ann sat down on the grass nearby. She didn't mind being alone, here, under these circumstances. Niki went to join the players, choosing the side opposite Hildy. A few of the girls greeted her, welcoming her onto their team. They made room for her in the row near the net. Ann watched lazily. Niki's coordination seemed better than anyone else's. Her muscular body was never caught off-balance. Hildy, on the other side, played a slower game. She moved in a more leisurely fashion, gracefully. As if every gesture was part of a whole, continued from the previous and leading into the next. But Niki, Ann thought, was the better player, the better athlete, quicker, sharper.

"Shall we begin?" Niki asked. The two teams of six each arranged themselves into front lines and back lines. Niki served, underhand and hard, into the opposite corner. The receiver touched it, but knocked it out of bounds. Niki's next serve went to the center rear. The girl punched it up and Hildy seemed to be waiting for it because she passed over the net. One of Niki's team ran for it, swung at it with a fist, but missed. Niki called out "One-nothing." Hildy's team rotated.

"Why not one-all?" Ann wondered. Each side had won a point. No, Niki said you have to win serve, so Hildy's team had only won serve, not scored a point.

Ann turned to see who was sitting down beside her. She recognized Eloise Golding, from the Hall, and swallowed back a groan. Eloise had been in her classes for three years and she had never gotten to know her, and she had never regretted it. Eloise was a square person, her head, her body, her chunky limbs. Her hair was straight and square cut. Her eyeglasses were square. Her white lips were square. Her mind—Ann assumed, for she knew only that Eloise got A's—was as square and pallid as her flesh. Eloise was always carefully quiet.

"Hi," Eloise said. Ann grunted. She was convinced that Eloise, if given encouragement, would become a leech.

In front of them the game went on. Finally, Ann felt she had to speak. A long-legged, long-haired blonde was serving on Niki's team. "I can't figure out what's going on. Can you?"

"Yes," Eloise said. "I'm familiar with the rules of the game."

Ann waited, then asked. "What's the score?"

"Five to one. The service team is ahead. The score of the service team is always given first, then the score of the receiving team."

"How come you're here?" Eloise was unathletic.

"I heard there was a game from someone—I don't know her name—who was asked to play. Since I had nothing else to do until the tea, I thought I might as well watch. My roommates were telephoning their boyfriends."

"How do you like your roommates?"

"They're tolerable," Eloise said. Then she added, as if surprised, "I just recalled that you aren't rooming with anyone from school either."

"No."

"Why not? I'd have thought you would."

Ann couldn't remember Eloise ever asking a question before, not even *What did you get on that test?* "If Sally had come here, I might have. But—and it was time to branch out I thought."

"I see." Another pause and then, rushing out, "Both of my roommates come from Houston. They requested to be placed together."

"Oh dear," Ann said without thinking.

"Just so," Eloise said solemnly. Ann, confused by having given away so obviously what she was thinking, wondered if there was a glint of humor in her companion. If she'd thought of Eloise at all, it had been to dismiss her, as a wispy person—like a tepid breeze on a summer day, uninteresting.

"How do you find *your* roommates?" Eloise asked. A second question.

"They're both here playing. That's why I came," Ann said.

"But I always thought of you as an athlete. How is it that you're not playing?" And a third. This wasn't like the Eloise Ann remembered.

"I've never played volleyball in my life," Ann explained.

Niki screamed: "Get your buns over there, dammit! You don't play the game standing still! Jackass." Eloise jumped.

"That's one," Ann said. Eloise smiled faintly.

"Her name's Niki. The other's the big blonde on the other side, with short, curly hair. Hildy. See her? in the middle." At that moment Hildy leaped up and placed the ball neatly at Niki's feet. Niki dived, but couldn't get to it. "Piss on it," she said, then, "Nice shot," then she screeched, "C'mon, we only need one point to win this game. Let's go! Close in." Her team inched toward the net.

"That didn't take very long," Eloise observed.

"How long is it supposed to take?"

"Ordinarily, if the teams are at all equal, a game will take between ten and fifteen minutes. This engagement appears to be a rout."

"Niki will like that. She creamed me yesterday at tennis."

"Didn't you play on the varsity tennis team?"

"Second string."

"Even so, I would have thought—" Eloise said. They had another silence while the game ended with Niki rushing to the net to spike a ball down into the empty forecourt (empty because the players had backed away at her approach). "I didn't know you had translated Catullus that way," Eloise said, not looking at Ann. "I mean, I knew we'd done him, but I wasn't aware you had executed poetic translations."

Ann flushed.

"Do you want to know what I thought of it?" Eloise asked.

Of course I do, you ninny, Ann thought, not wanting to have to ask. "Shoot," she said.

"You weren't precisely faithful to the syntax—"

"I know that."

"But you did it rather well I think. The scholarship, although not meticulous, is able enough. There's nothing specious in it. However, the feeling is what I noticed most. I think you really succeeded with the feeling. It's modern, but not too modern, and you have retained the fluency of the original. Though I wonder whether you should have used feminine rhymes. Do you know what I mean?"

A real criticism, Ann thought, nodding.

"Anyway, it is a sound translation," Eloise concluded pedantically, lamely.

"What are they doing now?" Ann asked. "I'm glad you liked the translation."

"They're changing sides."

"I *know* that," Ann's irritation came into her voice until she saw that faint smile. Dry humor? "What's Hildy doing?" Hildy was talking to her teammates. She held her arms up together, illustrating something and the girls nodded. Could you co-exist with someone for three years and not know if she had a sense of humor? and not know her? At the Hall you could, it seemed.

"Coaching, or so it would appear," Eloise answered.

Ann and Eloise attended more carefully to the second game.
Hildy's team served first. Hildy, in the front row, turned to the
redheaded girl and said, "Remember. Just keep it in play. Are
we ready?"

The girl's puffball underhand serve floated gently down. The
long-haired blonde on Niki's team hit an overhead shot, which
Niki seemed to be waiting for, because she jumped up with her
fist raised. A fraction of a second later, Hildy leaped. Her
hands met the descending ball above the net and snapped it to
the ground before anyone on Niki's team saw what had
happened. Niki glared at Hildy, who did not respond. Instead,
Hildy said to the blonde, "That was a nice set."

"Thanks."

"One-nothing," Niki announced.

When Hildy had successfully blocked two more spikes, as if
she could read Niki's mind and knew just where the ball would
cross the net, Niki stopped spiking. She called "Mine!" for
any ball anywhere near her and charged after it to get it back
over the net with all the power she could give it. The game
became schizoid: on Hildy's side the ball was gentled, made
soft; on Niki's it was energized and pointed. Hildy's team
would retrieve and pass it among themselves. If Niki couldn't
get to it for the first return, she was always there for a second
shot. "Look out!" she would yell to her teammates, who
backed away to give her room. Hildy too moved about,
although she did not range as far. "I'm behind you," she would
say softly.

"Nine-two," Niki called. "Let's get on it here. Wake up!"

Niki's team placed themselves for Hildy's serve. Unlike the
others, Hildy served overhand, a series of arcs, the tossed ball,
the arm, the body. The serve landed between two players,
equidistant from each. Neither moved. Each wore the same
expression of surprise.

Hildy served again. This time the ball was fast, speeding
into an uncovered corner. Niki dived for it, and missed. She lay
on the ground for a minute, as if thinking. As they waited for
the third serve, Ann noticed Niki watching her own team, not
Hildy. Hildy threw the ball up, over her head, and before her
hands touched it, Niki started to run. "Outta my way!" she
yelled and was there to receive the serve at the opposite side of
the court where there was a broad space between two players.

She got it, but could not lift it over the net. "To you, Sarah," she yelled. The blond punched it over to Hildy's team. The redhead received it at the net but did not return it. Instead she passed it overhead to a teammate beside her, who returned it to Niki's team. The ball landed softly on the ground.

"Twelve-two, dammit," Niki cried.

Hildy served again, this time another fast ball, landing low, just too far from the receiver's feet to be reached. Niki was there, again, her teammates having jumped back to give her room, and her shot went low and hard over the net.

"That's out," the redheaded girl called to the back row. They stood to let it go. It touched the end line before rolling out of bounds. "Hah!" Niki grunted. The team rotated.

"I'm sorry," the redhead said. "It looked out to me. Didn't it look out to you, Hildy?"

Hildy turned to face the girl. "I didn't watch it," she said. "When you called it I didn't watch."

"My fault," the girl said.

"Fault?" asked Hildy. "Why? You will be right more often than not, when calling a ball out. But you will sometimes be wrong."

Niki's team won two points, then lost serve again. Although Hildy was in the front row, she did not often spike. She sent the ball back, to her own team, over her head or sideways. She placed her shots when she made them over the net and ordinarily won the point. Her team won that game, and the sides switched again.

Ann and Eloise exchanged a glance, both with eyebrows raised. "I'm rather glad I decided to stop by," Eloise said.

Ann nodded. Niki's face was mottled with exertion, and so was Hildy's. All twelve faces were serious. The blonde, Sarah, served a moderate underhand. Hildy passed it overhead to a player in the front row. Niki's team shifted toward that side of the court. "To Carol," Hildy called, and the ball, instead of being sent over the net, was passed down to the opposite side of the front line, to the redheaded girl. She plopped it over for the point, into the emptied court.

The team rotated. To Hildy's serve. In silence.

Hildy served hard, and Niki returned it. Hildy's team passed it forward and over the net. Sarah returned it immediately, to the feet of a player who could not lift it back into play.

The team rotated. In silence.

A heavy, brown-haired girl, wearing boy's athletic shorts, served for Niki's team. The redhead, Carol, returned it easily, a long, high, floating shot. As soon as it left her hands, she slapped one palm against her forehead and looked about her apologetically, but nobody returned her glance. They watched the ball instead. Sarah moved to receive it. Niki poised by the net. The ball came off Sarah's hands at the same time that Niki left the ground. She executed the spike. Hildy dived for it, but missed.

Ann let her breath out.

Brownhair served again, across the court to the opposite side. Hildy's team passed it forward, then across the front to Hildy; who soared up to meet it with her fist, spiking it directly to Sarah; who caught it against her belly, surprised.

The team rotated. In silence.

Eloise crossed her legs beneath her and hunched forward.

The next serve was weak but accurate. Niki returned it to midcourt. Hildy crouched down to lift the ball enough so that another pass returned it over the net. Niki went to receive it, passed it to Sarah, who sent it back, deep and flat. The server ran to meet it and, with a frenzied fist, popped it up. Hildy was beneath it when it came down. She sent it to Carol who angled it across court. Sarah lifted it high, and Niki leaped.

"Hoo-aah!" Niki cried, as she fired the ball into the back of the court.

"All right! Now! We've got it!" Niki yelled. Her voice shattered the silence.

Ann repressed a nervous giggle. By a coolness at her back, she knew a third person had joined them. Word of this kind of contest must spread quickly. She turned her head to greet the newcomer, then scrambled to her feet.

"Miss Dennis," Ann said as Eloise, too, hurried to stand.

"Miss Gardner," the Munchkin answered. "Miss Golding."

Eloise bobbed her head.

Miss Dennis wore a navy shirt dress that emphasized her squat body.

"I was on my way to the tea," she remarked. "This seems to be a close game."

"It is."

"Yes. Well, so it appears."

"It's the third," Eloise volunteered. "Each team has won one."

They watched in silence for a while. The score crept slowly upward to five-five. As Niki's team prepared to serve, Miss Dennis stepped up to one of the poles. "Ladies," she announced. "If you continue, you will either miss the tea entirely or be embarrassingly late."

Eyes turned to wristwatches. "Hell and damnation," Niki said. Too loudly.

"Perhaps so," Miss Dennis' dry voice carried over the babble that hastily arose. "Ah, Miss Koenig. I see you have arrived safely."

Hildy's head swung around and she squinted toward the Munchkin. "Yes?" she said. She stooped and stepped under the net, coming to shake hands. "How do you do? It is good to meet you, yourself," Hildy said.

"It wouldn't do to miss the tea you know," Miss Dennis chided. "So I'll see you all there, in a few moments." She loped away, lopsidedly ascending a small bank of grass.

"We could finish," Niki said. But she knew she would not be heard. Girls were already running back to dorms.

"Dammit," Niki said. She flung the ball at the ground. "Who wants to go to this tea anyway?"

"Why, I do," Hildy answered. She picked the ball up and hurried off.

"See you there," Ann said to Eloise, as Eloise nodded. Ann hastened after Hildy, leaving Niki to make her own angry way.

Hildy and Ann took quick baths, by which time Niki returned, her hair damp from a shower. As soon as she had stepped into the room, she said, "Hildy? What if I played volleyball for my fall sport? There's a tournament—if we were on the same team, I bet we'd win."

Hildy had spread a brown cotton dress on her desk top and was smoothing it with the flat of her hand. When Ann asked what she was doing, she explained that this was her dress for the tea, but that she had worn it for two days' travel. Ann brought out a bright flowered Lanz, in the princess style. "Will you try this?" she asked. Hildy was taller than she but no broader. "Really," Ann insisted.

"Is it the custom to share?" Hildy asked.

"My sisters and I do it all the time," Ann said.

"Ah. I have only brothers," Hildy said. She put the dress over her head and pulled up the back zipper.

"Pretty," Ann said. The airy print and smooth lines of the dress suited Hildy's haphazard hair, her bright blue eyes and slender, tanned neck. It was a pleasure to see the dress on her. Both the garment and its wearer seemed fresh, accidental, and eager as a bank of daffodils.

Hildy smoothed her hands down the front of the dress. "Pretty," she agreed. "Isn't it too short though? You are several inches smaller than I. Am I immodest?"

"Never." Niki laughed sharply. "Besides, we're all female here, so who cares? What's to show? Who's to see it?"

Hildy stared at Niki for a moment, without seeming to see her.

"Anyway, what do you think?" Niki asked.

"About what?" Ann asked. They were all dressing.

"Playing volleyball for a sport. Me. And Hildy."

"I would not want to play on a team with you," Hildy said.

"What? What do you mean? Why not?" The air in the room crackled. Ann squirmed.

"You do not know how to play on a team," Hildy said. She apparently had not noticed Niki's fullblown reaction.

"What the—?" Niki said. "Holy pissing name of God."

Ann, whose squirming had intensified to acute discomfort, felt Hildy's wrath while the third girl struggled to find her tongue. Hildy's hands clenched. She stepped up to Niki, into whose eyes she could look as equal, and her own eyes were luminous. Her jaw moved, once. Her voice when she spoke was stony: "You will not use such language where I must hear it. I have heard enough."

Ann would have run from the room, had not her two roommates stood between her and the door.

Niki stood silent, sullen. Hildy faced her, implacable, not altering her gaze.

She spoke again: "You have not answered."

Niki could not possibly have mistaken the tone for a challenge. But she chose to respond as if it had been. "I guess you expect me to apologize, and wash my mouth out with soap because I'm a bad girl."

"You have not answered."

Ann almost admired Niki's stubbornness against the force of Hildy's anger.

"Just what am I supposed to say?"

"The truth," Hildy said quietly.

That stopped Niki. "Oh," she said. "OK," she said, "I won't."

Ann thought the argument would continue, but it didn't. Each girl retired to her bureau to brush her hair.

Niki spoke first. "Did you mean that about the team?"

"Of course."

"I can play anyway."

"I hope so."

"I'm better than you are, you know that."

"No, I do not know that. You are not, now, better than I; although you probably could be. You are much more agile, and your reflexes are quicker. But your emotion interferes with your play and with the play of your team. I am not confident that you are the better."

Niki fell silent. Ann did not speak. She sat on her bed, waiting for Hildy to be ready, thinking that her vocal cords felt entangled. She might never speak again.

But this is bizarre, Ann said to herself, mindful of the future weeks and months they had to spend together. Somebody had to speak. Somebody had to say something. She cleared her throat experimentally and then hurled herself into the conversational breech, firing off the first thought that came to her mouth. "I think I'll play volleyball too."

Hildy smiled, as at a child's foolishness, but Niki said, "Why?"

"Why not?" Ann answered, with a rhetorical waving of hands. "I don't particularly like field hockey and I don't enjoy playing it. It's time I tried something new. And besides, you two just blew up at each other and if I hadn't seen that game I wouldn't know why. So I have to take volleyball, to be able to keep up with your quarrels. And know when to steer clear of the room."

Niki grinned. Hildy protested: "But we were not quarreling about the game."

"You think not?" Niki asked.

"And we have understood one another, Niki and I," Hildy continued. "We have seen, each, what the other is."

"Speak for yourself," Niki muttered. "But there's more to me than meets the eye."

"Of course," Hildy said, surprised.

Ann's head turned from one to the other. "Yes, I think I'd better take volleyball. With you."

"If it is what you want, then that is fine," Hildy said earnestly. "But we have made peace with one another, if it is not what you want."

"Not what she wants? Peace?" Niki asked.

"What, volleyball?" Ann asked.

Hildy shook her head and her eyes peered at them. "You can't confuse me," she said.

"Peace *is* what I want," Ann babbled. "Serenity, security, balance— So, I'll take volleyball, whatever you say. How did that decision become so serious?"

"Ask Hildy," Niki advised, grinning and holding the door for them.

chapter

3

The first weeks at Stanton passed both quickly and slowly, as Ann tried to settle in and feel at home. They lived together, Ann and Niki and Hildy, and grew to know one another. There were classes to attend, professors whose methods had to be assessed, learning to accomplish. Ann worked at the ancient Greek declensions, neglecting science as much as possible, and finding the other courses rather easy. Hildy sat for hours at her desk, hunched over notebooks and textbooks; or she lay on the bed with a book up against her nose. Niki was frequently out.

They would get no grades until the results of the first set of tests, which were usually given three to four weeks after a course began. Ann studied regularly, as she had been trained to do, three or four hours a day given to preparation and review. Hildy rose with the sun, to sit over the books at her desk. Ann woke to see Hildy silhouetted against the desk light, her head low over papers, her fingers buried in her short hair. Hildy's hair looked ragged and unruly in the mornings, like a head just denuded of lifelong braids. Unprotected somehow. The same bent head, in more mellow light, was the last thing Ann usually saw before falling asleep.

Ann noticed in Hildy a consistent attitude, to every course, to every assignment. She approached all—even after several weeks, when Stanton had become familiar—with eagerness. What was odd was that her expectations were not disappointed. Hildy woke eagerly to each morning, turned eagerly to her studies, went eagerly to meals although she was neither a prodigious nor a fussy eater. About this last, Ann asked her. "I enjoy to be hungry," Hildy answered, "because—then I eat and I am no longer hungry. And it feels good not to be hungry." Niki snorted. Niki, opposite to Hildy in all things, criticized the food in language both imaginative and vulgar; she ate out frequently but seemed to enjoy discussing the dormitory food, as if she appreciated the opportunity it gave her to make Ann laugh. Ann saw herself muddling about between the two of them. "You cover all the extremes," she protested. "What about me?" And she would think, a little wistfully, about where she fit in, in this trio, before turning back to her own work.

Niki studied erratically and attended classes with notebook in hand. She was most often out of the room. She developed a wide circle of acquaintances, people she met in her restless search for something to do. Niki was always available to *do* something, tennis, touch football, softball, bridge, Clue, take a hike, or sit around the student center and talk. "You're making a lot of friends," Ann remarked to her. "Friends," Niki answered, not bothering to disguise her scorn. "They've just got a lot of time to kill—and they think if they're laughing they're having a good time—and they want someone to do their thinking for them. You can't be friends with people who don't know anything about you—and don't want to. Can you? Huh Annie, can you?" Ann turned away. They were alone together in their room because it was Thursday; on Mondays and Thursdays, Hildy walked up to the Observatory, two miles into the hills.

Ann tried to figure out what they were like, Hildy and Niki. And Ann. Niki wore her intelligence like her jeans, close and comfortable. Hildy held hers like a lantern, to illuminate. And Ann? Like a string of real pearls around her neck, in the dark of night on the wrong street, she nervously concealed her mind, her unquiet fingers both cherishing and proud. Was that what they were like? What she was like? During those weeks, and always afterwards, she considered this.

Niki demanded her attention but it was Hildy who dominated her thoughts. Niki made Ann uncomfortable, kept her alertly off-balance; but Hildy fascinated her, with her suggestion of mysterious possibility. It was Hildy she asked questions of, as if by collecting facts she could approach understanding. Hildy came from a family of four brothers and herself. Her father's farm was three hundred and two acres, her father's brother had a contiguous farm of four hundred acres, so that the family had substantial holdings. Hildy, as the only girl, had a bedroom to herself. She had taken the same five courses, all through high school: English, a math course, Latin, history, science. Her sports were volleyball, basketball, and track. her brothers were named Luke and Philip and Thomas and Matthew. Her mother had a vegetable garden and put up the fruits of it. Her parents were shorter than their children. All of this told Ann little. She could not attach Hildy to any of it. "What does your house look like?" she asked. "Is it a two-story one, with trees, among flat fields? With barns behind it? Is it white with a porch?"

"It is not like that at all."

"What is it like then?"

"I don't know how to describe it. What does it matter?"

"What about summers?" Ann asked. "What do you do during summers?"

"I weed, I harvest. My brother and I also raise chickens."

"Raise chickens? How do you raise chickens?

"Oh, well, we buy the chicks. There is a woman in Huger Ford who will hatch out the eggs for us in June. Then, we feed them over the summer as they grow. In August, we sell them to the dealer."

"What do you mean, sell them to the dealer, how do you transport them?"

"That is simple. We pack the truck bed with ice and straw, and put the chickens upon that. You must do it early in the morning, or they will spoil."

"They're dead?"

"Of course, she does not want them alive."

Ann couldn't see it. Hildy eluded her imagination. "How do you do it?" she asked. Meaning, how could you bring yourself to kill another living creature.

"I hold the chicken down and my brother cuts off the head. That is quick. Then we dip them into boiling water and pluck them. That is the part we don't like. You must work fast, and you are covered with sweat and feathers. Usually, he will gut the carcasses and take off the claws while I pluck."

Ann stared into Hildy's face, trying to see it in a place, the slaughter, the evisceration, the defoliation, and Hildy's face and hands working. Niki interrupted: "It's not the kind of thing our Annie likes to think about," she said. "Annie thinks chickens emerge, somehow, by spontaneous creation, as fryers and roasters, breasts and drumsticks. She doesn't want to hear about how they get to the grocer's, Hildy.''

"That's not it," Ann protested. Sometimes, she thought Niki deliberately misunderstood; only, of course, Niki was too close to being right.

"Isn't it?" Niki asked, her chin jutting at Ann. She explained to Hildy: "She'll never understand. She doesn't really want to."

"Then why does she ask about it?"

Niki couldn't answer.

But Ann couldn't have answered either, because what she had found out did not enlighten her about what she wanted to understand. She noticed, however, that Niki also questioned Hildy. In a different way but, Ann suspected, to the same purpose.

"Why do you talk so funny?" Niki demanded.

"Do I?" Hildy asked, looking up blankly at her dark roommate. Ann also lifted her head from a book to follow this conversation.

"Can't you hear it?" Niki asked. "You do. Ask Annie."

The face turned to Ann, who offered, "Not exactly funny, but—"

"You do talk funny and your mother dresses you weird," Niki announced.

"You understand what I say," Hildy answered.

"I wouldn't be too sure of that," Niki muttered.

"Why not?" Hildy asked.

Niki couldn't answer that, either. The expression on her face was part interest, part rage. Hildy went back to her work, but raised her head after a few minutes to say, "I think, sometimes, there is so much talking here. At home, we are working and there is no need to speak. In the evenings, my father will read to us from the Bible, while I sew and my brothers oil the machinery or replace the rushes on the chairs. Of course," she added, "that is only in the winter. In the summer we go to sleep."

"What about at school?" Niki demanded. "You must have talked to people at school."

"No." Hildy shook her head. "To my friend when she was free from class. Not often."

"What about the other kids?"

"What should I talk with them about? We were there to learn."

"Didn't anybody ever tell you you talk funny?" Niki demanded.

"Oh yes," Hildy said.

"What did you say?"

"I asked if they could understand me," Hildy answered patiently, "and like you, they said yes."

Niki snorted, shook her head either in amazement or affection. Ann wasn't sure.

"But," Hildy continued, "my mother does not dress me. I dress myself."

Days went by, weeks, and Ann continued to wonder. About Hildy. And Niki. And Ann.

They met people, they ate and slept and washed their faces, they read and wrote and sometimes thought; while around them the fall deepened its colors and brought variety to the landscape. Later, all this blurred together in Ann's memory, while the volleyball games remained vivid.

Ann did sign up to take volleyball. The freshman volleyball class met three times a week, as did all freshman sports classes, Monday, Tuesday and Thursday afternoons, from four to five. They shared the gym with the sophomore volleyball class. They also shared the instructor.

The instructor was a graduate student from the Education Department who knew, or so she said, "not much about volleyball but lots about teaching." On the firt day of class, she was joined by the chairman of the Physical Education Department, Mrs. Franklin, who coached juniors and seniors. Mrs. Franklin explained the volleyball ladder, its system of challenges and the time allowed for responses. All classes played within the ladder for the ten-week sports semester. At the end, the top freshman team would hold the Freshman Cup, the top sophomore team the Sophomore Cup, and so on.

Niki raised her hand. "The team on the top of its ladder. Can it challenge a team from another class?"

"Yes," Mrs. Franklin said. "You can challenge one step above you. Although I should tell you, such challenges are seldom successful, not even in some of the more popular sports, where the contest can be quite close. For example, many preparatory schools now offer good training in hockey and tennis, but even so, cross-class challenges don't succeed. And volleyball—well, it isn't the kind of sport taken by those who take athletics seriously, is it? Or by competitive girls. I'm not insulting anyone, am I?" She nodded her smiling face around the circle. Hildy raised her hand.

"Yes?" asked Mrs. Franklin.

"What?" responded Hildy.

"You had a question."

"No, I didn't."

"Why was your hand raised?"

"You asked if you were insulting anybody, and I raised my hand," Hildy explained.

The circle tittered. The chairman's face grew pink. The graduate student entered the conversation: "I'm sure Miss—"

"Koenig," Hildy said. She raised herself to her knees and extended her right hand. "How do you do?"

"Miss Koenig meant no disrespect," the assistant addressed the chairman over her shoulder, as she leaned to shake Hildy's hand.

"Of course not," Hildy said. "I would not mean disrespect. I meant to answer the question."

"Ah. Has the disrespect come home to roost?" Niki employed her stage whisper.

"Well," Mrs. Franklin said, her eyes searching the group.

"Does that answer your question about the ladder?" the assistant hastily asked Niki.

Niki nodded her head.

The chairman left them then and the assistant instructed them to form themselves into four teams. This they did, with five people left over. The assistant placed those five people on one team or another and tossed two balls toward the two courts. "Go ahead and play," she said. For good measure she gave a toot upon her whistle before turning her attention to the sophomore teams, who had a game in progress.

Niki's face gleamed with laughter. Ann, pulled into a team from the sidelines where she had been quite content, stood uselessly by a pole. Eloise was there, and the lovely blonde, Sarah, and Carol the redhead. Ann greeted Trudy Wallenbach, who had earned the reputation at the Hall of being the least athletic person there in its entire fifty years. On the same team as Ann was the brown-haired girl she had noticed at Sunday's game, Bess, and a friendly girl named Ruth whom she'd seen in her science class. They played out the remaining time of that first class. Ann volleyed two balls, both badly.

At the next session, Ann noticed Hildy talking with the assistant, who alternated shrugs with nods with glances at her watch with reassuring remarks to the sophomores. Hildy returned from the conversation and proceeded to divide the freshman group into beginners and experienced players. Ann, Eloise, and Trudy were among the beginners. They were instructed in the basic overhand and underhand shots. Ten of them practiced these, while the remaining nineteen played a game on the other court.

Midway through the class, Carol and Hildy came to the beginners' court. "We're going to play a game," Hildy said.

"What are *they* doing?" asked Trudy.

"Drilling, set and spike," Carol answered. "Can you get into your places? Do you know what the places are? There, and there; that's right. I'll play with this side, OK, Hildy?"

Ann stood between Hildy and Eloise. Hildy switched Ann and Eloise around. They began a point.

"Pass it forward," Hildy urged, while from the other side of the net Carol's voice advised, "Move where it's going to go. Hands ready."

The points they played were neither elegant nor exciting, but were played as well as their skills permitted. Ann enjoyed herself, concentrating on the ball as it descended to her waiting palms, trying to send it forward, then sideways to Eloise at the net. "Yes, that's it," somebody said.

On the opposite side, Trudy ran into Carol, toppling her over and then tripping, not over the body of her downed teammate but, incredibly, on her own ankles. "What are you doing?" Carol cried. Her face reddened, the freckles framed in white. "What's your name?" she demanded.

Trudy hunkered up on her hams. She twined her arms around her long calves. "Trudy. Wallenbach. I'm sorry. Are you all right? I just—"

"Try that point again?" Hildy called. "Our serve, isn't it? How about pulling your back line further forward?"

Carol nodded. The game went on.

With Hildy on their side, Ann felt an uplifting of spirits. She was able, she discovered, to think before she made a play, as long as she concentrated her eyes on the descending ball. Ann sensed that Hildy knew what she was thinking, what play she would make, not so difficult, after all, when Ann knew only two plays, sideways or forward. But the four other girls also seemed able to know what she was thinking. And more surprising, she was able to guess what they would do too. Ann listened for Hildy's quiet instructions. "Move up." "Cover me." "Somebody back Eloise."

They were winning, easily, until Hildy switched sides. Carol was not as good a player, missed more hard shots and passed less exactly. At the end of the session, Ann said to Hildy: "That was fun. Did you mind not playing?"

"I did play," Hildy said.

"When can *we* learn to spike?" Trudy asked.

Carol's eyebrows raised. "Ten years? Maybe eight."

"Next week, I think," Hildy said. "It's soon, but I think that's the way we'll do it. Don't you, Carol?"

"If you say so." Carol was unconcerned. "It's your problem."

They gathered up sweaters and jackets and said good-bye to the instructor. Outside the heavy gym doors, the evening was turning violet and crisply cool. "It's Thursday the next practice, isn't it?" Hildy said. "Shall we do it the same way?" Murmurs of agreement sounded.

Niki turned to Ann: "Stick around. I'll show you how to spike."

"Now?"

"We've got an hour 'til dinner. You could begin. You're coordinated enough."

"I'd like that," Ann said, surprised at Niki, surprised at herself. "I've only got Greek for tomorrow, and that philosophy reading. What about you, Hildy?"

"No. I must study."

"If I may, I think I would like to stay on a little," Eloise said.

"Who're you?" demanded Niki.

"Eloise Golding. Niki Jones," Ann introduced them.

"Another preppie," Nike said.

Eloise could make her face expressionless, more bland and square even than ordinarily. Ann had observed this and, for a second, despised Eloise and wished she would leave them. Then she despised herself. And Niki.

"I've got to go, I remembered," Eloise said.

"Stay anyway. What the hell," Niki said. "We'll need three people. You can fetch."

Eloise hesitated.

"C'mon!" Niki was impatient. "First you say you do and then you say you can't. What is it with you?" Eloise plodded back into the gym.

Niki showed Ann how to jump, revolve her body, and bring her hand down. She passed some balls to Ann, who attacked them. Sometimes Ann connected, sometimes she missed, sometimes she succeeded only in sending the ball weakly over the net. "It's like serving," Niki finally said. "You can do better than this."

"No, I can't."

"Then you can set for me." Niki was not interested in Ann's frustration.

"No thanks. I'll fetch. Eloise, do you want to set or go?"

Eloise agreed to try setting. Ann passed the ball over the net, to Eloise. Eloise hit it up, a low, floating curve; Niki pounded it into Ann's court. Ann gave up lunging for it after two tries, and just ran after it. They did this many times.

"I'm going to shower now," Niki said. "Thanks, Eloise." Eloise nodded.

Ann joined Eloise. Unthinking, Eloise sent the ball up into the air and Ann, recognizing it as an easy shot, spiked it. Her spike was the best she had yet done.

"Hey," Ann said. "Can you do that again?"

Eloise fetched the ball and repeated her shot. The ball came down at another point of the net, but it was where Ann could comfortably approach it and bring her fist down on it. They did this several times before Ann said, "Eloise, you're good at this. No, I mean it. You put the ball consistently into the right place. Spiking's like serving, where if you don't have the toss right, you *can't* serve well. Eloise, you're a secret weapon."

Eloise nodded solemnly. "I thought I might be," she said. "Or rather, I hoped I might. It seems quite simple to execute this shot properly. For me, so far, it's the only simple aspect of the game. However, it's dinnertime and I've got to get back to my dormitory. See you?"

"See you," Ann answered. "No—wait, I'll walk with you." She had a sudden mental glimpse of Eloise—standing aside, wondering if she did have this talent, silently examining the question. She had a sudden question in her mind about the nature of this unobtrusive, disciplined person; a question that blew across her mind like a cool, refreshing breeze.

In the darkness of the short walk, unable to see Eloise's face, she said, "Niki is—" but could not think of how to finish the sentence.

"I think I am beginning to understand," Eloise said, cutting off Ann's apology.

"And how are your roommates?" Ann asked.

"They're fine I guess," she answered. "I don't see them very often."

Directly after supper, Hildy left to walk up to the observatory. By the next day, Ann had forgotten that she wanted to speak to Hildy about Eloise's talent. But she did remember to look up Eloise's contribution to the freshman magazine. Eloise had submitted one of a dozen short essays they had been required to write for Problems of American Democracy. The teacher had called these essays legal opinion papers and required them to be written in a certain form, to present both sides of the argument. Eloise had chosen her paper on the Jones-Laughlin decision and had presented both sides of the argument with such clarity that Ann no longer felt sure that any decision was possible. She herself had come down strongly in favor of the unions' right to organize. Her paper had been more impassioned, and better written; Eloise's argument, on the other hand, seemed more careful, more thoughtful. More reliable, too, Ann thought. But she got from the writing no idea of what Eloise herself would have chosen to do, or of how she felt about the union-employer conflict. The essay showed nothing of the writer, gave nothing away about her prejudices, values, hopes; and in that careful impersonality it was, Ann decided, very like Eloise. Inexplicably, she both approved of that and was grateful for it.

For the next week the freshman volleyball class practiced with those divisions established the first day. It was all accomplished without benefit of instruction. Finally, at the end of the second week, Ann asked Hildy: "What about Miss Whatsherface. She never coaches us."

"She is angry," Hildy said. The group of freshmen listened, above the noise of a coaching session on the other two courts.

"Angry?" Niki asked. Hildy nodded.

"At us? But why?" Sarah asked.

Hildy shrugged, not looking at any of them.

"Does it matter?" Niki said, at the last. Her eyes beamed mischief, and celebration. "We haven't done anything, have we? *My* conscience is clear as a babe's. So what the hell? Let her eat cake. Or something else."

They were able to drill together by then, although the beginners were still noticeably weaker players. Hildy had set up fairly equal teams, for the ladder she said, with one substitute for each team.

"But *you* aren't playing," Sarah protested as she looked over the lists.

"We can't win without you," Niki said.

"Win?" Hildy asked. "But there are four teams—"

"The ladder," Niki interrupted. "Have you all forgotten? Didn't you see how it could work? With a good team, we could challenge the sophomores. If we took the best players: me, Hildy, Sarah, Carol, Bess. We could—our class—show everybody."

"Show what?" asked Hildy.

Niki made an exasperated noise. She chewed her nails for a minute. "Winning," Niki said. "That. That's why you play, isn't it?"

"What about the rest of us?" someone asked.

"I don't know, you'd keep playing with each other and that bottom sophomore team. We'd need two subs, probably."

"You've only got five on your prize team," somebody else said.

"I know," Niki said.

There was another silence. Faces were closed off, secretive. Niki's dark and urgent face looked into Hildy's unfocused eyes. At last Hildy answered: "It is time to begin. Let's drill the overhead pass today."

"What about that?" Niki insisted.

"Your team?"

Niki nodded.

"I don't think so," Hildy said, before turning to the others.

"Why?" Niki pulled her around.

"It is not the right way to play. Or even to win."

"Come off it, Hildy," Niki argued. "There's no wrong way to win."

Hildy didn't answer.

"I think we should do it, and I'll bet I'm not the only one," Niki said.

Hildy shook her head.

"Who put you in charge anyway?" Niki demanded.

"Let's *play*," Ann urged.

"Not me. Not today." Niki turned to go.

Cutting was not permitted.

"Niki," Hildy protested, warned.

"Tell them I've got my period," Niki said. "Tell them I'm bleeding like a stuck pig." She let the door crash behind her.

Practice continued. At the end of it, Hildy called them together to announce another practice, Saturday afternoon, following lunch.

"But why should we?" Bess wondered.

"We are not yet good enough," Hildy said.

"I'm not going to be here," Sarah said.

Freshmen were not allowed to go on weekends for the first six weeks. Sarah blushed. "A day trip. I have a friend coming up."

"Bring him with you," Hildy said. Everyone laughed. Hildy looked puzzled, momentarily, then as if she understood. "Well, and why not?" she asked.

"I'll try," Sarah said, smiling. "But it's bizarre."

So the practice was agreed on, to take place at the outdoor court if the weather was fair. Everyone agreed to attend. At least nobody said she wouldn't be there. "I'll talk to Niki," Hildy said.

"How about a Coke?" someone suggested. "Is anybody else thirsty?" Murmurs of agreement. They moved off, collective, but Hildy remained. Ann lingered: "Hildy?"

"I can't," Hildy said. "You go ahead."

Ann repeated the request, with a hint of pleading, but Hildy was obdurate, so they left her behind.

"What's with her?" someone asked Ann. "She's *your* roommate."

"I don't know," Ann said. "She works hard, all the time."

"My God, they're *both* your roommates."

Ann sighed.

The next Saturday was a mellow, golden day, the kind of day made to deceive flies into thinking spring has miraculously reappeared, against all ordinary limitations to things as they are. But, being fall, the day had lucid air, and colors were more brightly themselves, voices clearer, life more vivid; and in the evening chill the flies would die.

Hildy and Ann were first to arrive at the volleyball court. "Is Niki coming?" Ann asked.

"She wasn't sure."

"She'll be here," Ann told herself. The uneasy relationship between her roommates was a puzzle to her, as her continuing helplessness in it was a frustration. She never knew when Niki's temper would flare. Hildy paid little attention, so Ann followed her lead; but she would have preferred that they get along, that the relationship stabilize. They didn't have to be friends. Sometimes it seemed as if they were friends, and then Niki would find another quarrel. Hildy, after that first day, hadn't been angry, not that Ann could tell. The worst of it was, neither Niki nor Hildy seemed aware that they weren't getting along.

"I think she'll come," Hildy said. "She finds people disappointing. And difficult."

"I'd have said she's the one who gives everyone a hard time."

"You would be wrong to say that," announced Hildy.

Eloise arrived, announcing her intention of only watching. "I never have enjoyed playing in games," she demurred. Which reminded Ann to tell Hildy that Eloise could set. Hildy nodded her head and said no more. Bess arrived, jogging. She jogged everywhere, "Not to build muscles but to keep ahead of fat," she said. Ruth joined Eloise, without saying anything. Five minutes later, Sarah strode in. She began batting the ball over the net to Hildy, and gradually the others joined her, all but Eloise. They waited another ten minutes.

Then Sarah said, "I guess that's all. I guess *that* won't work."

"What won't work?" Ruth asked.

"Being better than you're expected to be. Much better. Making ourselves into genuinely good players. We can't do it in three hours a week. Can we, Hildy?"

Ann was stunned to find herself a member of that group of players Sarah spoke of.

"No. That wouldn't be possible," Hildy agreed.

Ann surprised herself by wanting to be included, even though she knew she would never be a really good player.

"We don't even have one team here," Sarah said.

"What about Eloise?" Bess asked. "Eloise? You've *got* to play."

"I really prefer not to," Eloise said. "I don't think I can," she said. Ann sympathized with her and found herself admiring Eloise's ability to stand up to pressure.

"It doesn't matter anyway," Sarah said. "I'm going back. My friend was going to study, but he won't have to now." She picked up her sweater, hung it over a shoulder, and walked away.

"Hey! Where you going?" Niki's voice blared out over the quiet scene. "I'm here now." Sarah ran back to the court. "Is this all that showed up?" Niki demanded of Hildy.

"Who is that masked man?" Ruth asked Ann, *sotto voce.* Ann grinned at her.

"Hildy? What did I tell you," Niki demanded.

"You were right," Hildy said, as if it didn't matter.

"I know I was," Niki answered, as if it did.

They started to play, with three on each side. Eloise watched. Niki and Hildy, as always, were on opposing sides. There was more running than usual, and less care necessary for moving around teammates. It was a more rigorous game in that, but less rigorous in the control needed to play the courts well. Hildy divided her side into rectangular zones. Niki divided hers into triangular pieces, increasing the frequency with which she could spike.

"It's harder to play in these triangles," Ann said, after a while.

"What do you mean?"

"Well it's harder to run backward. You know that."

"Yeah?" Niki said.

"Hildy has rectangles," Ann offered.

Niki considered this. She then cut a broad-based triangle

from the front of the court and took it for herself. The rest of the space she divided into rough rectangles.

These divisions did not last long, because the court gradually became filled, by girls who passed by and asked if they could join in. One at a time, Hildy took them onto her side and sent the freshmen over to play with Niki. "What're you *do*ing, Hildy!" Niki demanded. Then she seemed to understand something and patiently redivided her court. A sixth upperclassman came down the slope to ask if she could join in. Hildy crossed under the net. So that, when they began again, there was a mixed team and a freshman team. On the freshman team, Niki and Hildy both played, as well as Sarah and Bess, and Ruth and Ann.

These games (they played two, both of which the freshmen won) were exhausting to Ann. There was the opposing team to consider, points to be wrested from across the net. Then there was some kind of opposition between Niki and Hildy. Both voices gave directions to the team. Niki's orders were sudden, loud, last-minute. "Get it!" she would shriek. Or "Back! Back!" She accompanied her directions by running to do just what she was telling others to do.

Hildy's voice spoke softer and sooner, telling where to move or praising for having done so to Ann or Ruth, suggesting a set for spike to Sarah or Bess, yet silent to Niki.

Ann enjoyed herself playing, yet wished it would end.

End it eventually did, and Niki stood exultantly before Hildy. "Didn't I tell you?" she demanded.

Hildy remained silent.

"You see what we could do," Hildy said. "This was good playing. Competitive playing. We did all right, even Ann and Ruth. You didn't tell me what to do, you didn't have to. We managed, didn't we? And we won."

"If . . ." Hildy spoke slowly, looking off toward the tree under which Eloise sat, ". . . if you had Eloise to play instead of me—"

"Why?" The question hung in the air between them. "Besides that, I mean. Even Ann is better than Eloise."

Ann flushed.

"That team might work for you," Hildy said. "You might be able to do what Sarah wished."

"What was that?" Niki demanded.

"Be a good team, good enough to win games," Sarah said. She spoke enthusiastically. "Not just against the freshman teams. Sophomores too. It hasn't been done before."

"I'm with you. Baby, am I with you," Niki said. "But, Hildy, don't you want to win?"

"Very much," said Hildy. "A team."

Ann had a sudden vision of what Hildy meant, a wisp of conception as ephemeral as a fragment of mist, evaporating. For some endless fraction of a second, she saw the difficult and complex ambition of it. "I know," she said, "like ballet."

"Say the Rockettes," Ruth interposed, waggling a leg.

"Let's try it. You wanna? Eloise!" Niki bellowed. "Come here!" They waited for her slow arrival. "Would you be the sub if we were a team?"

Eloise looked ready to refuse.

"Don't be chicken. You probably won't ever have to play in a game. You like the game, don't you? *That* doesn't scare you? Eloise blinked, nodded.

"If she'll sub, and we all are the team"—Hildy was included in the sweep of Niki's arm and she did not protest—"couldn't we try it Hildy? We might just be good, really good. If we practice a lot and you coach them. Everybody wants to"—nobody would have dared to contradict her—"and we could, we could be good. By any standards, even yours."

"That's what I thought," Sarah added. "I thought we had a chance for excellence."

"Yes." Hildy nodded. "I think so too. I am willing."

"And will you sub, Eloise?" Ann asked. "Please? I'll feel more secure."

Under Niki's eye, Eloise agreed.

None of them wondered why it was they were so pleased with the agreement. They all felt excited by the prospect of this team. Ruth's throaty laugh floated over the afternoon air as she suggested they confirm the decision by having ice cream sundaes together. Only Hildy declined, returning to the room to study. The six others trooped down the street to the village, in the golden afternoon.

These times Ann remembered. And the stubborn way Hildy refused to alter that original team, despite Carol's arguments that she was "twice, thrice, ten times the player Ann is," and despite a jealous collective anger among those freshmen excluded from this team. These things passed, and Hildy's team played together, most often with Eloise in position and Hildy coaching. Hildy coached all the freshman teams. She coached everyone except Niki, whom she left alone.

They practiced on weekends too. It was not always convenient, but the girls always made their way to the court. Niki was sure they were ready for the first match game. Hildy agreed, but seemed unimpressed by the challenge. Ann was nervous. She hoped aloud she would sprain a wrist and so cause Eloise to take her place. Eloise declared her prayers for Ann's continued good health.

chapter

4

Niki's father wrote to say he had a new girl friend. He enclosed a photograph of her, and another of the two of them. Niki's father looked young, a handsome young man—slender, golden brown, muscular. He had a shock of brown hair and even, white teeth. Ann, whose father always looked like a respectable, responsible man, whose father would never have been taken for anything other than the Philadelphia lawyer he was, gaped. "He looks so *young*," she protested.

"Well he is. He's not thirty-nine yet." Niki studied the second photograph. "What about her?"

Ann looked at it. "How old is she?"

"He doesn't say. That means he thinks she's pretty young for him. Or he thinks I'll think or somebody'll think. Hildy? What would you say?"

"She looks sixteen, doesn't she?"

"He's not that bad. He doesn't seduce kids."

"Perhaps older than she looks? Where I live she would be sixteen or seventeen. But in California, where everybody stays younger longer—twenty perhaps."

"I can't ever tell people's ages," Ann said.

"Whatever, it's too young," Niki announced.

"What can you do?" Ann shrugged, thinking that this blasé pose rather became her.

"What I always do, tell him I'll go live with my mother," Niki said.

"Huh? You mean you'd go live with her? After all these years when you haven't seen her?"

"I haven't seen her and I don't want to. I didn't say I would go, I said I'd tell *him* I would."

"A threat?" Ann knew better than to try threatening her father. But she didn't have a father who looked, and apparently acted, more like a brother. You could threaten a brother. But a father. . . .

"A threat, Annie. Sometimes it's the only way to bring him around." Niki shrugged. "He gets fixated on these things."

"These women," Ann corrected.

"Not just girl friends. Matter of fact, he's pretty good about his girl friends. Jobs, attitudes, causes; those. He gets *idées fixes*."

Hildy's golden head turned toward them, a halo of lamplight behind it. "Your mother is not dead?" she asked Niki.

"Not a bit of it. They're divorced."

"I am sorry," Hildy said.

"Don't mention it, it's nothing unusual," Niki said, then asked, "Don't people where you live get divorced?"

Hildy shook her head.

"They do where I live," Ann said. "Some of them."

"My parents were divorced when I was about a year old. My dad has custody. He always did."

"How is that so?" asked Hildy.

"He wanted it," Niki shrugged.

"And your mother?"

"She didn't want it. Me."

"How is that possible?"

"Don't ask me. I was just a little kid. My mother lives in Mexico now, somewhere, on the alimony. She never married again, although she's had plenty of lovers. Or at least Dad says so. I don't know for sure. He hasn't married either. I've come in handy for that. If some dame gets serious, he just tells her I can't stand her and he has to put his daughter first. And I usually can't stand them, not as mothers."

"Do you ever hear from your mother?" Ann asked.

"Not since I was little. She stuck around the area when I was young, until I started school. After that she moved out into the Big Sur and I'd go spend a month in the summer with her. Her and her friends. We'd camp, do wilderness stuff. I don't know—I liked her but she scared me. She had this deep theatrical voice, and everything that happened to her was so serious. You know? Her life was a series of crises. I never knew what was going on. I don't know." She looked at the two photographs again, jabbing her finger at them meditatively. "I mean, Dad has his faults, but he's OK. You can figure out what he wants."

"Doesn't your mother—" Hildy began, but Niki interrupted her. "No. Not since she moved to Mexico. I was ten I guess, or nine. And I'm just as glad, let me tell you."

"That isn't right," Hildy said.

"It doesn't matter," Niki shrugged.

"A mother should not leave her child," Hildy continued.

"There's no law that says so," Niki said.

"She must be a strange woman," Hildy said. "Your mother. A bad woman."

"Now wait a minute." Niki's voice had shades of anger to it. "She had her own life to lead, didn't she? A husband and a child, especially the child, they tie you down. She needed to find herself, to know who she is. Women don't have a fair chance at life, you know that, Ann? You know it's true. Not a fair chance at a life of their own. Not tied down the way they are. Unless they're old maids. I don't blame my mother, not one bit. It's what I would do."

Hildy stared vacantly at Niki. "Perhaps. Would you like yourself for doing it? Leaving your child?"

"I don't know," Niki muttered. "How can you know ahead of time, a thing like that? Besides, who are we to judge?"

"Not to judge," Hildy said. "This has nothing to do with judgment. It is wrong."

"Nothing is that simple," Niki said.

"Yes. Some things are. People just—make excuses?—and this complicates things. But these excuses, they are not important. What she did, your mother, was wrong. If you did it, you would be wrong too."

"Well, I wouldn't want to do it probably. I like kids. I do. Male or female, I've got no prejudices. I'd take the kid with me."

"That too," Hildy said sternly.

Niki glared at Hildy. Then she turned her attention to Ann. "Do you know any divorced people?"

"Me? Or my parents?"

"Parents, of course."

"A few. Four, maybe six."

"Any relatives?"

"One of my uncles—his wife—I don't know." It was a

family secret; well, nor exactly a secret but something they preferred to keep private. "He married again."

Niki nodded. "How about you, Hildy?"

"None. Nor have I known any by hearsay." Hildy smiled.

"But what happens out there if the couple is unhappy? What if the husband screws around, or the wife? What if he's cruel to her, or to the kids? What if she drinks? Or takes drugs? What if they just hate each other and can't stand to live together and there is constant fighting and bickering with the kids in the middle all the time?"

Ann sided with Niki. "In some cases, people should divorce. It is so much easier, on the kids, everyone. Better than pretending that you're still happily married and the wife taking the kids off to a summer place; that's expensive too. And the kids play the parents off, one against the other. I agree with Niki."

"It is still wrong, however many agree," Hildy said. Her voice, for such a pronouncement, was curiously soft.

"My God, Hildy—'scuse the language. But listen. What's supposed to happen when a couple begins to fall apart? That can happen you know."

Hildy nodded. "I know."

"People get irrational. Nothing can save the marriage. They can't afford to live in separate places. That happens. What do they do then, in your never-never land? What does a wife do, stuck in the house with a man she hates?"

"She kills him," Hildy said.

Niki's mouth hung open for a second before she laughed. The tension in the room dissipated within the laughter, like a shriek dissipating into the clear sky. "But it's true," Hildy said, through her own laughter. "Why cannot people live apart? Even if in the same house. As if the other were dead. Only, one cannot remarry."

"What's the point in that?" Ann wondered.

"You keep your promises," Hildy said. "You have promised. To one another. To God."

Ann could not answer this objection, but Niki could make an impatient gesture with her hand. "Do you think He cares? If He's there."

"He's there. He cares."

"So He wants people to suffer," Niki pursued.

"That is not it," Hildy said.

"To resist the temptation? He puts the temptation there so we can pass it by? Is that it? A test?"

"No. He does not need to test. He knows."

"Then what's the point? Who put that tree in the garden of Eden?"

"God."

"Why?"

"I don't know. How should I know?"

"And the Jews in Germany? Or the blacks into slavery? Or a kid into a wheelchair, dying piecemeal? And his parents—watching, knowing. Or the Mexicans, the migrant worker. There's a life for you, a test of endurance. What about all of that?"

"How should I know?"

"Not to mention the Crucifixion," Niki continued. Her glance for Hildy was level, straight. "Do you *know* how people were crucified, exactly how they did it? Have you thought about the Crucifixion?"

"Yes. That one; and the many thousands of others so executed."

They looked into one another's eyes, searching. Profound bitterness reflected off, reflected in, profound sorrow.

"Then, what about it?" Niki asked.

"I do not know."

"What *do* you know?"

"There is a purpose. They purpose is good."

Niki shook her head. "That won't do."

"What do you think?" Ann asked Niki. "How do you understand it?"

"Chance," Niki said. "Accident. If I had been a boy for instance."

"Do you really think that?" Ann asked. "Does that mean you blame yourself?"

Niki shrugged.

Ann continued. "Maybe she would have gone anyway. Maybe she just used you as an excuse."

Niki shrugged.

"It's possible, isn't it?" Ann insisted.

"I guess so. But that isn't what happened. It doesn't matter anyway."

"Hildy?" Ann asked.

"It does matter," Hildy said. "And there is a reason. I must go to the observatory."

"A classic *non-sequitur*," Niki said.

"You should take a bike," Ann remarked.

Hildy protested. "It's not far."

"Want to use mine?" Ann offered. Hildy did not have a bike. "No, I mean it. Not tonight, because I haven't gotten a headlight yet, or reflectors. But would you?"

"I would like that," Hildy said. "But—"

"I was going to get that stuff anyway," Ann said. "I promised my mother I would. You know how they worry. She's sure to ask, and this will make sure I do it."

"What do you go twice a week for anyway?" Niki demanded. "There's only one lab a week up there."

"I'm learning to use the telescope," Hildy said.

"What for?" Niki asked.

"To study the stars. I really must go. I am expected." She buttoned a heavy woolen shirt, tied her shoes, and left.

Niki turned to Ann. "Do you ever wonder what will happen when she sheds her illusions?"

Ann nodded, disturbed by the appropriateness of the question. Whenever she thought she understood Niki, Niki threw her off-balance. "Maybe she knows something you don't," Ann ventured.

"Balls." Niki dismissed the possibility.

"I don't think she will," was the strongest defense Ann could make. "Besides, what do you care?"

Niki chewed on her nail and glared at Ann. "Sometimes, I think you're just another stupid preppy bitch," she remarked.

"What do you care?" Ann repeated.

"What do you care?" Niki mimicked her, in a nasal, whiny voice. "Nannynanny booboo and so's your old man," she said. "She doesn't have any money, you know."

Ann looked up. "What do you mean?"

"Full scholarship."

"How do you know?"

"Sarah said."

"How does Sarah know?"

"She knows these things. Don't ask me how. Maybe Hildy told her."

"But she hasn't told me," Ann protested.

"You her best friend or something?" Niki asked.

Ann had thought perhaps so. "I didn't know," she said.

"Do you ever see her spend money?" Niki continued.

"No, never. Look, I've got to read this."

"Why? We don't have class tomorrow."

"There's a test next week; and papers coming up," Ann remarked,

"Tough darts," Niki said. "But I'll leave you to it. We play our first game tomorrow, don't we?"

"Don't remind me. Please don't remind me."

All the match games were scheduled to be played on the gymnasium courts, indoors. As they walked to the gym the next afternoon, the three of them in a row, Ann tried to convince Hildy that Eloise was the better player. "Eloise will get to play," Hildy said.

"I don't want to play," Ann said.

"But you are on the team."

So Ann found herself standing between Hildy and Sarah, goosebumps on her legs. "Maybe nobody will hit anything to me," she said, more to herself than anyone else. The whistle blew.

Carol was serving for the opposing team. Her first serve went directly to Ann, who missed it. The second serve she also fumbled. Niki turned to glare at her. *"Annie."*

"Only lift it up," Hildy said quietly. Ann's cheeks burned. She could lose the whole game, without moving. She looked at Hildy. "Only lift it to me. Think only of that," Hildy said.

Ann concentrated. Carol grinned at her and waved a hand. The serve came to Ann. She thought only of getting it off to the right. Her hands clenched. Too late, she remembered her knees should bend. But she had her fists under the ball and it popped up, shoulder height. Hildy's left hand lifted it higher and sent it to Bess at the net. Bess batted it easily across. Carol ran out of position. "Mine!" she yelled. She hit it up, high and long, back to Ann.

"Only to me," Hildy spoke.

This shot was easier, because high. Ann popped it gently to her right.

"Good," Hildy said as she sent a high set shot forward to

Niki—who leaped up eagerly and hammered down on the ball. Niki turned back to give Hildy the thumbs-up signal. Hildy did not respond.

They rotated to Ann's serve.

"Sarah's beside you," Hildy said.

Ann did not relax, but her panic gradually faded. She managed to initiate a winning point before she served a ball out of bounds.

The game went on, on and on. Carol always sent her shots to Ann. Many, Ann still bungled. More she managed to lift sideways, to Sarah or Hildy. "You're getting it, Annie," Niki exulted. Ann knew better, but was too busy to argue the matter. Most of the other players were no better than she, so she could often play their shots passably. Once, she tried to set a ball for Hildy at the net. It was too low, but Hildy rewarded her daring with a satisfied nod. They won the first game, fifteen to thirteen.

As they switched sides for the second game, Niki called, "Close in," to the team. Nobody altered position. Everybody tensed. Niki was serving and earned seven points before Carol managed to return one of the straight, hard serves. This—Ann sensed it—dispirited the opposing team. Even Carol misplaced her shots, not caring where they went, no longer bothering to play at Ann. The second game took five minutes. Their victory was total, and Hildy's team cavorted about briefly. Then they remembered their manners and thanked the opposition.

"I want a hot fudge sundae," Ruth announced. "Anyone else?"

Everyone else. They trooped out of the gym on a wave of hilarity ("I *told* you, didn't I?" "We creamed them." "Did you see? We outplayed them.") and were seated around a large table at the student center ("I'm going to hate myself in the morning," Bess said as she lifted a spoon mounded with ice cream, dripping thick tears of fudge sauce) before anyone asked, "Where's Hildy?"

She had stayed behind to work with Carol's team on service return. "There was time left in the class," she explained, when Niki later criticized her absence.

Ann said, "I'm not complaining about anything you did— you know that, don't you, Hildy?—because you really helped me. I couldn't have gotten through it without you."

"Yes, you could have. It would have taken longer on your own. That's the only difference."

"But Eloise—she didn't get a chance to play."

"She will, the next game."

Ann was relieved. And chagrined. "Is it the day after tomorrow? Isn't that too soon?"

"No," Hildy said. "We'll practice tomorrow."

"Bess has two tests to study for."

"She will spare the hour."

Bess spared the hour, and then some. They met in the crisp air by the outside court. Hildy would not let them play a game, although Niki argued for it, as the best practice for a match. "But these freshman teams," Niki added as it became clear that the others would do whatever Hildy advised, "they're such creampuffs it doesn't matter." She stayed for about fifteen minutes before she drifted away. Hildy watched her go, eyes squinted toward the lowering sun. Niki walked away, not angry, neither discouraged, just unconcerned. Such drills had nothing to do with her, her narrow back said to those who remained behind.

Hildy had them do a passing drill, around and around the court. At times she required them to shoot only overhead, then only underhand. After that, she set them in one long line and passed shots to them with apparent abandon, because most of the balls fell low, close to the ground, out of reach. Bess was the only one who could tackle such shots, and she did just that: she dived for them. She tried only to get a fist beneath the ball and shoot it aimlessly up. Ruth tried diving, missed, and looked up with a grin. They all tried it. Sarah could save a ball that way, Bess could, and—to her surprise—Ann could. Eloise was hopeless, but when Hildy altered the drill slightly, having them in two lines with the second giving instructions to receive these frantic shots, Eloise proved more able.

One and a half hours later, with the sun's last rays semi-blinding them, Hildy set them up on the court and instructed them, as in the first drill, to pass the ball among themselves. "But I can't see a thing," Ruth protested. "Look," she declared, tapping the ball up and hitting it across the court. "Eloise? you over there?" Eloise was, and she returned the ball to the center front, identifying Ann as the receiver she intended; Ann angled it back to Bess, who sent it across to Sarah.

"I get it," Sarah said. "Why didn't you tell us, Hildy?"

"Tell us what?" Ann asked.

"We're good enough not to have to watch one another all the time. That's right, isn't it?"

"Yes. I thought you knew. I'm sorry, or I could have explained."

"It's amazing," Ruth said, her voice pleased.

"It's alarming," Eloise added, giddy. "Astounding, appalling, abounding, abashing—"

Ann joined in: "Incredible, ineluctable, intangible." She knew how Eloise felt, feeling the same way herself.

"What's all that about?" asked Bess. "Can we do it again?"

They could, completing almost twenty passes before Ann missed a shot that fell unexpectedly at her ankles. She had judged it to be nearer her waist.

"The next step," Hildy said, "is to do the drill without calling the names."

"Why is there always a next step?" Bess groaned. "And I've got two tests. Not today, Hildy."

"No, not today," Hildy agreed.

"Not tomorrow either," Bess continued.

"No, not tomorrow either." Hildy smiled.

They all waited. Smoky, slender clouds, patches of mist really, rose from the ground into the purple sky.

"But someday," Hildy said. "Is someday all right?"

Someday was just fine.

They were too late for dinner, served early and behind resolutely closed dining room doors. They planned to discuss their prospects over sandwiches at the student center and Ann tried to persuade Hildy to join them. Hildy was adamant. All the way back to the dorm, she resisted. She was not hungry, and she could ask the cook to give her a plate of something if she was, and she was putting on weight. It was when Hildy claimed any concern with weight that Ann knew she was lying. Even the intonation was Ann's own. It was not anything Hildy would say. Unless she was pressed.

Ann stopped pressing her. Instead, she returned from the student center with two tunafish sandwiches wrapped in wax paper. She placed these in the center of Hildy's desk and then, satisfied, returned to her own work. That evening it included reading over notes to write the outline for a history paper, as well as memorizing class notes from science.

Ann knew how to concentrate, and her mind was quite occupied by biologic terms when Hildy came back from the library. Ann had forgotten the sandwiches, until Hildy placed them quietly before her. "Thank you, but I cannot take these," Hildy said.

"Why not?" Ann asked. The girl did not answer, just smiled apologetically. Ann argued, "I can't eat them. I'm stuffed. They'll just get thrown out."

"What a waste," Hildy said.

"Are you hungry?" Ann demanded.

Hildy's clear eyes met hers: "Yes."

"Are you angry at me then, that you won't let me spend ninety cents on you and buy you a couple of tunafish sandwiches?"

"It's not that," Hildy said.

"What is it then? I mean, I really don't understand, Hildy."

"I have no money. Well, not much. None for extravagances."

"I know that," Ann said. "Why do you think I wanted to buy you supper?"

"For charity," Hildy said simply.

"Oh," Ann said, wondering if the accusation was accurate. It was an accusation. And Ann was, possibly, guilty.

"I am grateful for your thoughtfulness," Hildy apologized. "But I cannot accept."

"It's only two sandwiches," Ann protested. "It's not a big deal."

"Charity is a big deal, to accept it," Hildy said. "I will tell you something. When I received the scholarship to come here, and my father said I might come for a year, I promised myself that I would be careful of charity. I have had enough."

"You've earned it," Ann said. "They don't give scholarships away because you've got beautiful eyes or play a good volleyball game."

"Oh, I know that. But I don't know what they gave me a scholarship for. My SAT's were not high. Low six hundreds." No, that wasn't high at all. "My grades were good, not excellent. I am not brilliant. Other scholarships went to brilliant girls. Yes?"

Ann had to agree. "I just assumed you were that smart. I wonder why they did it?"

"I don't know. When I first wrote to the College, explaining why I wanted an application blank even though it was most probable I would not be admitted, the letter sent to me in return was most encouraging. I wrote to them, 'I don't know why you encourage me, but I am grateful.'"

Ann looked at her roommate, the blonde hair grown a little longer and now below her earlobes, curling unconcernedly. "I know why," she said, knowing. She couldn't have explained, except to say the words virtue, excellence, and to say them in their ancient Greek form—*arete*.

"Can you tell me?" Hilde asked.

Ann shook her head. Betraying innocence to itself, that must be wrong. She returned to the sandwiches at hand.

"OK. I can understand why you won't let me buy you dinner," she said, "and I won't ask it again. I understand, I do."

"I thought you would."

"But—"

"No," Hildy said, firmly.

"Not for charity." Ann pushed her chair back and stood, sandwiches in hand.

"For what else?"

"For friendship," Ann said.

Hildy's eyes widened briefly in surprise. She lowered her eyes, then raised them again. "Yes," she said. "I thank you."

She reached out for the two packages. Surely not worth such serious argument, Ann thought, and probably soggy by now. Taking them awkwardly, Hildy dropped one onto the floor and, in kneeling to pick it up, she planted her knee on it.

"Oh dear," she said.

"So much for pride and friendship." Ann grinned.

"It will still be edible," Hildy answered. "Only no longer attractive."

"Oh *that*," Ann said. She returned to work. Hildy went to her own desk. Ann heard the rustle of waxed paper combine with the rustling of a book. Ann recited incomprehensible terms, trying to implant definitions in her unwilling memory.

She muttered to herself, irritation barely losing out to training, and she was stopped by a thought: "Hildy, you said one year, why one year?"

"The scholarship is for one year," Hildy answered, without raising her head from the text. "That is one reason."

"Scholarships are renewed, unless something unseemly happens."

"I know. I have been given one year."

"By who? Whom."

"My father."

"Why only a year? What'll you do when you go home?"

"Marry."

Ann turned to stare at her. "Marry? Marry who? Whom."

"I am promised to a man. A widower with young children, a neighbor. A good man."

Ann couldn't think about that. "Do you want to stay here? I mean, would you rather?"

Hildy turned clear eyes to her. "I didn't ever think of it. Why should I think of it?"

Ann couldn't answer that. "They won't like it."

"Who?"

"The College. The Munchkin, for one."

"But she knows. I knew when I filed my application that it must be so."

"Oh," Ann said. "Did you tell them?"

"Of course."

"How much money *do* you have? I mean spending money, for the year."

"Ten dollars and fifty cents. If there is an emergency, I can cash in my return ticket, which should be worth over twenty dollars. I am just fine."

"Good," Ann heard herself say. She was having an idea. She was having two ideas in fact, two possible ideas. For one, she needed her parents' advice and help, so she couldn't think about that until she had written them, or called, or gone home for a weekend.

She worked in the silence of the room for another hour. Hildy sat motionless at her desk. At such times, when Hildy and Ann were alone in the room, Ann felt as contented, as relaxed, as she had ever been, except within her own family. The light in the room was yellow, warm. The sound of quiet breathing or murmuring memorization suited the light. The dark outside the window did not enter, but remained afar, tame as a painting.

At such times, Ann concentrated deeply and swam upward into self-consciousness refreshed. This night, however, she was continually diverted, until her restlessness drove her out of the room to find Niki. At the door she looked back to Hildy, who peered into an English textbook, squinting at it as if by such narrowing of the field of vision, she might hone her understanding.

Niki was in the living room, engrossed in a game of Clue.

"I thought you might be out," Ann said, sitting down by Niki. The six girls were playing on the floor, each hiding her sheet of information behind a large book, each busy with a pencil.

"Damn you Ann, do you have to come barging in like that?" Niki greeted her.

"I'm sorry," Ann said. Always sorry. Even though Clue, as far as Ann could see, was never a serious game.

"Fat lot of good your being sorry does me. Kathy, what did you ask for? And Marsha, you showed her something, right?" Niki's eyes glazed in concentration. Her eyes crackled and her teeth showed.

"I want to talk with you," Ann said.

"For God's sake then—will you wait? It won't be long."

"Won't be long! Niki, have you been cheating? I don't even know *one*."

Niki rolled the die, moved her piece, asked her questions, then made an accusation. It was correct, Ann knew, by the blank looks exchanged around the table. If an incorrect accusation was made, it showed immediately. You could feel it in the air. Then, if you looked around, you could see who held the card you'd named, the person with a little smug smile on his face.

Niki threw down the three cards triumphantly.

"It's a system," she answered their cries of protest. "All logic, logic and careful notation. I'll be back in a few minutes, OK?"

She whisked Ann into the dining room, where they sat at a corner table, far from the girls who were typing papers or letters. "OK. What is it? It must be something, for you to come to me. You need an abortion?" Niki leaned toward Ann, who sat back, away from the thrusting face.

"No, no," Ann said too quickly, inwardly angry at being off-balance again. "It's Hildy," she went on.

"What about her?" Niki's interest faded.

"She really doesn't have any money. Really. Like, ten-fifty for the whole year."

"One thousand fifty? Or ten dollars and fifty?"

"Ten dollars. That's not right is it?"

"I don't see that it's any of our business."

"But there are so any things she can't do. Movies and dinners, weekends. Books."

"Not that I think it's any great loss, but what do you want me to do about it?"

"You've got money, haven't you?"

"Oh no. Not that. Not the Lady Bountiful act. You can masturbate yourself with it, but you're not going to get me to play too."

Ann's cheeks flamed. "You're not being fair."

"Annie. I'm not rich, to begin with. My dad has a good income and he spends most of it. Some on me, yeah, but it's not like we have oil wells or hosiery companies. That's one thing. But I don't give charity—on principle. What are we going to do, go trundling up to Hildy and say, 'Oh we are so sorry you don't have an allowance like everyone else so we are going to give you an allowance Ann and me aren't we wonderful?' Holy crap, Annie. I'm not wild about you, but I never figured you for such an ass." Niki put her finger in her mouth and watched Ann's face.

Ann's enthusiasm gave way before Niki's negative force: she was close to tears, baby tears, whiny tears of frustration. "You're right," she said, quite adult. "Of course, you're right. I should have thought."

Ann started to rise, but Niki's long arm shot out and held her wrist to the table. "Why do you give up like that, so easily? So what if I'm right?"

"What are you doing?" Ann pulled her wrist free. She had had about all she could take, she felt sure of that.

"Think you'll cry?" Niki needled. "Annie?"

Tears welled up behind Ann's eyes.

"You're a quitter, Annie." Niki stood and left the dining

room, deliberately not closing the curtained doors. The two typists raised irritated faces, and Ann hurried out, her head bobbing apologetically.

Ann went out outside. The air was cold, iron-edged. Ann's lungs were offended at it, but she remained on the porch, breathing deeply. "Ohellohell," she crooned to herself, until her emotions settled. The leaves rustled in a light breeze. The grass looked purplish in the artificial light. Ann stepped off the porch and onto the grass. She moved away from the light into the dark created by the tall presences of oaks and maples, sycamores, birches, beeches. She rubbed at her upper arms, to warm herself.

The bleak sky was sprayed with points of light, and the arc of the new moon hung close to the earth. Ann turned her face to the stars. Specks of light, bright, white, crisp—*golden fire*, Shakespeare had said, and *fretted*. Fretted had two meanings. Fretwork, as the filigreed Indian screens. And to fret, to bother, irritate, annoy.

Was Niki right? Was she a quitter? It could be. Niki seemed to enjoy causing pain, but she was usually astute about people. She had a good sense for where a person was vulnerable, and she would go for that spot, like a dog leaping for the jugular, clamorous in attack. Not silent, skulking. Niki wouldn't skulk anywhere, not after anything.

So she might be a quitter. But what more could she do? She had thought that if she and Niki together did it, then Hildy couldn't refuse, but if Niki wouldn't cooperate—there wasn't anyone else. Roommates were different. She had wanted to do something good, something kind and generous. And Niki made her feel—awful. And then told her she was a quitter. A tear was running down her nose. What more could she do?

Two juniors walked toward the house, talking loudly. Pride dried Ann's eyes and spirits. She would have been so ashamed, caught sniveling—the very thought humiliated her.

"Hey, Ann. What're you doing?"

"Taking a break." Ann kept her voice quiet. "Smelling winter coming down." She smiled, because she had thought of something else she might try, if she could work herself up to it.

Ann would talk with the Munchkin about Hildy. Miss Dennis would know if anything could be done. Hildy was virtually teaching the freshman volleyball section. She set up all the matches, saw to supplies, kept the balls inflated, took attendance, everything. Hildy was coaching them.

Ann ran back inside the house. It was *cold* out there. She stopped in the reception area where the girl on watch commented on her nuttiness in going out without a heavy sweater. Niki emerged from the living room, a few Clue cards clutched tight. "You know what worries *me?*" she said, walking with Ann to the stairs. "Not this surface crap. Money and clothes, they're not worth pissing on. You know what I wonder?"

"What?"

"Look at me, will you?"

Ann turned.

"The way she reads with the books so close to her eyes."

"I haven't noticed," Ann protested, trying to move away.

"I'll tell you what," Niki said. "When you go in, see how close her eyes are to the page, then try reading with yours that close. I think she needs reading glasses. And ten dollars and fifty cents will not buy you those. Not in this world, Annie." Niki clapped Ann on the shoulder for emphasis and loped back into the living room, shrieking, "It's my turn! Mine!"

chapter

5

Ann made her appointment with the Munchkin for one evening when Hildy rode off to the observatory. Hildy would never ask where she was going, but Ann opted for secrecy. It rained that night, a dark storm rending leaves from trees, bending supple branches, driving the water before it. Ann's raincoat was soaked through after a five-minute walk. She dripped on the Munchkin's porch for a desolate time before ringing the bell. To be bedraggled made her feel at a tangible disadvantage.

Miss Dennis answered promptly. The light behind her was dry and warm. "Miss Gardner. Do shake yourself."

Ann complied. She hung her coat on a wall hook and stood, awkward.

"I have a pot of tea. And a fire."

The Munchkin wore trousers and a shapeless beige sweater, which made Ann feel overdressed. She followed the small figure down a short hallway to a small study, a mannish room with its leather, wood, and books. A comfortable room, not an attractive one. There were no curtains.

Unable to begin speaking, Ann accepted a cup of tea and sat gratefully in the warmth pouring from the deep fireplace.

The Munchkin sat facing her, in a matching leather chair. Her eyes stayed on Ann's face, unblinking. She waited.

Ann began: "You said we could ask advice."

A pained expression, quickly disguised into irony, passed over the round, wrinkled face.

"In your opening day speech."

"Not a speech. I did so hope not to give a speech."

"No, of course not, I didn't mean *that*."

"Was it so bad?" the Munchkin demanded quickly.

"I didn't mean that," Ann said again. She blushed. She saw

that the little woman's feet did not touch the floor, and looked
quickly away. "Miss Dennis, I . . ."

"Want some advice," the Munchkin finished, after a bit.
"Not about men, I hope."

"Of course not," Ann disclaimed quickly, and felt her face
grow hot again. She lost her train of thought.

Miss Dennis waited, again, then asked again. "Advice, you
said."

"It's my roommate," Ann said. Her approach to the
proposal had been so clear in her mind.

"You can't get along with Miss Jones."

"No. Not that. Give me a chance," Ann protested.

The gray eyes twinkled at her. "All right, here is your
chance."

"Hildy. Miss Koenig."

"I remember."

"She has a scholarship."

"I know."

"She has no money."

"Yes?"

"I shouldn't be here talking about this, should I? I'm
meddling, I know that. I'm not a meddler."

"I will assume that your intentions are good ones. Let that
conclude the ethical quibbling. Just what is your point?"

"Ten dollars for the whole year," Ann continued. "And fifty
cents."

"Ah. Not an abundance. Is she concerned about this?"

"Hildy? No."

"But you are. Why is that?"

"She can't do things with us, like going downtown. But
that's not important. And it doesn't bother her at all. She'll
have to stay East over the vacations, but she can come home
with me—I'd like that, so that doesn't matter. But Niki
noticed—Miss Jones—that Hildy's eyes are bad. When Hildy
reads, the book is no more than three inches from her eyes.
Even then she squints and wrinkles up her eyebrows. You can't
read from that distance. She couldn't afford glasses, you see."

"Or an eye examination."

"And she doesn't like taking things, presents. Charity, Hildy calls it." Ann debated adding this next, but decided to. "Even the scholarship."

The Munchkin nodded. "I'd be inclined to trust Miss Jones's observations."

Ann agreed eagerly. "She told me and I watched Hildy. When Hildy writes, her face almost lies on the paper."

"You have an idea, I think," Miss Dennis suggested.

"Yes, I do. I don't know if you know that Hildy has been running the freshman volleyball classes."

Miss Dennis smiled. "I heard something of it. Some words were spoken. Miss Stookings—you won't remember her?"

Ann shook her head.

"The graduate instructress. She came to see me. More in sorrow than in anger, it seemed. However, since she had to agree that Miss Koenig was capable, I could see no objection to what had clearly been a successful plan. The decision was, as they say, in my province."

"I didn't know that," Ann said. "It all happened so easily."

"Thank you," Miss Dennis bowed her head. Ann had relaxed enough to smile.

"Niki will like that."

"You will not tell Miss Jones."

"Oh."

"Oh, indeed. But, your proposal is?"

"Could Hildy be paid for that work? Could the College pay her for what she's doing? Or, I could ask my parents and they could give you the money and you could say it was from the College."

"I think we can discount the latter, don't you?" The Munchkin's gaze brightened. She refilled their tea cups and sat looking into the flames. "What were you thinking of?"

"I beg your pardon?" Ann asked.

"How much money were you thinking of?"

"I wasn't," Ann admitted.

"Right and proper, if foolish." Miss Dennis said. "What is the usual monthly allowance?"

"I have no idea."

"Surely you have an allowance."

"Not exactly. My parents put money into my account when I need it."

"I see. Well then, I'll think about the suggestion, and do what I judge is correct."

"Is it within your province?"

"I believe so. I believe it can be put there. I am not so certain that Miss Koenig will consent to see an optometrist."

"Why shouldn't she?"

"I don't pretend to understand Miss Koenig. But let me make a deal with you. I will do what I can about remuneration, and you will do what you can about an optometrist. Agreed?"

"Agreed."

They shook hands, leaning toward one another before the fire.

"Mine may well be the easy task," Miss Dennis warned Ann.

"It would be silly not to, and Hildy isn't silly." Ann stood up, to leave. Miss Dennis did not protest. It had all been so much easier than Ann had hoped. At the door, her sodden raincoat cold around her body, she turned to try to express her gratitude. Miss Dennis raised her eyebrows, forbidding.

"I just want to say," Ann said, then—unable to halt the stumbling words—"that I am really enjoying your course." She walked out quickly into the cold rain, mumbling her thanks, wondering if she would ever be able to say things as she wanted to.

Ann decided she would give Miss Dennis a week. If she had not heard about her proposal within a week, she would assume that the Munchkin had decided it was not suitable or had been unable to convince the College. Two days later, Hildy approached Niki with a typewritten letter. It was the long hour before dinner and Niki was working out a math problem. "What of this?" Hildy asked. Niki turned. Ann watched the scene.

Niki read the letter. Her expression was puzzled. "Was there a check?"

Hildy produced it. Niki looked at it, then reread the letter. Ann, shading an inner glow, said, "What's going on?"

"I am not sure," Hildy said.

"It seems," Niki said, "that Hildy's work with the volleyball class has not gone unnoticed. The Munchkin's all-seeing eye has fallen on her."

"And?" Ann prompted.

"They will pay me," Hildy said. "That is what the letter says, isn't it?" Niki nodded.

"Generously," Niki added. "They worked it all out, hours in class, hours extra."

"May I see?"

The letter was from Miss Dennis. It was short and simple. The College considered a trained Physical Education Instructor to earn twenty-five dollars per class, plus twenty-five dollars a week for preparation, maintenance, etc. Hildy would be paid for half the work, by virtue of talking on half of an assignment. The enclosed check represented the salary for the past four weeks of classes. Henceforth, she would be paid by the week.

"That *is* generous," Ann said. She looked at Hildy.

"They think of me as a trained instuctress," Hildy said.

"Apparently," Niki said. "Nice going."

"But I didn't *ask*," Hildy said. Her eyes were puzzled. "I wonder if it is right to accept this."

"Hildy!"

Niki silenced Ann with a dark glance. "Why not?" she asked. "Look. You didn't ask, so they must have thought it was the right thing to do. There's no reason why you shouldn't get the usual pay, is there? You should get more than usual— you're much better than Whoozis was. They're just playing fair."

"But I have already a full scholarship," Hildy argued. "Surely that is enough. I would think of the volleyball class as a small return to the College."

"Ah." Niki grinned. "That's it."

"What?" Hildy asked. "What is? What is what? Tell me."

"I was wondering why the Munchkin didn't do this in person. Now I know. You'd have gone all righteous on her. You would have refused the payment—now be honest about it, Hildy—and say something devastatingly simple about your gratitude."

"Perhaps I would. Is that righteousness? I am not righteous, am I?"

Niki looked at Ann. "Annie?"

"Not righteous," Ann soothed Hildy. "But all the time Right. Do you really think Miss Dennis couldn't face Hildy? That doesn't seem like her."

"I'm sure she had some deep and complex plan," Niki said, "which comes down to—she didn't want to face Hildy."

"Why not?" Hildy wondered.

Niki shrugged. "You're too tall, I guess."

"Not in the brain I'm not, and that is how she measures. I do not understand what she says in Philosophy lectures. I read and read and do not understand what she says. In the section meetings, Miss Dennis will answer my questions and those answers I understand. But I know she spepaks only from the surface of all her knowledge. To make things easy for me to understand." Hildy considered, and concluded, "No, she would not be afraid of speaking directly with me."

"But that's not as official," Ann said. "Official things are what is written down and put on the record."

"Yes," Hildy nodded. "So I should write and accept, to be official."

"There's no question of acceptance, is there?" asked Niki.

"Not in their letter," Ann agreed. "Maybe just thanks?"

"Are you sure? Then I will write to thank them."

"What're you going to do with this new-found wealth?" Niki asked.

"I shall open a bank account," Hildy said. "I will be able to return to my family with some money. My father will approve of that. I will have a small dowry."

"You're just going to bank it? All? I'm disappointed in you," Niki said.

"Not all. I'm going to buy myself a dress. Like that one Ann has, the one I wore to the tea. Will you come with me, Ann?"

"Of course." Ann was flattered, flattered and pleased.

Niki said, "Tell you what I'd do, if I was you."

"What?"

"Have my eyes checked."

"My eyes checked? But why?"

Ann looked at Niki.

"You hold the book too close when you read. Something's wrong."

"No, nothing's wrong," Hildy said. "I have the eyes I was born with. The expense of an eye doctor—" Hildy shook her head. "I will get some school stationary from the house-mother." She left the room.

Ann and Niki kept silence for a moment.

"I'll keep after her," Niki said, watching Ann's face. Then, shockingly, she grinned and hugged Ann, hard and brief.

"What?"

"I knew you'd think of a way," Niki said. "Good job, Annie."

Ann allowed the glow of pleasure to spread through her before she resolutely put it aside. "There's something I want to tell you," she said, remembering what the Munchkin had said about Miss Stookings. "But I can't until we graduate. Remind me on graduation."

"You'll have to do it by mail," Niki said. "I'll be in California. But I'll remind you—even if we haven't kept in touch. Let's go eat."

The second volleyball match was easier than the first and Hildy's team won quickly and easily. After this match, Sarah told Hildy that she would be away for the next but one, scheduled for a Saturday. "I'm going down for the Yale-Princeton game," she said. "Couldn't you change the match date?"

"I don't think so," Hildy said. "You will have to change your plans."

"I'll need to think about that," Sarah said.

Niki kept after Hildy about seeing an optometrist. The variety of her approaches dazzled Ann. She spoke of a cousin who had to undergo expensive surgery after ignoring weakness in his eyes. "He'd have gone blind," Niki said. "Hildy?" "I will not go blind," Hildy said. "My eyes are as they have always been."

Niki inquired about Hildy's regular checkups. "I have never had one." "Didn't the school require it?" "Why should they?"

Or, at breakfast, "What do you see?" Niki would ask Hildy. "Tables, eggs, Ann," Hildy answered.

"What do you see?" Niki asked, as they walked to classes in the morning. "The sky gray and low, heavy with rain," Hildy said. "Trees in before-winter bareness. The sidewalk white, almost as if snow had already fallen."

"Who is that?" Niki pointed to a distant figure. "Someone glad."

Ann tried once, when they were alone in the room. "What if Niki's right about your eyes?"

"You think she is?" Hildy asked.

"Yes."

"You don't often agree with Niki," Hildy observed before she returned to her studies.

Studies took a great deal of Hildy's time. Their first set of tests and papers had not been graded, so Ann had no plumbline for judging Hildy's abilities, but the amount of time Hildy spent at her studies roused Ann's curiosity. However, Hildy did find an hour, her first free afternoon, to go shopping with Ann. "Find me a dress like yours," Hildy directed her.

Ann protested.

"You'll know it," Hildy argued. "I was pretty in that dress, but I could not find it for myself."

"You're pretty in anything," Ann said. It was the simple truth.

"That dress was particular," Hildy said.

Ann agreed, and found Hildy a Lanz of similar style and fabric. Hildy did not like the price ("That is three times what I have ever paid"); because it was what she wanted, she bought it.

The third freshman volleyball match was another easy victory. After it, Hildy formally challenged the lowest sophomore team, for the next Saturday.

Sarah came over in the evening to talk with Hildy. "I can't play," she said.

Hildy nodded.

"No, you've got to listen, Hildy. I called and asked if he'd understand. I tried to explain how I felt, and how you feel, and who you are and what you're like. But he—Timmy, Timmy said that the weekend was important to him."

Hildy nodded.

"He doesn't say that lightly. And Hildy, it's the only time I'll get to see him before Christmas. He's—I couldn't go all the way until Christmas vacation without seeing him. I miss him, do you know what that means?"

"Yes, I know," Hildy said. "I can understand."

"So you understand why I can't play?"

"No," Hildy said. "I can understand that it is a difficult choice for you."

"Are you angry?"

"Not angry," Hildy said.

"Fat lot of good that does me. Ann?" Sarah asked for help.

"Couldn't we change the date?" Ann asked.

"No," Hildy said. "It is worked in among many other matches."

"Why don't we play it Sunday afternoon. You could get back by late Sunday, couldn't you, Sarah?"

"If I left early in the morning," Sarah said. She turned the idea over in her mind. "I'd do that, Hildy. Can we play it on Sunday?"

"Not Sunday," Hildy said.

"Why not?"

"It is the Sabbath."

"But we've practiced on Sundays," Sarah said.

"We do not play matches on a Sunday," Hildy said.

"That doesn't make sense," Ann said. "Be fair. You're not being fair."

"I am. Sarah has made her choice. I have said nothing to sway her."

"Does this mean," Sarah stood at the door, "that I am off the team?" She put her hands into her pockets. "I really don't want to be dropped."

"Why should you be dropped?" Hildy sounded surprised.

"Hildy," Ann said, "what about those people who didn't come to the first practice? Remember?"

"They had said they would come and then did not," Hildy explained, as if it were the most obvious distinction imaginable, as if surprised that such a thought should not cross their minds. "Sarah has not done that. She has merely made a choice."

"Boy, I'm glad I told you as soon as I knew."

"Who'll take her place?"

"Eloise will."

"Who will take Eloise's place?"

"No one. We do not need seven players, only six."

"That's OK then," Sarah said. "I'm sorry, Hildy."

"I know that," Hildy said.

After Sarah left, Hildy did not return to her work, but remained facing Ann, her face puzzled.

Ann tried to explain: "You were so unyielding, that other time. I can see why she thought she'd be dropped."

"Then you also did not understand?"

"No. Was I supposed to?"

"It doesn't matter. Am I allowed to ask you to help me?"

"What?" Ann said. "What are you talking about."

"I wrote a theme. In English. The professor has given it back to me. He has instructed me to rewrite it."

Ann had never heard of such a thing.

"He says it is not good enough. I must do a better job," Hildy said. "But I can't do better: this was the best I could do. I wonder if you could read it and help me make it better. Is that allowed?"

"Of course. As long as you're the one who writes it. What do you want me to do?"

"Read it, I think, don't you? And then tell me what the mistakes are and how to correct them? And then——"

"Just give it to me," Ann said. "We'll get to the *and then's* later. You're a babe in the woods, Hildy."

"I think so," Hildy said. She gave Ann three handwritten pages. "It is also too short, he said. I've never had themes to write for English before. So I don't know what is expected. Can you tell me that? And explain how I can learn to do it?"

"Stop talking," Ann said.

The paper was untitled. Hildy's topic was, apparently, names in the *Odyssey*. Ann read the paper slowly. It wasn't about names, by the time she got to the end. What was it about? Recognition? Self-knowledge?

Ann read it through again.

All of the paragraphs could be tied in with naming, if she thought about it. But as to what Hildy had actually *said*, Ann was not sure. Hildy's use of language was correct. It was the jumble of ideas that confused.

"What was your outline?" Ann asked.

"I do not know outlining. I thought to write about the unveilings. The professor mentioned that one day. It had to do with the theme of human excellence. He said—the professor— that the most important question for the book is: Why did Odysseus refuse Calypso's offer of eternal life?"

Ann nodded. She remembered.

"Can you help me?" Hildy said. "If you could tell me what to do?" She waited, with bright expectancy.

"I don't know, Hildy. You see, I can't understand what you are trying to say in this."

Hildy shook her head.

"I can't follow your ideas. And sometimes, you seem to lose the thread of what you're saying so that all your grammar indicates that *this* is the main idea of the sentence, but what you actually say indicates that *that* is the main idea. Does that make sense?"

Hildy's color was higher. "Yes," she said. "No. I think I understand, but I do not know how to fix it. All the spelling is correct?"

"That, yes. And the grammar. But— You see, I could write it myself—"

"No, no. That is plagiarism." Hildy took the paper out of Ann's hands.

"Let me finish the sentence. I could write it myself, but I can't figure out how to explain what I'd do, or why I'd do it."

This Hildy did understand. "Make it as simple as you can. What is the most basic thing I do wrong?"

"Basically? I think . . ." Ann hesitated and then continued. "I think that you don't consider words real. Not real as things are real. Not like desks or volleyballs or eggs. Does that make sense?"

Hildy nodded. Watching her face, Ann felt that Hildy understood everything she was saying, and much of what she was trying to say.

"If grammar is the orderly presentation of ideas, you don't use words and grammar to present your ideas," Ann said. "You write as if the two were not related."

"What two?"

"The idea, and the tools you use to express it."

Hildy mused: "I think I see. If words are real, like stars, absolutely there. . . . Good. Now, what do I do?"

Ann considered. Hildy needed quotes in the paper and to recast most of the sentences. She needed to put in transitions and to write an introduction.

"Make an outline."

Niki burst into the room. Ann immediately felt foolish, but

Hildy ignored Niki's presence. Niki listened for a while, then sat at her desk, unexpectedly muted. Ann forgot she was there.

"Why do I need an outline?"

"For a plan. Everything you write about should have to do with your topic."

Hildy's face grew puzzled again. She shook her head and looked at Ann.

"Look," Ann said. She pointed her pencil at a paragraph. "What does this have to do with unveiling? With showing who someone truly is?"

"Oh," Hildy said. She turned to her desk. Ann sat and watched the back of her head, bent low over the paper. Ann did not move, because a fragile picture was forming in her head and to jar it would be to destroy it. Hildy's mind was clumsy, cumbersome—like what, in its befuddlement with abstraction, its lack of polishing technique? Also, its abundance of possibilities. Her perceptions were true. Like a forest, perhaps, wild and profuse in its growth, some several strong and noble trees growing above a tangled floor. Like a forest, accidental, at least in human terms, in its self-management. And large: one did not weed a forest to bring order. A forest was too complex an arrangement of livings, too tough in its own right, for garden management. To improve a forest one would have to deal with the essential ingredients, and be patient. Like, adjusting soil balance or planting seedlings, and then waiting to see. Because what you planted would be altered by the nature of the forest into something other than you had imagined.

Whereas Ann's own mind was water, a lake held within controlling banks, sensitive to induced changes, but always with unexpected water-promises. Things would float to the surface and, within limits, move free. You could easily see how to alter and improve a lake, although you could not predict what it might give up to you from its unseen depths.

How would you teach a mind like Hildy's? Not by piddling weed-pulling points. And how teach it without changing its real nature?

Hildy returned with a new sheet of paper, topic and subtopics.

"That's it," Ann said. "Can you see it now?"

Hildy shook her head, apologetically.

"Wait," Ann thought. "How long was this supposed to be?"

"More than five. Less than ten."

"Typwritten?"

Hildy nodded. "I can't type. I don't have a typewriter. He said it had to be typed too, the rewrite."

Niki spoke: "Did he write this down, or just tell you?"

"He spoke to me after class."

"I could have guessed he'd be too busy," Niki said. "Don't worry about typing, OK? I can easily knock off ten pages."

"That's fine," Hildy said.

Ann had been thinking. Hildy's outline would produce only two or three pages. "What does it mean about Odysseus if nobody recognizes him?" she asked, trying to show Hildy that there was more to write about.

"But that is not true," Hildy said. "His wife does."

"What do you mean Penelope does?" Niki interrupted. "She's the worst of the lot. She doesn't know who he is even after he tells her. Not until that stupid test about what their bed was like."

"Oh, I think she does," Hildy said. "He is her husband and she loves him."

"If she loves him, why did she send her suitors those secret love letters?"

"For her son. And for her husband, her son's father. She is in a difficult position, you see. He has been away for so long, her husband; the suitors no longer fear him or they would not be there, living in his house. If the suitors understand that she will not marry any one of them, they will take the property by force. Her son's property. And maybe take her, too, by force. So she must make each man think he is the one she would choose, when she can lawfully choose. She must encourage them just enough, each one. And she must stay firm until her son is grown to manhood and can fight for himself and hold his father's property. Or until Odysseus returns."

Ann looked up from the outline. "Hildy, did your professor tell you that?"

"No. He did not like Penelope. He liked, I think, Calypso for Odysseus. He said Odysseus was diminished at the conclusion, in his woman. I do not understand what he meant by that."

"The idea about Penelope," Ann said, "is it your own?"

"Yes."

"Can you prove it?"

"How should I prove it? It is clear to me. The kind of woman she was."

"Can you take that idea and show how it explains the way she acts in different scenes? Can you show how she shows she knows, by referring to things she says and does?"

"Of course."

"Then that's your paper."

"What of these?" Hildy pointed to her outline.

"It's not as good, not nearly. Why did you take that topic anyway?"

"The professor talked about things like that. Unveiling, diminishing, the function of the gods. I thought these were the kinds of ideas I should be having."

"They're OK," Ann said. "But that's not the way *you* read the book, is it? Hildy, when you pick a paper topic, you should always pick something you're good at. I'd guess you're good at character. At people."

Niki asked Ann: "You've studied this? You seem to know what you're talking about."

"A couple of years ago."

"Good memory."

Ann nodded. "I told you, it's a talent."

"You recommend that I write about Penelope," Hildy said.

"Try it. Try it and see how it goes. Make an outline and all that."

Hildy nodded. "I think so. Will you read it when I am through?"

"Sure," Ann said.

For a brief time, Ann thought about Penelope. If she had recognized him. If she was the master, not the gull. Then Penelope too had excellence, human excellence. And there were some scenes of high comedy. Ann knew how she would approach the paper, how she would place fact atop fact and have an impregnable wall built, before she named her thesis. What would Hildy do, being earth and not water? Ann cleared her head and turned to the Greek middle and passive voices.

But Niki interrupted her concentration by slipping a sheet of paper before her eyes. It was labeled *The Socrates Award*. Niki had drawn a prize ribbon, then shaded it in with blue pencil. *To Ann Gardner,* the writing went on, under the ribbon. *Here's to you, Annie.* At the bottom of the page a hand held out a crude goblet inscribed with the word *hemlock.*

If she and Hildy were water and earth, then Niki was fire, Ann thought. Crackling, hot, destructive. She put the award into the center drawer of her desk, considered a minute, and pulled out a blank sheet of typing paper. *Thanks, Niki,* she scrawled. She dotted the i's in Niki with circles, in which she drew little smiling faces, each topped with a curlicue of hair. This she placed on Niki's desk.

Niki looked up at her, "Sweet, very sweet."

Hildy was bent down over the paper on her desk, her pen moving methodically along.

Ann read this second paper. The ideas were orderly and strong. They were not skillfully presented, but the argument was clear, direct. It sounded like Hildy. "Penelope is always in control of things," Hildy declared in her first sentence.

"Is it good enough?" Hildy asked.

"I think so," Ann said. "You need to rewrite it for polish—"

"No," Hildy said. "I could not. That is the best I can do, for now. I think my next paper will be equally good, so I have learned. I cannot yet polish."

Niki typed it up and the next day Hildy handed it in. She told Niki and Ann that the professor read it through while she watched, nodded his head, and said he would accept it although it was not in the style he understood all Stanton students had mastered.

"But he took it," Niki said to Hildy. "It'll be all right. I was afraid, from what you said about him, that he'd refuse it because of the ideas."

"Why should he do that?" Hildy asked.

"You said he didn't care for Penelope. Your paper contradicted him."

"He told me my thesis was an interesting one," Hildy reported.

"I'm glad," Niki said. "Really I am. I'm just surprised."

"You shouldn't be," Ann remarked. "This is the Northeast."

"No gloating," Niki answered. "Gloating's not allowed."

Inevitably, the next Saturday arrived. Ann found herself surprisingly calm before their match with the fourth-ranked sophomore team. Eloise was pale and speechless. She polished her glasses vigorously. Niki bounced onto the court with taut energy. She stared at Eloise before she spoke: "You're a fledgling Munchkin," she announced. Eloise smiled a little. Niki punched her lightly on the arm. "Buck up. We'll murder them. You won't have to do a thing: I'll be right beside you."

"Is that supposed to make me feel better?" Eloise asked. Niki laughed. "To make *me* feel better," she answered.

"You'll be fine." Hildy spoke from behind Eloise. "You know how to keep the ball in play if you can't make a shot." Elois nodded and polished her glasses again.

An audience had come to this game. It was mostly freshmen from the volleyball class scattered sparsely over the benches, but the Munchkin's gray presence occupied one end of the front row.

The first few points were played tentatively, by both sides. The sophomores had played together for almost two seasons, and that experience showed in their control and confidence. Even Niki was subdued by this. The score was tied at five-five when the sophomores quickened the pace. They gained five more points, in quick succession. Ann felt herself growing still more calm. This was what she had expected, to lose.

Niki's face was dark as she served. She seemed about to explode, all knotted muscles and angry eyes. Ann looked around. The faces of defeat, she said to herself, heavy, expressionless faces. Hildy alone held her body ready to move, her face alert.

Niki tried for too much power in her serve, mis-hit the ball, and gave the opposing team an easy return. They sent it floating over to Ann, who debated seeing if it would go out of bounds, then moved too late to save it.

"You twit," Niki muttered. "Annie. Even you could get that." Ann responded with familiar sullen self-pity and anger.

"She is right," Hildy's quiet voice remarked. Ann flooded with shame. "We should win this match, but we cannot if we *expect* to lose it."

Her voice carried around their court, no further. "OK," Ann said to herself. "OK, OK."

Eloise flexed her knees and polished her glasses, yet again. Bess straightened her shoulders and spread out her strong arms. Ruth touched her toes twice, quickly, and all the laughter was gone from her face when she raised it the second time. Niki crouched, fiercer, if possible.

They won back the serve. Then Hildy served for them, the balls placed so as to force the opponents to return shots from off-balanced positions. Eloise executed a perfect set, which Niki drove into the feet of the sophomore facing her. Ann returned a long shot to an unwary back linesman. Ruth passed quickly to Bess who as quickly sent it full across court. The score was tied. More important, they had assumed control of the game.

The sophomores spoke among themselves. "When that tiger moves off the front line," they said. "Hit to the one with glasses, they're protecting her." But Eloise could keep a ball in play most of the time, and the girls beside her and behind her covered efficiently. Niki spiked, time and again. Hildy spiked seldom, but blocked with dazzling accuracy. Once she called to Ann to block with her and, to her own amazement, Ann did. She did not touch the ball, nor did she jump as high as Hildy; but it was as if Hildy could pull her upward. "I see," Ann said to herself, "I see how." This too she would practice.

Eloise muttered Latin declensions to herself, dried her hands on the seat of her shorts, and played with unwavering steadiness. Niki perspired abundantly. Hildy, like a beam of light, moved among them.

They took the first game seventeen to fifteen. The teams changed courts without speaking. Ann muttered to Eloise, "You might move on to conjugations." Eloise nodded her head, but could not answer.

It was halfway through the second game that the opposing team creaked, cracked, and crumbled. Ann felt it. The freshmen did not relax their efforts, but all sensed the collapse. More and more, individuals tried to take shots, crowding the net to spike, or calling for returns that were not properly theirs.

After the freshman victory, the sophomores congratulated them. "Good game," they said. "We'll try again."

Niki shook her head. Sweat flew off her face. "You won't have a chance," she said.

"Eat it," a sophomore muttered.

"Watch your language," Niki snapped, and Ann suddenly understood how Niki was keeping faith with Hildy.

"What are you, a bunch of effing saints?"

"You're that ashamed of losing," Niki observed. "Is it humiliating?"

The sophomore glared. "We'll catch you on the way down."

"Hold your breath. Apoplexy becomes you."

The girl turned angrily away. "Gracious me," Niki said.

Ann answered her: "I thought it was more of a meeting of the minds."

"Annie. You, vicious? I never would have thought it."

The Munchkin approached their team. The girls fell silent. "You have done well," she said. "I shall make a point of seeing more of your matches." She left abruptly.

Eloise still sat where she had collapsed at the end of the last point. "That was terrible," she said. She took off her glasses and polished them. "Look, I'm trembling."

Hildy gave her a hand up. "You were fine."

They showered and agreed to eat out. Hildy said she would join them. She had never had pizza, so they walked to the local pizzeria.

Ruth wolfed down two succulent slices before she asked. "Could you feel it? Everybody. I want to know, could you feel them giving up?"

"Yeah," Ann said. "I've never felt that happening before, even when I was winning a tennis match. Which wasn't often," she hastened to add.

"People will always give up," Niki said. "If you go at them hard enough, long enough. That's right, isn't it, Annie?"

"I guess so," she said. "I do."

"We know," Niki said.

"Lay off," Bess directed mildly. "This is a celebration, remember?"

Niki continued. "The secret is to hate the opposition. There's only so much hatred people can withstand."

"You're kidding," Ruth said.

"No. I always do. Don't you, Hildy?"

"Why should I?"

"Because you have to break them in order to win," Niki said.

"They will lose when we outplay them. To break them? I don't want that. Then I have not won, but destroyed."

"And it's only a game," Ruth contributed. "It matters not if you win or lose," she sing-songed at them, "but how you play the game."

"Hah," Niki said.

"Anyway, I could feel them giving up, or seeing it slip away from them." Ann continued her own thoughts. "What happens in professional sports?"

"The same thing," Niki said.

"How can it, when everybody has that drive? When everyone feels the way you do?"

"One team or even one player has it more. The killer instinct."

That evening, Sarah called long distance and asked for Ann. "What happened? How did we do? We've only got a minute or two."

"We won."

"How was Eloise?"

"OK, she was OK. Poor kid, it gave her the fidgets. She was a brick."

"How many games?"

"In two, like before."

"Then we still haven't lost a game."

The operator interrupted.

"Having a wonderful time?" Ann asked.

"Now I will," Sarah answered. "Tell Hildy I'm glad."

Ann gave Hildy Sarah's message later that evening. Niki sat up in bed to greet the third girl and remarked: "Have you ever thought, Hildy, that if there is something wrong with your eyes and you had glasses, you might spend less time studying?"

"I enjoy studying," Hildy said. "The library is quiet, as a church."

"You ought to think about it, at least," Niki said.

Hildy shook her head, patiently.

Niki threw back the covers and jumped out of bed. She pulled on jeans and a shirt. "You know how to give orders but not take them," she said. She slammed out of the room.

Ann watched Hildy's smile. "You don't mind her being angry?"

"That is not anger. That is acting."

Ann found Niki downstairs, dealing a hand of bridge, entirely cheerful.

The next morning, Sunday, Niki woke Ann. Hildy had already left for church. "Ann? Wake up. How can you sleep through those bells?"

The music of the bells reverberated among the hills. Ann listened.

"Seriously. Tell me. Don't they drive you crazy?"

Ann fixed Niki with a beady glance. *"They* don't wake me up. *They* don't drive me crazy."

"I'm gonna get those bells before I leave," Niki said.

Ann closed her eyes, then opened them to remark, "The sun's out."

"Yeah. It feels like a warm day. I always thought once fall began the weather here just gave up the ghost." Niki paced the room. "Don't go back to sleep. Are you going back to sleep? Let's play tennis."

Ann sat up. "The courts will still be damp from dew."

"Even after breakfast?" Niki pulled down the top section of window and stood looking out, her arms resting along the window top, her chin resting on her arms. "Is this Indian summer?"

Indian summer it was, a sun to bake crisp the fallen leaves. Indian summer is internal weather. Slow, mellow, golden hours, daylong. Ann lifted her head and smelled the air. "I've got some reading to do," she said, "and we're having practice this afternoon."

"That's this afternoon," Niki protested. "Why not one quick set?"

"The courts will be wet, I said that. Clay absorbs water. And think of the leaves all over them. Besides, it's the wrong kind of morning to hate the opposition. Take a bike ride."

Niki had purchased a racing bike, with ten speeds. She took long rides on it, although she never used it for short trips. "Maybe I will."

"We could eat breakfast," Ann said. "I think I'll read outside."

"Reading is not doing anything," Niki said.

"Says you," Ann answered placidly. "Besides, we'll have a day off soon. Bell Day."

"You said the magic word!" Niki shrieked. "Where is that duck?" She hunched her body over, waggling her eyebrows in imitation of Groucho Marx. With one hand she groped at the ceiling to pull down the duck, with the other she mimed the tapping of a fat cigar.

"No," Ann giggled, "it's a tradition."

"Oh goody."

"They ring the bells at breakfast. All classes are canceled for the day. The student center packs free lunches and you can take off, for anywhere you want."

Niki stared at Ann. "Are you telling me that there is another day besides Sunday when these damned bells will rouse me from my honest slumber?"

"Yep. Always during Indian summer."

"Is there always an Indian summer?" Ann nodded. "It could be tomorrow? It could be that the bells will ring two days in a row?" Ann nodded. "Out in civilized country we don't do that, you know. We don't ring bells. Nobody would dare even suggest it—he'd be lynched."

Niki was engaged in glaring back at two fried eggs the next morning when the bells rang outside the closed windows. Somebody rose to open a window and let the sound in. The housemother entered, in a long sateen robe, to make the formal announcement.

"We will miss our classes today," Hildy protested.

"I'm ready for that," Niki said. "I've been a model student too long."

"But I go to the observatory tonight."

"I know the classrooms are closed. I don't know about something like the observatory," Ann said. "Anyway, what do you want to do with the day?"

"I shall go to the library," Hildy said.

Niki groaned.

"Closed," Ann said.

Niki grinned. "Tradition."

"I shall study in the room then."

"We're supposed to do something outdoors," Ann said.

"Why?" Hildy asked.

"Yes, why?" Niki turned on Ann.

"I don't know. It's traditional, my aunt said. The dining room is closed for lunch and the box lunches are ready at the student center. We're supposed to go on picnics and hikes. Maybe as a last blast before winter settles in. I don't really know why, and I don't much care. I'd like to do something, wouldn't you?" Ann noticed that they were all three assuming that they would do something together.

"We could ride up to Falls Park," Niki suggested. "Hildy, you could borrow a bike, couldn't you? I've been there once. It's only five miles and there's a good waterfall."

"Five miles uphill," Ann said. "Why not? Even for a bad waterfall. Anyway, it'll all be downhill returning."

Hildy considered this. "If we could leave later in the morning, I would like that. There is work I must do."

"There *are* a few short downhills going up," Niki said to Ann. "It's worth the trip. We'll walk most of the way, how's that? You can walk five miles."

Ann looked out the window. It was a honey-colored day, the shadows lying cool on the ground. "OK with me. Hildy?"

"Could we leave at noon?"

Niki jumped up. "I'll get the bike if you'll get the lunches for all of us, Ann."

The narrow road wound up from the College. They coasted downhill and, after a few muscle-straining attempts, walked their bikes up the long grades. There was almost no traffic, an occasional car, one or two trucks making deliveries to towns further up in the hills. The observatory was half an hour away from the College, Ann noted. She saw the telltale dome among pine trees. A small wooden sign announced its presence, where the gravel driveway entered the road.

The park had no guard house, just a wooden gate and a map etched into a slate stand. They left their bikes and followed a short path toward the sound of water.

Niki led them to a clearing at the top of the falls where a broad creek tumbled down over a cliff into pools below. "Here it is," she said.

Hildy squinted.

"I thought waterfalls were supposed to be deafeningly loud," Ann said. "Roaring thunder, and all that."

"It isn't Zambesi," Niki allowed. "But it does spray up rainbows; isn't that good for something?"

"Maybe I'm too hungry to appreciate it," Ann answered. They ate sandwiches, fruit, cookies. They scooped out handfuls of icy creek water to drink. Hildy took off her shoes and waded away. Niki crouched in uncompanionable silence, tossing stones into the water. Ann followed Hildy, going along the damp mossy bank. She stopped to bend down and watch water beetles busy at something incomprehensible in the eddies that preceded the rapids at the top of the falls.

If she watched long enough, Ann thought, she might figure out what the water-skaters were doing. The gliding circuits they performed couldn't really be as random as they seemed. She looked back to where Niki sat, tossing stone after stone. Ahead, Hildy stood in calf-high water that foamed at her knees and burst gladly up around her legs. At that part of the rapids around Hildy some larger rock had been caught and lay partly exposed, partly covered with moss. Hildy bent to touch the rocks. Behind her, Ann saw the distinct line of the falls. Hildy moved forward.

It seemed to Ann that she stood up from the bank in slow motion, but her mind worked rapidly, checking her eyes' perception of how close Hildy was to the edge of the falls. Where the rapidly moving water swept over, and down.

"Hildy!" she called. Hildy hesitated. "Hildy, don't move!"

Hildy's puzzled face waited for Ann, where she clambered through the icy water. Ann's sneakers slipped on the bigger stones beneath her feet. The water pulled at her legs, to take her off-balance.

"What is it?" Hildy asked, as Ann approached, but not yet to arm's reach.

"You're too close to the edge," Ann panted, holding out a hand.

Hildy smiled and shook her head. Turning away, in a motion as smooth as daffodils bending under the wind, she lost her footing and fell forward.

Ann grabbed at the arm Hildy flung out for balance. She caught Hildy's forearm in both of her hands and pulled the girl back.

"Wait," Hildy said. "My leg is over—" She put one hand down into the water and brought her leg back under her. She stood up beside Ann.

Ann legs were shaking, whether with cold or fear, she did not know. She could see the height of the drop now, down six feet into restless black pools of water. It wasn't Zambesi, but it was dangerous enough.

"I thank you," Hildy said.

"You couldn't see it, could you?" Ann demanded. The worst damage to a falling body would be done by the boulders it hit, tumbling down among the waters. "You couldn't see it and you were going to just ignore me. Goddammit, Hildy, tell the truth."

"I always tell the truth," Hildy said.

"And you refuse to have your eyes examined," Ann cried. She held tight onto Hildy's arm as they waded back to the bank. Hildy tried to pull away, but Ann wouldn't let go. "Well, I won't have it. Do you hear me? Damn you, answer me."

Hildy's face was dimmed, meek. "You are right, of course. I will make the appointment."

Niki ran up. "What appointment? What happened? Are you OK?" She looked at Ann, then at Hildy. "You didn't see how close you were, did you?" Niki asked quietly.

"I have already given Ann my word that I will go," Hildy said.

"Why will you do it when Ann tells you and not me?" asked Niki.

"She was so very angry. She swore at me."

"Hell, if I'd known that would work, I'd have done it long before," Niki said.

"It is not the same for you," Hildy answered.

Niki grunted. And grinned. "All's well that ends well?" she suggested. "Except, both of you are wet and shivering." She jabbed Ann in the shoulder with her finger. "You're it," she declared, and ran away.

"I don't want—" Ann protested. Then she quickly reached out for Hildy, before the blonde girl could realize the game; but Hildy had swept away and was running back toward their empty lunch boxes.

They played a senseless and exhausting game of tag until they all sat, flushed with heat, beside the creek.

"I don't know about you," Niki said, "but that makes me feel better. I got a letter from my dad this morning," she announced without transition. "It seems I may have a stepmother. Replete with three ugly step-siblings. I've never thought of myself as the Cinderella type."

Ann grinned. Hildy spoke from Niki's opposite side. "Will he marry her?"

Niki shrugged. "It's none of my business. Only she's not as young as we thought. I figured it out and she can't be. The youngest she can be is twenty-six because her oldest kid is ten. Her husband is a barber, Dad says. They want to go to Acapulco during Christmas to get her a divorce. Among other things. He didn't exactly say he was going to marry her, but it's in the cards."

"You haven't even met her," Ann said.

"Don't think I want to." Niki let another handful of pebbles slide back into the icy water.

"Would he marry someone you haven't met?" Ann asked.

"He thinks I won't like her. He hasn't said so, but it's pretty clear. I mean, I'm not invited to Acapulco."

"What'll you do over Christmas?" Ann asked.

"Who knows? I've got a couple of friends in New York. Let me ask you, both of you, don't you think eighteen is the right time to lose your virginity?"

"What? Why?" Ann said.

"I've got a feeling. If you hang onto it, it gets to be a bigger and bigger problem. Lots of women aren't virgins before eighteen—Kinsey made that clear enough. Eighteen is well away time to learn what it's like, sex. If you don't want sex to take over your life. I mean, I want a lot of it, I expect I will, but not to tie me down. Hildy? What do you think?"

"I think this woman of your father's is married now. While he is taking her out. Is that so?"

"Sure. What does that matter? Before or after, what's the difference?"

"What of her husband?" Hildy asked.

"Dad says he's stupid."

Niki thought, "That could mean anything," she went on. "It could mean he's a failure. Or slow-witted. Or that he works hard and is the reliable sort. Or just that he doesn't like Dad."

"I can understand *that*," Ann said. "What does your father think you're supposed to do?"

"He doesn't," Niki said. "I'm on my own."

"They are adulterous," Hildy said, in continuation of her own thoughts.

"Root word adult, as in consenting adults," Niki responded.

"That is wrong," Hildy said.

"Spare me the fundamentalism." Niki dismissed her. "My problem is more immediate."

Ann felt sorry for Niki. "Come home with me," she said. Then she felt sorry for herself.

Niki shook her head. "Your mother would have fits. It's a bitch of a problem."

"Hildy could come too."

"And we could continue our gay camaraderie unabated through the entire year? No thanks, Annie, it's not my idea of a vacation."

"You should not let him do this," Hildy said. "He is your father and you are responsible for him."

Niki's laugh contained no mirth. "You've got it backwards. He's responsible for me."

"As you say, you are on your own, and he has permitted this. You should stop him."

"How? I've played my ace. As far he's concerned, I can go live with my mother. He said I'd like her, Letitia—*Letitia,* can you believe it?—when I got to know her. That's the kiss of death."

"He holds his soul in jeopardy," Hildy said.

Niki looked at her. "Yes, I think maybe. But not in the way you mean."

"That doesn't matter, does it?" Hildy answered.

"Oh, I hope not," Niki said. "But—what can I do?"

"Go and stop him."

"You know, you're right." Niki stood up and stretched. "I'd have a couple of days with him before they're scheduled to leave. Maybe I'll try it. Although what the hell I'll say I don't know."

"You'll think of something," Ann remarked.

"Yeah, I will, won't I? Right as always, Hildy, and you too, Annie. Right as always. I owe it to him to try at least. He's taken some trouble over me, in his day."

"Maybe she'll be nice," Ann said. "Maybe you'll like her when you meet her."

"More likely, maybe she'll be after his money and I can explain how it's not as much as she thinks it is and a lot tied up in a tidy little trust for me."

Niki walked away, upstream. She kicked at stones as she went.

"I meant that about Christmas, Hildy," Ann said. "I'd like it if you would come home with me."

"I know," Hildy said.

"Think about it, OK? I've got to check it with my mother first, of course, but I'm pretty sure you'll like her."

"And she'll like me?"

"Of course."

"She did not like Niki?"

Ann shook her head.

"And you, do you like Niki?"

"I haven't thought about it," Ann answered. "Not recently at least. We're getting along all right, all of us. Why? Do you?"

"Of course."

"Sometimes she embarrasses me. Sometimes she's pretty funny. Sometimes she makes me angry. Sometimes she scares me. I don't know. I haven't thought about liking her. I'm kept busy living with her."

"Niki dares much."

"I think she plays it safe," Ann said. "In a backwards way, that's just what she does."

"No," Hildy said. They were silent.

Evening was drawing in when they returned to their bicycles. Hildy asked if Ann and Niki would like to come to the observatory with her. "Saturn will be visible," she offered them.

Niki refused, saying she was going to make a call to New York. Ann thought it sounded beautiful, Saturn surrounded by its blazing rings.

Niki rode off fast, pedaling to gain all possible momentum for the roller coaster return. She waved a rodeo rider's hand as she disappeared around a sharp curve. Ann kept Hildy right behind her and held them to a carefully controlled speed. Hildy did not protest.

chapter

6

Hildy went to an optometrist late the next afternoon. When she returned, her pupils were dilated but her step did not waver. She seemed unexcited by the experience, although perhaps a little amused. "He was first angry," she said. "But not at me, I think. He says what you say, that I cannot see. I asked him then, *What is it I have been doing all my life?* He stopped being angry and became curious. I am a challenge he says."

"Why?" Ann asked.

"He says there are so many things wrong about my eyes."

Niki tried to peer closely at Hildy's eyes, to descry the flaws.

"You cannot see it, he said. He said astigmatic in both eyes. It is so serious for me because of the other flaws, which cause one eye to be nearsighted, the other farsighted. He said that he will have the glasses ready on Friday, because I am in mortal danger until I get them."

"I'll vouch for that," Ann remarked. "Can glasses correct the errors?"

"Big glasses," Hildy said. "Thick glasses." She was silent. Ann tried to reassure her. "You'll look fine in them."

"What does that matter?" Hildy said. "I was remembering. As I left he said that my eyes looked perfect to him. He said he was sorry to say I must have glasses. Isn't that strange?"

"No," Niki said.

"So I told him if he would write a note to my roommates that I was all right, I would not need them. And he put me in his car and drove me here. So that is done."

"When do you get the glasses?" Ann asked.

"Friday at four."

"Then I won't see them until Sunday when I get back. You

111

won't schedule a game for the weekend, will you? Remember, I have to go home—it's my father's birthday."

"Our only match this week is Thursday," Niki said. "No problem."

"No bike riding until you get the glasses. OK, Hildy?" Ann asked. Hildy nodded meekly, but spoke softly to herself as she lay down on her bed.

"What?" Ann asked.

"Nothing. Nothing. How old is your father to be?"

"Fifty-four."

Niki joined in. "That's not young."

"No. So what?"

Niki shrugged. "I just thought. People, when they get older, into their thirties, they don't want the inconvenience of small children. I just thought that."

"I've got a younger brother too," Ann said.

"What's he like, your father?" Niki asked.

This time Ann shrugged. "I don't know. He's strict. He's conservative. He's a pretty good lawyer, I think. He doesn't care anything about art or literature. Cultural stuff. He says he lets Mother dabble in all that. We don't have these incredible father-daughter talks. I don't tell him—you know, we're not intimate. I mean, what does he need to know about my first menstrual period, say, or Greek verbs? He's busy. We get along OK. I like him." She thought. "I don't know him well. Not nearly as well as I should, do I?"

"What's it matter," Niki asked.

"Do you know your father, Hildy?"

"I have worked beside him. He has taught me patiently. But as a man—no, I do not know him, and that is proper. He is my father."

"He's just a human being, like every other," Niki argued.

"His seed made me. His blood flows in my veins. His work feeds me, clothes me, shelters me. How am I to think of him as I do other people?"

"Do you like him?" Ann wondered.

"We work well together, my father and I."

Their second sophomore match went smoothly. Ann played the first game, Eloise the second. Watching, Ann could see a coordination in her team that she was not aware of when she was playing within it. Most of the crowd at this match rooted for the freshmen, although a few partisan sophomores hooted, jeered, and called out to their own team, praising and pushing them on. The gym walls echoed the spectators' enthusiasms, magnifying them.

Miss Dennis slipped onto the bench beside Ann during the second game. She did not take off her heavy jacket, although Ann offered to help her. "This game will not last long," she said. "You won the first, didn't you?"

"Fifteen—eight."

Ann was too constrained by the Munchkin's presence to shriek eagerly, as she would have, say, when Sarah rose to spike a ball. Miss Dennis applauded a good play, a sound undistinguishable in the general noise, a little Munchkin sound of fingers on palms.

"I want to thank you—"

"For the grade?" Miss Dennis cut her off, leaning slightly toward her. "You disappoint me, Miss Gardner. I had thought you capable of accurate self-evaluation."

"Yes, of course," Ann said, flushing as she realized what she had almost said.

The woman smiled at her and inclined her head. It was a gesture Ann knew from Philosophy lectures, perfectly ambiguous.

Grades were announced at the middle of the week. Carbon copies of the reports that were being sent to parents were mailed to each student. Ann had a B + in Philosophy; what she would have guessed. The rest of her grades, even the A in English, were not surprising either: except for a D in Sciences. Ann looked at the slip of paper and then at Niki. "I must have flunked the unit test."

"What?" Niki was displeased about something.

"Science. I got a D. I've never flunked anything before."

"What about the rest?"

"B's and an A."

"Don't sweat it. D is passing and you won't have to take another science."

Ann bit her lip.

"Annie—are you really upset?"

Ann nodded.

"Why? You don't want to transfer out of here or anything. No graduate school will look at a freshman science course."

"I'm not worried about *that*. I've never flunked. Not even a quiz. I didn't think I'd done that badly. I don't understand how I could have. It's the only thing I could count on being good at, school."

"Don't worry. It doesn't matter, does it? Now, I've got a real problem. Look at this."

"That looks pretty good. How did you get an A-minus in Math?"

"What kind of question is that?" Niki mocked hurt feelings. "No, you're right. We did some Calculus last year and this first section has been review for me. The A will go down, I promise. But English—"

"C-plus? That's all right."

"I need at least B's to get into Berkeley. Nothing lower. They got a lot of transfer applications."

Hildy entered, bearing her grade slip, serene.

"And how'd you do, Hildy?" Niki asked.

"I have passed everything," Hildy spoke lightly. "Not well, but I did not expect to do well. See? So that is all good."

Ann noticed that, although she had received permission to take two sciences, Hildy had C— in both.

Niki was not to be distracted from her own interests. "The English professor doesn't like me. To begin with. She'd like you, Annie—you're her kind. She's a bastard."

"Maybe if you worked a little harder?" Ann returned. "Maybe if you worked a little?"

"Nope. I keep up, and that's enough for an English course. She says I don't think about the stuff. But it's English. You don't think about English, you have opinions. What do I do, Ann?"

"How can I tell?"

"Would you look at my papers?"

"What's wrong with them?"

"I don't know."

"Is the professor right? She is, isn't she? You don't think about it, do you?"

"It's boring. It's all so . . . undefined. You can prove almost anything, if you twist and turn it enough. And why bother? That's what I want to know: why bother? I can't think about that stuff. Just getting the reading done—I have trouble staying awake for that."

"Well then," Ann said.

"There's got to be a way around this. If I could get an A on the long paper, I'd get a B for the semester. Don't you think? Even if all the rest of my papers are C-plus? How do you get an A?"

"I don't know."

"You helped Hildy."

"Hildy was in trouble."

"Will you just read one paper? That's not so much trouble is it? Just one? The *Odyssey* one. I'm not asking you to do very much, just tell me what you think about a paper. It's not hard, not for you. I'm not asking you to like me, Annie, just read a paper."

"All right. I give up, I will. All right."

Niki opened a drawer and pulled out a paper. "Here, I happen to have it handy. Hildy? What did you get on your Penelope paper?"

"C."

"That's two letter grades up. You can do it, Annie. You can do it for me."

"What do you think of this?" Hildy asked. "If each game a different person sits out. In rotation."

"Eloise is our sub," Niki said.

"She improves," Hildy said.

"How about, everyone but you and me?" Niki suggested.

"I thought everyone. You do not have to though, that will make no difference."

"I have no objection to the idea," Ann said.

"Why wouldn't I make a difference?" Niki asked.

"You play by yourself."

"Balls," Niki said. "The team needs me. And you. The team needs us."

"Not me," Hildy said.

"Then me," Niki said. She turned on Ann, "I know how that sounds so don't bother saying it."

"You make many of the points more quickly; you make them more easy for us," Hildy said. "They would still be made."

"Piss on it."

"I do not understand," Hildy said in a genuinely puzzled voice, "why you use such words. If you have chosen them for their meaning, you are either deliberately rude or simply stupid. If for any other reason, you are a hypocrite."

Niki fumed. Her mouth opened on unuttered responses. Finally she slammed her hand down on the desk. "What am I supposed to say?"

"Nothing. I did not ask a question."

"You know, you may be right, capital-R Right. But you won't break me." Niki's voice was steely.

"I know," Hildy spoke softly. "I do not want to. But you cannot know that."

"I don't care. That's the truth of the matter. All I want is to get my English grade up. So I can get the hell out."

"I'll read the paper right now," Ann said, seizing the diversion. "Look, I'm starting. I'm reading the title." *Adultery*. Ann read through the seven pages, noted and agreed with the C+ grade, and was surprised at the flat though workmanlike content and style.

Niki, she became aware, had watched her throughout. "Well?"

"I need to think," Ann hedged. *Interesting* is the comment by the grade. Is that all the professor said?"

"Ah. You think that, as a critical analysis of the paper, as the response of a trained intelligence seeking to enable improvement, for example, that as such it is not incisive enough? Maybe a little lacking in constructive criticism? Although it is succinct."

Ann said, "What strikes me is that interesting is the one thing it isn't."

Niki threw back her head and laughed. "You're right, of course. Bizarre, yes? Talk to me after dinner, OK? Annie—I knew you could put your finger on it."

Later, Ann tried to explain to Niki that it was a matter of the quality of the idea and the complexity of dealing with it. "You've missed so much," Ann said.

"But I only had ten pages."

"Yes. And you plumped for the most pedestrian use of them. That surprises me."

"Why?"

"This paper is so safe."

"When you're going for the grade—"

"Admit it. You got the grade you got by going for grades."

"OK, OK. So I've got to have better ideas."

"And deal with them more thoughtfully. That may be hard for you."

Niki looked down at her paper. "I guess that makes sense. OK. I see what you're driving at Annie. I owe you one. Want me to help you with science?"

"Eloise said she would."

"Eloise? Why Eloise? Is she smart? I don't believe that, Annie. She's such a wimp, how can she be smart?"

"The real thing," Ann said, sure of it. "Not like us. She may even be a scholar. She has that sense for—perfection in detail, is that it? You're underestimating her, Niki."

"But I bet I could show you better than Eloise. She won't know how to yell at you. We'll try it together."

Ann was not up to arguing about that, not even for the sake of her new, burgeoning friendship with Eloise.

Ann went home for the weekend, riding the express bus. Ann's home, altogether, in all respects, reflected the kind of polishing that makes silver shine and wood gleam. Mrs. Gardner had a rib roast, Ann's favorite, for Friday dinner. Her two older sisters had also come home for the occasion, and one of her older brothers. The next day, her father's birthday, lobsters were served. Sunday morning was filled with leave-takings; only Ann and her younger brother would stay through Sunday lunch. It was a typical weekend at home: logy with food, passing the time slowly in a kind of contented haze, making desultory inquiries about other peoples' jobs, schools, activities.

When she had a moment alone with her mother, Ann asked whether she could bring her roommate home for Christmas. "Niki?" Mrs. Gardner inquired. "Or the other girl, Hildy."

"Actually, I asked them both."

Mrs. Gardner raised her eyebrows.

"But Niki has to go out to California to keep her father from getting married, if she can. She didn't want to come anyway."

"Why should she want her father not to remarry?"

"It's complicated," Ann said. There were some areas of the

world her mother could not understand. "Anyway, I asked Hildy."

"Before you had spoken to me?"

Ann knew she was in the wrong. "I thought—you'll like her, I'm sure of it—it's Christmas and she can't get home herself—"

"Why not?"

"She doesn't have much money."

"So, you've been feeling sorry for people again," her mother said.

Ann left the room.

Ann's green and white bedroom felt strange to her, for the first time in her life. She had lived in this room for much of her life. Its corners were cluttered with pieces of her childhood and with personal treasures. But she was no longer entirely comfortable there. On Sunday morning she packed a long stuffed snake into her suitcase and rolled up her Kennedy campaign poster; she picked out her first edition of *The Secret Garden*. She set her suitcase in the hallway, ready to go.

At lunch, a large platter of chicken salad sandwiches, her mother answered her. "I've been thinking about Christmas. Ann wants to bring a friend home with her for the holidays," she announced.

The suggestion did not seem to evoke much interest.

"I've decided that it's all right with me," Mrs. Gardner said. "When you shop, remember that there will be one more person. Her name is Hildy. She plays volleyball—isn't that right? She comes from a modest background—that's correct, isn't it, Ann?"

Ann protested. "It wouldn't be like that. It wouldn't be right to give her presents the way we do each other. That would embarrass her."

"I think the question is," Mr. Gardner said, "whether it would embarrass us *not* to do so. Or are you suggesting that we celebrate differently this year?"

"No, not at all. Hildy wouldn't mind. She wouldn't even notice. She doesn't notice stuff like that. Are you trying to tell me it's a bad idea?"

"Of course not," Mrs. Gardner said. "I'll admit I'd have difficulty welcoming Niki. But Hildy, when you write of her, seems quite nice. A little simple. Though she might feel uncomfortable here. Have you thought of that?''

Ann, feeling at that point uncomfortable herself, nodded.

Ann's brother joined in. "Let's do it. But play it by ear and not make a big production out of it. Is she pretty?"

"Very."

"She'll be bound to have a good time then. Don't get in a tither, Ma."

"You know, if you wanted to, you could come up and meet her first. Maybe that's the way to do it. And if it feels OK to you, you could invite her yourself."

"Now that's a workable idea," Mr. Gardner said. "A very good idea. I'm glad to see our money is not being wasted. We could have a day's quiet skiing, just the two of us, and take the girls out to dinner. Some time between Thanksgiving and Christmas, don't you think?" He talked down the length of the table to his wife.

"That does seem better. We should do it quite close to Thanksgiving, though."

"Niki too, let's include her in the dinner," Mr. Gardner said. "I was taken with her. She put spokes in your mother's wheels, if you can imagine that," he said to Ann's brother.

"Of course, Niki might not care to dine with us," Mrs. Gardner said.

"Yes, but she might. I shall attempt to charm her, if she hesitates."

"You'd do better to bully her," Ann advised.

"That too," her father agreed.

"Is *she* pretty?" the brother inquired.

"No," Ann said.

"But, Ann," her mother said. "Niki could be quite striking. Dramatic. She has lovely hair and a fine figure."

"What's Hildy like?" Ann's father asked. "Besides pretty."

Ann tried to think of what to say. "She's sort of—unusual. I like her."

Mrs. Gardner smiled patiently. "What's her background, what does her father do? Where did she go to school?"

"Her father's a farmer. She went to a high school. She works hard, she goes to church every Sunday."

"Catholic?"

"No, she just—worships." Ann struggled to find the detail

or description that would explain. "I don't know—she's just herself. You'll have to meet her. She's sort of the volleyball coach. I really like her, everybody admires her."

Ann's brother changed the subject. "What *is* this I hear, you're playing volleyball?" Ann nodded. "I never figured you for a jock," he remarked.

"I sort of fell into it," she justified herself. "I kind of like it. We're playing on an all-school ladder and doing pretty well." This much boasting she allowed herself.

"Volleyball?" His opinion of the sport was obvious in his tone: low.

"Mens sane," Ann answered, knowing how weak his Latin was.

"We know you're the brainy one," he responded equably. "But it isn't like you to play a sport—it isn't, is it? You won't even go off the high diving board, Ann."

Ann giggled, remembering. "OK. I'm no athlete, I'm not even competitive—"

"Hot news flash," he announced to the table.

"—but you should understand this: I feel like I know how to get better at it. Do you know what I mean? I can almost feel— see—what it would be like to be really good. Like you are at tennis. I never will, of course, but—listen."

"I'm listening. I can eat and listen."

"I've always been good in school, but I never had to work that hard, especially for the things I liked, like languages and English. It was all sort of accidental. I did the only thing I could think of to do and it was excellent." She didn't care if she was boasting, because she was figuring something out. "But in the volleyball, because it's a team maybe and there are other people. . . . Always before, I never tried for anything I wasn't naturally good at. Maybe I figured I'd lose anyway, or maybe I was too scared of looking stupid. But now, in this, I'm really working hard even though I know I'll never be as good as I'd like to be. Doesn't that happen to you in school? Don't you know what I mean?"

He looked thoughtfully at her. "You must have a good teacher," he said.

"Hildy," Ann said. "She and Niki are really good players. Really good. I'm the worst on the team." That was true, Ann realized, and wondered why she had never thought of it that way before. "Except maybe the sub. Eloise." She forestalled her brother's inevitable question. "No, *not* pretty. But Hildy . . . well, just wait and see."

He groaned and smote his breast. "If I were only two years older."

The room was empty when Ann returned. She unpacked quickly. The snake coiled in furry indolence on her bed. The poster, with its photograph of JFK, she tacked over her desk. Ann changed into trousers and walked over to the gym, to see if there might be a practice. She wanted to see Hildy in her new glasses. But nobody was at the gym, so she went back, drew herself a bath and lay in it, sketchily reading *The Secret Garden*.

A steamy and silent time passed before Niki rapped on the door of the cubicle. "Ann? Is this where you are?"

Niki entered and sat on the little white stool, moving Ann's towel and underclothes onto her lap.

"I'll be out in a minute," Ann said.

"You're not embarrassed, are you?"

"Yes. I am."

"Don't you want to see Hildy? We were looking for you. I saw your suitcase. We've been walking around. It's like having a baby in tow. Shall I call her?"

"No! Just give me a minute to get out and clean the tub."

"OK. OK. Keep your hair on."

Ann padded down the hall expecting—what? Some great surprise. But there was not that, only alterations. Hildy's glasses were thick, gold-rimmed. They magnified her corn-flower eyes, giving to her face a slightly befuddled expression. "So you see," she said, self-consciously.

"*You* see," corrected Niki.

"I am clumsy still," Hildy said. "It is the change in depth perception. I fell off your bike, but there was no harm done. I have been practicing."

"She can recognize people at a hundred yards," Niki reported, "and read a book at arm's length. Leap tall buildings at a single bound."

Ann studied Hildy's new face. Its simplicity was made more obvious by the thick lenses. There was something helpless about it, appealing—like a startled elf. "What do you think?" Ann asked. "Do you like them?"

"I grow accustomed," Hildy answered. "There is so much—I did not know. Colors, and light. Everything is cluttered."

"Don't tell me," Ann said. She lay on her bed and crossed her ankles. "I've just spent an hour washing the city off myself."

"Do you ever think about how much garbage a city makes?" Niki asked. "Picture it. The garbage from your own house, multiplied times a million, all piled up, on the streets say."

"That's depressing," Ann said.

"It's terrifying. Garbage will take over the world, poured into rivers and lakes and the oceans, dug into marshes and meadows. Now there's a problem with a future. Turn your mind to that one, Annie." She bit a nail. "I hate cities. Where'd you get that?" She pointed at Ann's poster.

"From home."

"I wouldn't have figured you for a Kennedy fan."

"Why not? He's—educated, witty—"

"Rich, good-looking. In short, an aristocrat. I guess I can see it."

"Well and why not?" Ann challenged her.

"You really buy all that stuff?" Niki asked her. "You don't know anything about what really goes on?" Ann squirmed. "His daddy bought the nomination for him." Ann had heard that story. "He's not even faithful to his wife."

"You don't know that."

"Not from personal experience, no. And what about the Bay of Pigs?"

Ann couldn't think of a rebuttal.

"You've fallen for a pretty face and a quick wit—charisma, that's all."

"I don't know," Ann said. "But you can't tell me you would have voted for Nixon," she attacked. Niki waved that objection away. "Besides," Ann said, "when there is someone you can be proud of—yes proud, because he speaks well, because he picks intelligent advisors, not political ones—"

"—that's another of his mistakes," Niki said.

"Who reads books and treats them as if they're important, somebody better than the ordinary. It gives you—it gives me at least—the sense that excellence is possible. That it's not just in stories, or in somebody long dead, excellence; but now. I don't know, I like being a citizen of the country he's president of. It's like—being at Stanton."

Niki snorted.

"Or like the volleyball team, our team, that's doing something well. Or even being a member of the class that has that team, even if I didn't play on it." She thought. Niki chewed on a finger and watched her. "Besides everybody makes mistakes. Napoleon should never have gone into Russia, but that's not important. Neither is the way he made his brothers emperors."

"What is then?" Niki asked.

This time it was a question Ann had hoped for. "The Code Napoleon, he revised the whole legal system of France."

"Good point," Niki approved. "But what does it have to do with supporting Kennedy?"

Ann couldn't say.

"My father does not vote," Hildy volunteered. "He says they are all great liars and out to deceive, and he will give no one his vote."

Ann and Niki exchanged a glance.

"What does that look mean?" Hildy asked.

Ann flushed. Niki remarked, "You begin to see how things have changed?"

"It means, in my case," Ann told Hildy, "that it is a privilege of democracy to vote and that the system rests upon each person using his vote."

"That little speech is enough to keep me away from the polls forever," Niki said.

Hildy was watching their faces. Her eyes were—inscrutable.

"My dad is a Republican by reaction," Niki said. "All the screaming liberals in California make him nervous. But I'd have thought the Gardners were Republicans by choice."

"The rest of my family is. I'm a heretic," Ann said. "My grandmother, do you want to know all she had to say about Kennedy? *'All that hair, my dear, and all that money.'* "

"The real question is, can he govern," Niki said. "What history will say about a man who calls his kid Jon-Jon, I don't know. But it's history's verdict that will count, and that'll take a hundred years. If we have a hundred years. Nobody's managed to ban the Bomb yet."

"It is in God's hands," Hildy said.

"Do you think so? Do you really think so?" Ann asked, because if Hildy thought it, it might be true.

Hildy nodded.

"In the meantime," Niki announced briskly, "we have here Hildy, no longer half-blind, in need of some care. Can you ride with her to the lab tomorrow night, Ann? I've got a lot of math. All the assignments for the last three weeks, if the truth were known, all due Tuesday."

"Sure. I'll take some work. What is it like with glasses, Hildy? What do you see?"

"I cannot tell, it is all so confusing."

"Let me try them?" Ann held out her hands. Hildy took off her glasses and became herself again.

Ann could see blobs of color and light. Areas in shadow. A pale shape, framed in fluid black, Niki; her tensed body as if— Ann lost the thought. Ann stood up and put out a hand to steady herself. The light from the hall swam before her eyes. The little muscles that control focus strained to make details clear. She turned a head grown suddenly cumbersome to where Hildy sat. Light there, and two deep, darker circles that must be eyes. The body sure and strong there, firm as a tree, supple as spring wood, silent.

Ann rubbed her temples and took off the glasses. "Wow they're strong," she said. "It makes me dizzy."

"It makes me dizzy also," Hildy said. "But I will adjust."

"Think of what it'll do for your volleyball game," Niki said. "You'll blast us off the court."

Oddly enough, just the opposite happened. Hildy, looking out-of-proportion with magnified eyes and long legs, played an altered game. On serves, she brought her arm forward with less assurance and power, with more conscious care. She watched the passage of the ball and the expression of the receiver and was, thus, late into position for the return. When her team passed the ball forward, her head followed its progress. Her spike was improved, her blocking hampered. When she made a poor shot, she would shake her arms and stand puzzled, her hands clenched. It was as if her entire internal tempo had shifted.

"You'll get used to it," Niki assured her. "You didn't play badly."

"I know that," Hildy said. "I must try harder. It is noisy here."

"It's always been noisy."

Ann rode with Hildy to the observatory Monday evening. While Hildy looked at the stars, she sat in an empty office studying Ancient Greek. Her absorption was so complete that it was not until a shadow fell over the page of the textbook that she knew lab was over. Hildy leaned down to touch the Greek letters. "What does it say?"

Ann translated: "Whom the gods love, die young." Then she read the Greek aloud.

Hildy's eyes stayed on the page. "Those would be cruel gods, to love so," she said, and her fingers moved over the lines of exercises, as if it were Braille. "People spoke this language."

"Yes. Although nobody now knows for sure how it was pronounced."

They walked out to the bicycle rack. Clouds scudded over the stars. "There are lost languages, ancient ones," Hildy said. "Languages—how many?—there are also, other than our own. Some spoken only by members of isolated tribes. Each with its own vocabulary. Why is that?"

"Some are cradle-of-civilization tongues," Ann explained. "Like Indo-European, which has word forms, roots, that appear in many languages. Because of that, many languages are quite similar, and in grammars too."

"Does that make it clear to you?" Hildy asked.

"No. Especially when I think of the infinite variation," Ann said. "It's like thinking about stars and space."

"It would be better if we all spoke the same language," Hildy said. "How could so many differences exist?"

"The tower of Babel?" Ann suggested.

"Is that possible?" Hildy wondered. She looked at the sky, where the few visible stars seemed snared by bare branches. "It seems a heavy punishment."

They rode down the mountainside together, in windy

silence. Hildy had Niki's bike. She did not use the gears. Neither did she ride quite steadily. Part of the reason for this was her constant turning of the head, to see Ann, to look up, to look back.

"May I come with you Thursday too?" Ann asked. "I got a lot of work done. There's no distraction at all, up there."

"Of course. I would be glad of the company and I am not yet, as you can tell, riding well. But I am so much better than on Saturday, when Niki first took me out."

They played the third sophomore match that Thursday. They had practiced every day, and her team had adjusted to Hildy's new limits. They covered for her more and counted on her less to back them up. This was no sharp alteration, merely a shift.

The gymnasium stands were full. The audience screamed approval, disapproval, general excitement. Hildy's team played softly and accurately, except for Niki whose shots had still the old force and crispness. They won the first game, lost the second.

"Push it a little," Niki urged the team. "Try it a little harder and faster. You've got to."

They nodded.

They concentrated, they forced the ball over the net at unexpected moments, they set up more spikes for Niki and Hildy, and they won the game. For some reason, victory did not elate them.

Eloise, when she came to see what Ann was doing wrong in science, expressed her understanding of the difference in the team to Ann and Niki. She had stood in the doorway, wearing a skirt and sweater, her feet in penny loafers. "Me and my brace of preppies," Niki greeted her. Eloise sat on the edge of Ann's bed, tentative.

"We have all lost confidence in Hildy, so we are unsure of ourselves," she said. "Except you," she added to Niki. There was approval in her voice as she said that.

"She's changed," Ann said. "You must have felt it."

"But not that much," Eloise protested. "Not as much as we have. I didn't know I was doing it while I was in, but when I watched I could see—you'd look at her, as if you expected her to say something, or you'd move closer to her if the ball was going there. And now move back into position. Everything was taking you by surprise. I don't know. I'm probably wrong, but that's the way it seemed to me at the time."

"You're probably right," Ann said.

"Bess remarked," Eloise went on, "afterwards, that she felt as if she were playing alone."

"Me too," Ann said.

"I always felt that way," Niki said.

"There's a message in that," Ann answered.

Eloise looked from face to face, as if dreading Niki's reaction. It was Niki who reassured her. "We deal directly with one another, me and Annie. I'm not conversant with your prep school subtleties."

"And proud of it," Ann said. "Anyway"—she changed the subject and gave herself the last word—"I have this problem."

The two looked over Ann's notes and her tests. They muttered over her lab reports and laughed at her drawings. Eloise and Niki were in complete agreement that Ann needed to devise memorization tricks for science. They worked through a vocabulary list at the back of her notebook, grouping the words, making associative connections, connections so outrageous that they were memorable. Some were classical, some literary, many simply obscene. Then Niki fixed Ann with a truculent eye and announced: "You've got to stop writing this way."

"What?"

"She's put her finger on something rather important," Eloise agreed, reluctant to offend Ann. "I'm afraid I agree with her," she apologized.

"Nothing's wrong with my writing," Ann said. After all, *she* was the one with advanced English placement.

"It's too good," Niki said. "Too subtle. Too complex. Too thoughtful. Too much dependence on idea." She grinned. "Make it flat. Stop using verbs well, use *to be* instead. Be pedestrian. No joke, Ann. I'm succeeding in biology with just that style."

"But that would make it so dull," Ann said.

"C dull, do you think?" Niki asked. "Maybe even B-minus dull? Think on it, Annie."

The shame of a D was great enough to bend Ann's pride. Niki had a bridge game at ten—"I'm working up to playing for stakes. Money, eventually; they're coming around"—and Eloise lingered, reluctant to leave. Ann, who thought she would let her new resolution settle in for a night before she got down to work employing it, welcomed the distraction.

"Where's Hildy?" Eloise asked.

"In the library. She studies there."

"Is this her bureau?"

"Yes. Why?"

"I thought so; it's peculiarly bare. Doesn't she have any photographs of her family?"

"I've never seen any. How are your roommates?" Ann hadn't thought about them for weeks.

"They're fine, I presume. We don't encounter one another frequently, and when we do— They like having me be on the volleyball team, do you know that?"

"We're getting a reputation. Some of the people in my Shakespeare class said they were going to come to a game. Do you like that, being famous?"

"Yes," Eloise said firmly. "Yes I do. I never . . ." Her voice dwindled off.

"I know."

"We've really left the Hall behind," Eloise said. "Not just me, you too. Doesn't it seem a long time ago, if you remember last fall? Like another country."

Ann agreed, and added that she was not sorry. "But I loved it there. If I have a daughter, I'll send her there. If I get married."

"Is Niki being humorous most of the time?" Eloise asked. "I'd never realized that before. Now it seems possible. Is it all intended to be amusing?"

"Who knows?" Ann said. "I doubt it, but I can't be sure. Sometimes, I think maybe. It's easier to take her that way, so I try to. You should too."

"I'll try," Eloise said.

They chattered and gossiped until a few minutes before the dormitories would close. Then Eloise started to leave. "It's pleasant here," she said.

"Even Niki?" Ann grinned.

"Try my terrible twosome from Texas. Niki's not so bad, not so bad at all."

They met Hildy on the porch, and she and Ann stood

together watching Eloise trudge down the path between the trees.

"You like her," Hildy said to Ann.

"Yes I do," Ann answered.

"But you didn't always?"

"No. But I didn't know anything about her, not really."

"You are a good friend for her," Hildy said finally. "And that is right."

chapter
7

The match against the top sophomore team took place on Tuesday afternoon. When the freshman challengers arrived at the gym, the benches were full and people had overflowed onto the floor. Ruth was the one picked to sit out the first game, glad to do so. She watched tensely from beside the center pole, where the Munchkin, in a heavy camel hair coat, sat behind her.

The first game did not last long. The freshmen never took control of the ball. Nothing went right for them. Balls they sent close to the end lines seemed to float out of bounds. Sets were too low. Passes wobbled across the court. Balls popped up off the palms of their hands erratically. Ann felt herself closing into herself, lowering her expectations to the most basic elements of her game, trying to just hold her arms correctly and receive the shot, trying to find the point at which she could begin to play again. But every time, she slapped desperately at the ball. She lost her sense for what the others were doing, so focused was she on her own part of the court. Her confidence waned, dwindled, then fled. During the last points, she even began to shy away from the ball, leaving Niki more room to play in.

"Let me go out," Eloise asked Hildy. "Please. It's too tense. I can't when it's so tense, I just can't." Hildy agreed.

That was not like Hildy. A further change. Ann, waiting to be called into position, looked at the sophomores. Their eyes were smug.

Niki harangued the team. Her hands waved impotent fury, her fists pounded the air. Ann did not listen, thinking that in ten minutes it would all be over, and ten minutes was not so long. "And Annie"—Niki's voice broke into her thoughts— "Annie's quit. Sarah's playing like a pregnant cow. You can't do this. Hildy—watch the ball, for God's sake. For somebody's sake. Bess, you've got to move. Not stand there like a lump of lard. Ann, you're wallowing in self-pity. You can't do this to me, you hear? If you do, so help me I'll—" her teeth clenched around unspoken thoughts—"I'll find a way. Every one of you. And you'll be sorry."

Ann felt a silly smile spread over her face, prelude to a giggle.

"Try me, Annie, just try me," Niki growled.

Her fierceness was like a slap in the face, a direct physical assault. Ann was sobered, even frightened.

"All of you," Niki said. She glared at five pale faces, each pair of eyes staring at her. Only Hildy's were unshocked.

They trotted out onto the court, with Niki behind them. Ann was dreadfully aware of where Niki stood and where Niki looked. She did not dare return a glance.

Hildy served. The sophomores passed the ball forward and sent it to rear center, low, curving away. Ann's ball. It was too far away to be fetched, but Ann dived anyway—because Niki snarled—and, incredibly, she got a clenched fist under it. Ann struggled to put any kind of punch into her shot, to lift the ball high enough, just that much, so that Hildy or Bess might pick it up. The sinews of her shoulder twisted.

She managed it, and Hildy managed a shot forward, and Niki slammed the ball into the vacant center of the opposite court.

"All right," Niki muttered. Not in approval but in continued threat.

The next point went on for minutes. Ann strained after the ball, her eyes fixed on it, her muscles always ready. She could half-see Hildy, beside her, moving as she herself moved, in parallel. She was aware of Niki at the net, her eyes (her whole will it seemed) bent on the receiver of the ball. When Ann was that receiver, she could feel the hot anger Niki emanated, hanging over her, like a curled tidal wave.

This point too, they won.

After five points Hildy was still serving. The sophomores played well, but the freshmen played hard, as if something stood behind, pressing them.

After ten points Hildy was still serving. The sophomores were less smug now. The freshmen were desperate, as before;

but careful too, as if they knew that a slip would put them at a greater disadvantage than slackened effort.

Hildy served the fifteenth and final point. The sophomore receiver muttered to herself, drew back with arms raised, and caught Niki's glare through the net. She fumbled the ball. It sailed out of bounds.

The stands erupted into cries and cheers and the incongruous small sound of applause. Ann had played the long game in a vacuum of concentration. She awoke and looked about her. The same dazed expression she saw on Ruth's face was probably on her own.

"Change courts," Niki ordered. They obeyed, like automatons. "You're not through yet," she warned them. "You hear me?" Five heads nodded. "Annie?"

"Yes?"

"You serve next. When we get it."

Ann nodded. She had heard the threat. She swallowed twice, thickly, bent her knees, and looked up to the whistle. The sophomore served to the center rear. Ann fixed her eyes to the ball, and silence descended upon her again. She could hear nothing except Niki, and she only imagined that Niki spoke to her.

Ann served, not boldly or powerfully, but with unfailing accuracy. Time and again, Ann pulled back her clenched fist to drive the ball at the opponents. Always, as she knew it must, it stayed within bounds. She was hard, she was relentless, she would make no error.

The silence within Ann spread to the audience. The gym was empty of sounds, except for the grunts of the players and the slap of palm against the ball. Through the silence moved Niki's anger and Niki's will. She was darker, by degrees, than anybody else playing. She sweated more profusely and gnawed on her lower lip. She swiveled her head with sharp, vicious motions, watching the members of her team make their shots. And when she leaped to spike, you could see her exert her strength to snap gravity's hold, as if actual hands twisted around her ankles, to seize the height, to make the play, to win the point.

Hildy leaped with a diver's ease, as if those fingers that clutched at Niki turned light and springing for her. She soared up, a temporarily winged being, overreached the ball and gave to it her own curve, descending. Her head was touched by the beam of sunlight that wafted in through the high windows and her hair turned the pale, fading light into fire. Hildy spiked often, to countereffect the lackluster quality of her other shots, her passes that did not fall into receivers' fingers easily, blocks that misfired as often as they won the point.

Ann had not kept score—she bent her head, gathered her resources, looked up to serve again—and was surprised that the other team was not there to receive the ball. Silence dissolved into a roar of approval from the audience as the freshmen won the third game as they had the second, fifteen— zero. Miss Dennis was on her feet, clapping.

The crowd drifted away, leaving the freshmen alone with Miss Dennis. They did not notice her, however. They waited for Niki to dismiss them. But Niki lay belly up on the floor, her eyes closed. Her skin was blotched, mottled.

Finally the Munchkin spoke. "Miss Jones?"

Niki opened her eyes.

The Munchkin nodded her head, up and down, twice. "I congratulate you." She held out her small hand to Niki, who reached up to shake it. "That was well executed. Crude, but having signs of splendor."

She turned from Niki to smile at the others, but warmer for Hildy. "Miss Koenig. How do you find the glasses?"

"Confusing," Hildy said.

"One becomes accustomed," Miss Dennis said firmly.

"Yes," Hildy said.

The small woman left. She hurried to the exit, without looking back.

Niki looked around her. "God damn but I'm tired. Sorry, Hildy. You know the thing about the Munchkin? She is perfectly laconic, but never without the right word to say. Let's get out of here."

Later, after baths, after dinner, Hildy asked Niki: "You sent Eloise from the game?"

"Did I?" Niki asked.

Hildy's eyes flashed. "Don't lie. You spoke to her. I could see."

"If you say so," Niki answered.

"You knew that you could not drive her so?"

"That. I also thought she might collapse. I didn't know if she was too strong or too weak. It wouldn't have worked with her. Like it didn't work with you, only you permitted it."

Hildy continued to study her.

"That's all. That's the complete truth," Niki said. "It's almost Halloween."

"So what?" Ann said.

"So I'm going to New York."

"When?"

"Tomorrow afternoon. A guy I know at Columbia—they throw a big party for Halloween. He said he didn't have a date for it so if I wanted to come down I could."

"You'll miss classes," Hildy said.

"Not English, and that's the only one I need to keep a perfect face for. When do you think we'll play the juniors?"

"Not until you return," Hildy promised. "Saturday afternoon, I think. Eloise must play."

"Fine by me. I'll be back Friday. I've got English Friday."

"I will give up wearing these glasses," Hildy said.

"Don't you dare," Niki said. "Don't do that. What's the point of the technological nightmare if you don't take advantage of the little it can do for you?"

"I cannot say that," Hildy said, "but—"

"No buts."

"Perhaps. In any case, I will need them for the writing of my long paper, if I am to type it myself."

"But I'll do that if Niki can't," Ann offered. Hildy shook her head. "What are you writing on?"

"*King Lear*. Cordelia."

"Why her?" Niki asked. "She's such a weenie."

"A what?" Ann giggled at the sound of the word.

"A weenie." Niki waved her hands. "You know. She trundles across the stage and you say to yourself weenie-weenie-weenie. You know what I mean."

"No I don't," Ann said, "and I'm not sure I want to. Cordelia should make a good paper for you, Hildy. You should put some quotes in, to prove your points. Do you know how to do that?"

Hildy said she did.

Ann loved *King Lear*, although she could never feel she

understood it completely. There were always new and unexpected facets, she felt.

"You know what my favorite line in *Lear* is? When he meets Gloucester on the beach and says, 'If you would weep my fortunes, take my eyes.' The play turns on that line."

"How is that?" Hildy asked. Niki listened.

Ann summarized her notion of compassion in *King Lear* and showed how the characters fit into it. She discussed the theme in relation to plot, especially the irony of Edmund's capitulation at the end. She tied it into tragedy, the alternate themes of power and justice, and the parent/child motif. She found herself excited by her own idea, delivering a small lecture to her roommates, without realizing what she was doing. Until Niki began to applaud. Then, Ann smiled foolishly and apologized.

"Well, except for the beginning, with that lamentable favorite-line gambit, I'd say she's done a creditable job." Niki said. "Wouldn't you, Hildy?"

"Oh yes," Hildy said. "I could understand only a small part of it."

"Maybe because the rest was hot air," Ann suggested.

"Don't do that kind of stuff, Annie. Don't cover yourself in that way."

"Yes, dear," Ann spoke meekly. Then Niki thought her ideas were good?

"Which is not to say I'd sign up to take a course," Niki said, answering that unspoken question. "But again"—she grinned—"I might."

Niki departed for New York on the afternoon of Halloween. She had rented a car. "But that's against the rules," Ann protested, although Niki argued that her father had given her the credit card. She did not sign out until just before she walked out the door, so that nobody could stop her. Ann, looking at the signout book, noticed that she had left no destination, no address or phone number where she could be reached. This too was against the rules. Ann could now perceive Niki's code of behavior: Niki would not lie, but she would not volunteer the truth.

They practiced every day that week, grimly. Hildy took part in those practices, but did not seem able to recapture the

authority that the glasses had taken from her game. Ann
thought she was philosophical about the loss. She stayed late
after practices with Hildy, drilling shots that had previously
been reflex actions. Hildy worked patiently, calmly, without
irritation at herself, without relaxation of discipline.

"Although it disheartens me," she said.

"I wish I could help you, the way you did me," Ann said.

"You can't," Hildy said. "Not in this."

"What about this junior match?"

"The juniors and seniors have each only two teams," Hildy
answered; or rather, did not answer, as Ann thought. "Because
sports is not required in those years. So, those who continue to
play are highly motivated."

"Oh, dear," Ann said. "How will we do?"

"I do not know," Hildy said.

"Will we be horribly outclassed?"

"I do not know."

"You aren't making me feel any better about it," Ann
complained.

Niki was away for two nights. During that time, Ann and Hildy
grew into a chatty intimacy that surprised Ann. She had
thought that Hildy was above gossipy, speculative, superficial
conversation. She was delighted to be wrong.

They exchanged opinions of Miss Dennis. "I admire her,"
Ann said. "Her life is clear and uncluttered. High."

"Does she fear people?" Hildy asked.

"What do you mean?"

"When you say high—elevated?—you might also say she
isolates herself. She builds around herself a wall, with
knowledge and with age, to keep people away. It is not just
with students, I think, but also with other adults. She is always
alone."

"Maybe she doesn't like people close up."

"Perhaps."

"I mean, close up people aren't—you notice body odors and
little personal flaws."

"You think she is protecting an ideal?"

"Or she sees through to the heart and doesn't want to be
distracted from the vision. I think she's consciously chosen
solitude, and she accepts the limits imposed by that choice."

But it could be fear, Ann recognized, a sense of insecurity, inadequacy. Could the Munchkin think she was inferior?

In the quiet darkness of the room before they fell asleep, Hildy said, "Do you think Ruth is Jewish?"

"Of course."

"She does not say so."

"Why should she?"

"Because she is."

Ann switched on her light and leaned her head on one palm, to look at Hildy. "Does that bother you about Ruth?"

"Why should it? She is a good friend."

"You make things so simple," Ann said. "I wish I could."

"You are not often sure of things, are you?"

"Not often. Not nearly often enough. Except what I've learned in school, I don't think I'm sure of anything. Not like you and Niki."

"You would like to be sure." It was not a question.

"Life would be easier," Ann said.

Hildy was looking at her, her eyes quizzical, but Ann knew that Hildy without her glasses could not see her, not as Ann understood seeing, and she did not guard her face.

"What does Ruth believe in?" Hildy asked.

"In one God. In the law. I guess."

"The commandments?"

"Those, and the books of law. In the Messiah maybe."

"Why do you say maybe?"

"Because I'm not sure if it's only Orthodox Jews who still believe in the Messiah. Do you know about Orthodox and Reform?"

"What does that mean?"

Ann started to answer, then stopped herself. "I was going to say it was like Catholic and Protestant, but you know what? I don't know. I mean I know about it, vaguely, enough to catch references, but not really. I'd better take a religion course next year. That sounds like fun anyway, doesn't it? All I do know is that Jews don't believe in the immortality of the soul."

"If they do not believe in heaven, what happens to them when they die?"

"How would I know that, Hildy? How do any of us know?"

"Do you believe in it? In the immortality of the soul?"

"I'd like to. I'd like it to be true."

"It is," Hildy said.

This was forbidden territory, and Ann turned the light out again.

Hildy spoke out of the darkness: "But how is it that you should know that? Where I live, the sky is closer to the earth than it is here in the east. Closer than anywhere else."

"That's impossible, Hildy." Ann said.

"I know, but it is so."

What had Hildy's life been, to make her so sure of things; Ann wondered, but did not ask. Maybe it was living on a farm, seeing things grow. Maybe when everything you did was important to the family life—milking the cows for instance— then you wouldn't spend so much time thinking and worrying about yourself. Hildy always did what she thought was right, but she didn't do just what she wanted. She wasn't selfish, the way Ann and her family understood that word; and Niki too. What had Hildy's life been, that gave her the confidence to know, without question, things that Ann and everyone else questioned. Except Niki, Niki didn't question, so it couldn't be just living on a farm, it must be something more. How could Ann find it out, so she could know? "What's your family like?" Ann asked. "Hildy?" But Hildy was asleep.

"Why does Bess not stand straight?" Hildy wondered, after a practice. "Why does she stand with her arms folded before her?"

"She's overweight," Ann answered.

"You also stand so."

"I guess so. I hope that it minimizes my belly."

"But it doesn't."

"You sound like my mother."

"Is she ashamed of her breasts, Bess?"

"She could be. People tease you, you know, if you've got large bosoms. Boys. Kids."

"She shouldn't listen to them."

"Easier said than done," Ann said.

"Inside, she is quite proud," Hildy said. "Inside, she thinks she is beautiful."

"How do you know that?"

"In the way her eyes seek notice. She says she is fat but does not believe it."

"Volleyball has been good for her. For me too," Ann said.

"Bess is vain," Hildy continued. "That is a degrading characteristic."

Ann considered that. "Hildy, did you always have all these thoughts in your head?"

"Yes, of course."

"I never thought you did. I always thought you were too good to notice what the rest of us notice."

"These things seemed unimportant before."

"Before what?"

"Before I could see so well."

"What was important then? What did you think of Bess before?"

"Like a goddess, but a sulky goddess. Zeus' wife I think, the jealous one. I thought she needed to honor herself."

"And now?"

"Now I see—it will be harder for her than I thought. She does not understand herself."

"Do you understand *your*self?"

"Yes."

They rode together to the observatory, although Hildy no longer needed accompaniment. Ann had grown accustomed to the evening rides and the silent hours of study there. She liked the change, and the cold, dark air. She found she could ride the bike almost all the way up to the observatory now.

"How did you manage this ride before?" she asked Hildy.

"That was easy. I could feel the road beneath the wheels and the hills flowing down to it, in their curvings. A car I would hear and pull off the road until it passed. And the sky above was lighter, not so heavy as the land. The center lines, like a ribbon of light, led before. I rode on its path as through clouds of darkness. It was easy."

"But unsafe."

"I suppose so, yes. Now I can see—everything. Every tree, every curve. The center line is not elusive. And yes, I can see the stars now, too. I am always looking about and seeing. The moon does have a face."

"I know."

"Not as I had seen it before."

* * *

One of those evenings, Ann invited Eloise to come back from practice with them for supper. "But you haven't signed for a guest," she protested. "Have you?"

"You can be Niki."

"Where is she?"

"Out," Ann said, but Hildy answered as quickly, "In New York."

"She's cutting classes?"

They nodded.

"A law unto herself, is that the idea?" Eloise said, adding: "I can't help admiring her. But I don't see why I should."

The dinner achieved its usual level of mediocrity, but Eloise said she didn't notice it. "It's no worse than I'm accustomed to," she said. "Nobody in my family cooks well. I suspect I'm doomed to a life of mediocre sensual experiences, a chicken-a-la-king life, lived over Minute Rice, with frozen peas and box biscuits."

"Jello for dessert," Ann added, "and fake whipped cream."

"Precisely," Eloise agreed.

"Does food matter?" Hildy asked.

"In a world where there is rare steak—" Ann said.

"Or a smoked ham, sliced so thin you can't chew it but just let it lie on your tongue until every part of your mouth can taste it—" Eloise added.

"Yes," they answered Hildy.

Eloise pushed at a mound of whipped potatoes with her fork. "Oh well."

"Maybe you aren't," Ann said. "And besides, there are compensations, aren't there?"

"I hope so," Eloise said, wistful.

"Food doesn't matter," Hildy assured them.

"We were speaking metaphorically," Ann protested. Hildy looked puzzled.

After coffee they went upstairs to the room, where conversation floundered. Eloise admired the view and the Kennedy poster, then went to the door. "Well, thanks a lot," she said.

"Why are you leaving?" Hildy asked.

"You have work. You always have work to do. I don't want to disturb you."

"But you won't. Not tonight. Not for half an hour, anyway. Have you something you must do?"

"No, I don't have anything particular."

"Do you *want* to leave now? I thought we would visit."

"Visit?" Ann asked.

"The way women do at home. They visit with one another, of an afternoon. When there is an hour or two between dinner and supper and chores are completed. They sit and talk."

"What about?"

"Children, men, diseases, recipes. Whatever is uppermost in their minds. It does not matter what they talk about, just to visit."

"My mother visits," Eloise sat cross-legged in the middle of the floor. "She visits the sick or the grieving, or anyone else she can find who is needy."

"Good lord," Ann said, "why? I'm sorry, Eloise, that was rude. I didn't mean to be rude, just curious."

Eloise understood all that, and answered. "My father is a minister. My mother sees it as part of her work, as his wife, to dispense comfort and consolation wherever it's needed. She used to take me with her when I was a child. I hated it."

"Why did you do it then?"

"What else could I do? Anyway, since I won that first scholarship, I haven't been home that much, which has caused them no consternation. A ministerial scholarship," she explained to Ann's questioning face. "Churches tend to have money. It's the clergy that don't. Of course, they prefer you to attend Christian school, but I chose the Hall and waited them out. It wasn't so difficult to do. The committee wasn't accustomed to rebellion of any kind, and that gave me a certain palpable advantage. I needed any advantage I could get."

"Was it worth it?" Ann asked.

"The Hall? Yes, I think so. Don't you?"

"You know how I feel about it," Ann said. "But you——"

"Even so, I liked it. Friends aren't everything. I've been alone wherever I lived, partly because of being the minister's child, partly because of what I'm like." She dismissed Ann's protest with a wave of the hand. "But you, you're so ordinary—no, that's good, Ann; I don't mean it with insulting connotations, not at all. I mean you're what someone is supposed to be like. You're easy to be with, because you know you're all right. I'm surprising you."

"Well, yes."

"Hildy, don't you think I'm right about Ann?"

Hildy nodded agreement, then asked, "Have you quarreled with your parents?"

"Not exactly that. They don't quarrel, of course, and consequently we don't fight. They don't understand—what I want to get away from. Or to."

"To what?" Hildy asked.

"I'd like to teach. If I can get the degrees, I'd like to teach in a college. Failing that, I'll go somewhere like the Hall, somewhere removed from the hurly-burly."

"You already know what you want to do?" Ann demanded.

Eloise apologized. "I had to make plans early, or I'd have been trapped in an intolerable life. My parents don't discourage my desire to teach. They merely want me to work somewhere I am needed." She shook her head. "I don't want that kind of life, the constant battle. I'm not even convinced that good can be done, that way."

"I have no idea what I want to do," Ann said. "None. I guess I should."

"Of course not," Eloise soothed her. "You'll work for a year or two, at something you like, then get married and have children, whom you will raise well."

"That sounds horrible," Ann said. "Isn't there anything more interesting, or purposeful, in your crystal ball?"

"It sounds interesting to me," Eloise said.

"To me also," Hildy said.

"You want more glamour?" Eloise asked. "Romance? Excitement? Originality? I'm original. Niki's original. Hildy's original. Are we what you want to be?"

"No." Ann shook her head. "But sort of. I mean, Niki's right about you, you're like the Munchkin and I really admire her. She's a scholar. Her life is dry and solitary, but it has integrity. So will yours. Whatever else happens or doesn't. I can't imagine you—belying your intelligence. That's what I mean by integrity. My life won't have that. And Niki has all that energy and will. I'd like to have that. Wouldn't you? She doesn't bend before anything. And Hildy—Hildy's wonderful. You know I think that, don't you, Hildy? Everybody thinks that. So I wouldn't mind. Although—" She thought of what she would have to relinquish.

"Yes. Although," Eloise echoed her. "What is it that Niki wants to do?"

"Who knows?" Ann asked. "To go to Berkeley."

"Niki wants to relieve the misery of the world," Hildy said, "but she does not want to wait to do that. So, she is angry and impatient. She wants to be where the institutions are under attack for their blindness and crimes. Where she can make changes happen."

"Then what is she doing here?"

"She didn't get into Berkeley," Ann explained. "She's going to transfer."

Eloise nodded. "What about you, Hildy?"

"I will marry."

Eloise raised her eyebrows.

"My husband to be is a farmer and has two children. There is much to do. I would like to raise chickens, I think, and have children of my own."

"You sound so definite about it. When will all this take place?"

"July."

"Next July?"

Hildy nodded. Ann nodded too, although she hoped something would occur to alter Hildy's plans, or at least postpone them.

"That rather depresses me," Eloise said, voicing something Ann had never had the courage to put words to.

"I have this year for my own," Hildy said. "You cannot understand."

"But you know, I can understand it, better than most people," Eloise said. "I've lived most of my life in rural towns. And I did make those calls with my mother. I am neither deaf nor dumb, so I understand quite clearly the terms of your choice. Of course, I wouldn't think of attempting to dissuade you—but I can't like it, can I? Not for you. Besides, what about the volleyball team?"

"You will find others," Hildy said.

"It won't be the same," Eloise said.

"How could it be? And why should it be?"

"You can't argue with Hildy," Ann remarked to Eloise.

"Moreover"—Hildy ignored Ann—"it is the same thing, in

the microscope and the telescope. The details differ, but not the essential order."

Eloise changed the subject. "Ann. Let me look at your science notes."

"Want me to recite for you?" Ann offered.

"Please, not that."

Niki returned on Friday, during lunch. Ann went upstairs after the meal to pick up books and notebooks for her afternoon classes and saw Niki on the bed, her legs stretched out, her arms folded under her head. "Hi there," Niki said.

"Hi. How was it."

Niki waited for Hildy to enter, then, still supine, made her announcement. "I am a woman."

Oh, no, Ann thought. Here it comes.

Hildy did not speak.

"I agree with you both," Niki sat up. "It's not worth discussing. I had hoped, I must admit, for more. The earth to turn, transcendental experiences, two becoming one, lightning bolts. Something. But it's just another cheat, sex."

Good, Ann thought, then we can drop the subject.

But Hildy took it up. "You think so? Truly?"

"Truly, truly. I wouldn't lie to you."

"What then did you expect from it?"

"Honestly?" Niki asked.

Ann wondered if by remaining in the room she was behaving in bad taste.

"I expected something great. Something to take me out of myself. Or overwhelm me." She shook her head. "The more fool I, right?"

"But that is what happens to animals," Hildy said. "They come into season and give themselves over to their matings."

"I kept wanting to laugh," Niki said.

"And you did not?"

"Of course not." Niki actually sounded shocked.

"What kind of man was this, when you could not laugh?"

"Hell." Niki got off the bed. "What do you know about it anyway?"

"Something," Hildy said. "More than you, I think."

"Come off it. Ogling barnyard activities doesn't inform you about people. People are supposed to be different."

"And they are," Hildy said.

"Hildy, do you mean to tell me . . ." Niki asked, slowly. "Tell me just what you mean."

"I have lived with a man for more than a year. The man I am to marry when I return. He hired me when his wife died, to keep the house and the children. We have loved one another."

"How did you keep it from your parents?"

"My father knew it must be so."

"That's unbelievable."

"But you see, I do know. And you do not, not yet. It is not an exercise you do, to learn how. It is not like practicing volleyball. It is a human experience. When you ask it to be something other, you cannot have it so."

"You're saying it's my fault," Niki said.

"No," Hildy said.

"You're telling me you got there first and did better."

"No."

"Then what are you telling me?"

"You cannot separate the body and the soul. You make love not with only the flesh."

"Oh come on. It's just nerve endings."

"You know that is not so."

"All right, lubricated nerve endings."

Hildy shook her head.

"Anyway, I've got a class to make." Niki pulled on a denim jacket and was grinning by the time she reached the door. "I'll tell you. They talk about California," she said. "If they only knew."

Ann congratulated Hildy. "You certainly took the wind out of her sails."

"Did I? I hope not. I wanted to put the wind back into them."

They held a final practice early Saturday morning, just after breakfast, to prepare for the match with the juniors. They played for an hour, drilling passes, sets, serves. Afterwards, Hildy sat down on the floor of the gym, to discuss tactics.

"But what do you think, Hildy, how will it go?"

"I do not know. I have never seen the junior teams play, although I expect they are good. I cannot guess just how good."

"How good are we?" Bess asked.

"We are solid," Hildy said. "But there are so many small weaknesses—"

"And I'm one," Bess said.

"In a team, weaknesses of that sort do not exist," Hildy answered. "We have also strengths. Each player has strengths she gives to the team and takes from it."

"And weaknesses," Bess said.

"Yes. It is a matter of fitting those together. That is what I cannot see, how we will fit the parts together."

"You're gonna have to make this on your own," Niki said, not inappropriately.

"Look at it this way," Ruth remarked. "We've already broken the pattern. So even if we lose today, we have reason to be satisfied. What did we expect, after all?"

"I expected to get about this far," Sarah said. "I won't be unhappy."

"But I will," Hildy said. Even Niki looked surprised. "At first it seemed we could do well, but I was not sure how well. Then, I could see—so far ahead for us."

"You *do* care about winning," Niki crowed.

"Of course," Hildy said. "Because it means you have done the best, because you have taken what you are and practiced until you are more. I cannot explain it. Except that when we all play together—then it is right. I had thought we might win though."

"To the very end. Even the seniors," Niki said. "Right? That's what I thought. That's what I want. And who says we can't?"

"Nobody says *you* can't," Ruth answered. "It's the rest of us that hold you back. Except Hildy when she's on her game. If wanting it would do the trick, then you've got enough wanting to do it on your own."

"You don't?" Niki asked.

"It looks impossible," Ruth said. "Doesn't it?" she asked the others. "It's not just me, is it? Don't the rest of you feel that way?"

"That last game," Ann said.

"Don't remind me," Sarah said. "It was a miracle that we pulled it off. Niki's miracle, and none of my own." She picked at the soles of her sneakers.

"Oh well," Niki said.

"Yes. So what?"

"What is impossible?" Hildy said. "If it can be imagined, must it not be possible?"

"I don't buy that," Niki answered. "Dreams aren't powerful, not in that way. The way we wish it would be. That's part of what's bothering us right now, that we had begun to dream and now we've begun to accept the loss. To dream the loss. Not only have we not lost it, we haven't even played for it yet. No dreams please."

"But I could see it. I could see us doing it. I could see it for us. Not dream, see," Hildy argued.

Niki stared at her a moment. "We know about the clarity of your vision."

"Can you still see it?" Bess asked, hopefully.

Hildy shook her head.

chapter

8

Another large audience awaited this match. "Come to see the kill," Niki said. "People are more interested in the kill than the chase."

"I wish they would go away," Ann said. "I wish we could all go away."

"Soon enough, Annie," Niki answered. "Who knows? We may cream them. This is the bottom junior team, remember?"

"Or we may hold our own," Eloise encouraged.

Holding their own was difficult. The juniors were well drilled and accustomed to playing matches. They made mistakes, but did not become disconcerted by them. The freshmen were tense. They talked among themselves, quietly, usually to reassure.

The first game went slowly, serve frequently changing, teams frequently rotating. Both teams accumulated points steadily. Hildy's face held a constant vigilance. She was clearly enjoying herself, even though her game was still flawed by those slight miscalculations. The freshman team felt itself performing at a peak of concentration and skill. This was the high reach of their abilities. They won the first game, fifteen to thirteen.

Ann felt drained, but satisfied. Ruth trotted on the court to let Bess take her place by the benches.

"It's a good match," Ruth said.

"It's a tough one," Niki answered.

The second game started badly. Sarah lost service and the juniors kept it for a three point lead. After that, Ann fought off distraction and fatigue to keep up her level of play.

Like tennis players who have allowed their serves to be broken early in the set, they could maintain their progress, but not make up the lost points.

The score reached nine-six, juniors leading. Niki won serve back with a spike. The juniors won serve with a quick-time pair of passes. The serve careered back and forth, from team to team, never settling long enough to enable either team to gain points.

Ann strained to keep up, to play well, to predict accurately, to cover where she was needed. Beside her, sometimes in front of her, sometimes in back of her, Hildy, too, strained for the lost precision of her play. Out of the corner of her eye, Ann saw Hildy's chin grow determined and yet more determined. She heard grunts of disappointment as a shot went too wide or a block angled imprecisely.

Ann had the serve. She looked at the floor for a few seconds to gather herself together and make no careless error. She looked at the spot where she wanted the serve to go and judged she had room for some lack of placement. The serve arced perfectly. The receiving junior passed it forward. The setter at net sent it high up. The spiker rose with it and brought it down hard. Hildy moved too late into the block.

For a second Hildy stood where she had landed. She raised a hand, fist clenched, and hit herself on the thigh. She raised the other hand and removed her glasses and hurled them into the stands. They spiraled through the air, winking in the light.

Ann's eye did not follow them. She watched Hildy stretch, up, onto her toes, her hands large and strong, her legs spread apart. Then Hildy bent her knees and prepared for the next point.

The serve pelted toward Ann, low to the net, hard. Ann could do no more than block it with her forearms, a shot made as much from defensive reflex as from any choice. The ball flew off toward the center of the net, angled toward the floor. Hildy slid underneath it and not only saved it but passed it well to Sarah, who returned it to the juniors.

The juniors set up a spike. Hildy blocked it, beautifully, without hesitation sending it back to the one uncovered place in the opponents' court.

The freshmen smiled, relaxed, and continued play. They were each as careful as before, only each seemed to have more skill in her hands, more craft in her placement. They were vigilant, but vigilant to win not defend. They had, it seemed, all luck with them—or so the juniors said. "Everything started to fall your way," they said, the juniors, after the second game. "You couldn't make mistakes. I've never seen such luck—no, really—it's enough to make you believe in fate or predestination or divine guidance or grace. But it was a good game."

"Yes," Hildy answered happily. "It was good to play such a game."

"You're good," this team also said. "But our number one team—they've been undefeated for two seasons. That's a match that'll be worth watching."

"This match also was worth watching," Hildy said.

"Yeah it was, wasn't it?" they agreed. "When's the next?"

"In a week."

"Next Wednesday? Well, we'll be here. But where is it all going to lead?"

"To the top," Niki answered. "To the very top of things."

They all laughed and shook hands.

"We're not usually this good," the juniors confided. "It was fun to play you. How do you do it?"

The freshmen knew how, or at least why, but did not care to discuss it. Instead, with a kind of solemnity, they accepted the congratulations of the opposition, fans, friends, Miss Dennis.

Even when they were alone together, they did not talk of it. Each player felt a pride and pleasure beyond words, an interior glow she could recognize in her teammates, that did not need explanation. Bess returned Hildy's glasses. "I would not just throw them away," Hildy answered Ann's look. "They were expensive."

"I'm glad to hear that," Niki said. "You will still wear them, won't you? Only not for volleyball."

"I think that is how it should be," Hildy agreed.

"But how do you do it?" Niki asked. "I mean, you're nearly blind, so how can you play? How do you see what's going on?"

"It is easier to see the play when I cannot discern faces. It is all soft, smooth, simple. I see what will happen and what has happened. The ball floats to me, like a little cloud. It is still, without glasses. There is no winning, no losing, just the play itself."

"Well, you break all the rules," Niki said. "You're the exception."

"I would not do such a thing," Hildy denied. "The rules must include me, I think. If we knew them."

"Whatever," Niki said impatiently. "This is too big and furry a discussion for me. As long as you can compromise with the glasses I'm happy. It's lovely to see you play. I mean that, Hildy, I really do."

The team had asked Hildy, as a special favor, to schedule few matches during the next couple of weeks. Freshmen English classes traditionally had a long paper, due at the end of that time. This paper was the single most important section of the first semester's work. Except for Ann, they all needed more time to work on it. "And less time at practice," they said. "Not to mention the nervous strain. Especially the nervous strain."

So they did not play the second junior match until the middle of the next week. They still held frequent practices. Hildy said they could use them. During that time, Ann was often alone at odd corners of the day that she was accustomed to fill with companionship. Hildy was out of the room until she returned at ten to bathe and go to bed. Niki worked in fits and starts, starts and stops, concentrating intensely over her typewriter for a time before she slammed her hands down in exasperation and pushed the chair back and fled, downstairs or outside.

One night, when Ann was waiting for Hildy to return from the tub, Ann picked up the glasses Hildy left folded on her bureau.

They were heavy on the nose, those glasses. It would take a while to become accustomed to the weight balancing there. Ann closed her eyes, then opened them on the room.

Yellow lights swam, liquidly. The spaces in the room seemed indefinite, motile. But the furniture, beds, desks, bureaus, bookcases, stood firm. Not clear, but stable, and possessed of a brown trustworthiness.

Ann moved her head slowly, for to switch attention quickly dizzied her and made her feel physically disoriented. Her bed, with the slash of yellow that was her stuffed snake, pulled the proportions of the room off-balance. Niki's, covered by a bright, striped Indian spread, had the same effect. Hildy's, having only blanket and sheets, seemed repose made concrete: the beige blanket and creamy linen had no separating edges, but flowed, one into the other, inviting a deep and restful slumber.

The poster above Ann's desk was bleak, one-dimensional, flat, empty. So too seemed the photographs on Niki's bureau and on her own. Meaningless blurs.

Ann moved tentatively across a floor gone askew toward the window. She had looked out on the night; it had a lucid November darkness. Through Hildy's glasses the night blurred to mystery of an ancient sort. What Ann knew to be there were spiky, grasping fingers of bare trees, and the distinct triangles of pines; these disappeared into equality of clouded darkness. The darkness of these lenses suggested infinity and might lead to a sea of darkness. If you could sail into it, you would be driven by winds of emotion, winds so strong that you would need all your strength to follow them and survive. To arrive, where? At dawning, at the source of light?

Ann took off the glasses and the night receded into itself, in the proper chiaroscuro, with the known details. She rubbed her eyes and temples.

Hildy came in and Ann handed her the glasses. "What do you see without them? Is what I see when I put them on what you see when you don't wear them?"

"I don't know," Hildy said.

"I looked out the window," Ann said.

"What did you see?"

"I'm not sure. I can't put words to it."

"I don't mind if you want to try them on," Hildy said.

The glasses continued to intrigue Ann. She put them on whenever she could and tried to assimilate the information they gave her. Niki, having watched this, tried them on once. "I can't see a thing," she said. "What's the fascination?"

"I don't know. Didn't you ever pretend to be blind? Wonder what it was like?"

"When I was a kid. I figure, it's hard enough to see the world as it is. Who needs to go around trying to see it as it isn't?"

"What if it is as it isn't?"

"That's a damnfool thing."

"No I mean it. How do we know?"

"All this kind of argument is sophistic," Niki said. "We have only the evidence of our senses. The rest is—taradiddle."

"Is what?"

"Taradiddle. It's one of the words my mother used to use."

"Your mother might be OK."

"Yeah. I think she probably is. On her own terms. Sometimes I think I'll get to know her when I'm living on my own and all. I mean, she is my old lady, the thing itself. That's a fact."

Inevitably, the second junior match had to be played. That it was an iron cold day, with air that iced the lungs and made your nose start running when you got inside, did not excite Ann with its promise of deep winter as it would have on any other day that week. She was to sit out the first game of the match, a position that ordinarily filled her with relief. This time, she found herself thinking that to watch was worse than to play.

Ann watched intently, even before play began, holding Hildy's glasses in moist hands. She knew them all, her solemn mind told her, seeing them as if for the last time. Hildy, Eloise, Sarah. Niki, Ruth, Bess.

The stands filled. Ann could not sit still. She turned to see the faces behind her. She greeted friends. Her feet jiggled against the floor. She passed the glasses back, from hand to hand. Then she breathed on them and polished them on her cotton shirt.

At last the game began.

Ann was so nervous that she could not see what happened. She leaned forward and her mind whirled, projecting the number of points from the last played to the end of the game, debating who would win. If the juniors won, then Ann would have to play in the deciding game. If the freshmen won, then the next game would not be as crucial, but the one after that would be deciding.

"What's the score?" a latecomer leaned down to ask her. Ann did not know.

Fidgeting, she put on Hildy's glasses. The world blurred, receded. Even sounds seemed muted.

Through the glasses, the freshmen were difficult to distinguish, except that Ann knew in memory who each was. Who they were in the glasses, though, she did not know at first.

Watching the play, she knew somehow that the freshmen were winning. She leaned back without taking her eyes off the play, queried, and discovered that that was the case.

She could see how things would go, one or two plays ahead of each particular shot. She saw the juniors move together for defense, the freshmen move forward for offense. Then the patterns would alter slightly, and the freshmen were in danger. It was as if she could see through to the essence of the game.

Only Hildy was unaltered in this new vision. As always, she was light, leaping up to join the cloud of brightness that floated above the court (from the high windows, Ann remembered), arising to rejoin her own element. The four others—Niki excluded—moved with Hildy, around Hildy, as planets around the sun. Independent, dependent.

And Niki, like some lost soul among the angels, cut across the light—but made a part of it, as shadows define brightness.

If I wore these before a mirror, Ann wondered, what would I see? What am I?

Somebody sat down beside her on the floor; this she registered without interest. "They are playing well." A familiar voice spoke softly into her ear. "They will take the game soon, I think. But these juniors don't look defeated yet." Ann did not respond. "Miss Gardner?"

Ingrained courtesy toward adults and teachers pulled Ann out of her own thoughts. She turned her head quickly, to apologize for not responding more immediately.

But she could not speak the words. Through the glasses, so close, you could see, she could see, into the eyes of Miss Dennis. Ann there saw—falling into it: the depth of the other, down a gray tunnel drawing inward. She had not thought there was so much to any other, or to herself. Such inward spiraling shades or layers of gray, unfolding. The eyes grew startled and sent up lighter flecks of color, as if to close doors or build defenses to repel the invasion. Ann's vision moved too swiftly to be checked.

"Miss Gardner? Is something wrong?" the Munchkin's voice recalled her. What would she discover if she followed the cool gray corridor far enough?

Ann took off the glasses and reentered the recognizable world.

"I'm sorry," she said. "I wasn't paying attention."

"I thought not," Miss Dennis said. "Is it quite safe for you to wear those?"

"I don't see why not."

"You'll be going in soon, to play. You'll need to readjust your vision."

Ann agreed.

"It is most exciting, isn't it?"

Ann agreed.

"Fourteen-twelve," Miss Dennis informed her briefly. "In favor of the freshmen." She sat up, back onto the bench behind, smiling. Ann grinned sheepishly and watched the next point. Hildy served. Sarah won the point.

Ann went onto the court as Hildy came off. Niki was muttering and bouncing on the balls of her feet. Her face was ominous. "They're tough," she said to Ann. "They're good. I don't know why Hildy had to go out."

Ann, still bemused by her recent transition, did not answer. She did not even feel distracted by Niki's emotion. She shrugged and looked about her at the team.

"Are you awake?"

"No." Why take the trouble to lie?

"Wake up then. You'll blow it for us. Every one of us has to be playing at peak. Even with Hildy here. So you better—or I'll stick pins up your nose."

Ann giggled. "Pins up your nose," she repeated with pleasure. Her head cleared and she poised her body for the game.

It was a match between equally determined opponents. Both teams were alert to defend and attack. Points were won, not given away. The juniors won the second game, seventeen to fifteen. Hildy came in and Sarah went out. They switched sides again.

It was Hildy's presence, as much as her skills, that made the telling difference. The freshmen assembled around her and became unbeatable. The juniors did not give up; they fought every point energetically. But Hildy's team stood firm, placed winning shots, received and returned difficult passes, played with one another as if they were all parts of one body, even Niki, if you allowed that the left hand might not know what the right is up to. They were the better team. At the last shot, the gym rang with cheers. The spectators cheered the freshmen and the juniors, they cheered the game itself. The two teams remained on the court, applauding one another. Then the crowd dispersed, and the players drifted reluctantly off the court.

"Yeah," Niki said. "That's it. That was OK. I'm going to shower here."

Ann and Hildy returned happily to the dorm, to bathe. Ann walked, undressed, sat in the hot tub, toweled, and padded down the hall in a haze of self-satisfaction.

Hildy had finished her bath. She stood naked, except for glasses, by Niki's desk. Her flesh glowed pink and white. My God, women are beautiful, Ann thought.

Then Hildy spoke. "No," she said. Her voice was harsh, angry.

"Hildy? What's the matter?"

"This. This." She picked up Niki's paper.

"I don't get it." Ann looked at the stapled pages. "Compassion in *King Lear*," she read. "Oh. She wouldn't do that," Ann said. "Niki doesn't do things like that."

Hildy had tears in her eyes, magnified by the glasses.

"It's OK, Hildy. You know Niki, it's OK."

Hildy did not answer.

"Look, she'd have hidden it away if she'd felt guilty. Isn't that right? But she didn't hide it, she left it right out on her desk."

"I would not have seen it, not to read, without the glasses."

And I am trained not to see what is not on my own desk, or has not been given to me to read, Ann thought.

"What then? Should we read it?"

"No," Hildy said.

"You'll ask her?"

"I do not have to," Hildy said.

"Well, I do. You can't condemn her without knowing for sure."

Hildy nodded, replaced the paper, and turned to dress. Fear sat on Ann's stomach.

Niki dashed into the room and chucked off her shorts. She opened a drawer to take out her denim skirt. Her hair was damp. She snapped happy fingers as she changed. Then she heard the silence of the room.

"What's with you two?"

Ann swallowed. Hildy's back was to them. "May I read your paper?" Ann asked.

Niki froze. Her eyes turned agate and defied them. "Judge and jury—is that what it is? And Annie for a fair trial."

They did not respond. Hildy did not turn.

"Sure, what the hell, read it. But I'm OK, you hear? I'm on the right side of the law." Her voice was bitter. "You should be flattered really, Annie. It's a compliment if you think about it. That I remembered so well what you said. It means, if you think of it, that you said it well. Really. You could try looking at it that way. Your words were burned upon my memory. But I tell you"—she spoke to Hildy's back—"I know the rules and I'm OK."

She left the room abruptly.

chapter

9

Ann read Niki's paper and judged it a good one. The thesis, her own after all, had validity. Niki's examination of it was thorough and well documented. "It'll get you an A maybe," Ann wanted to say to Niki. But she did not see Niki, except in passing, in bed asleep or pretending to sleep; at a distance on the way to or from class; across the dining room. Ann wanted to say to Hildy, "You were right," but Hildy maintained a troubled silence. Ann slept badly in that room those two long days, could not concentrate on her studies, could not see her way through to any resolution. The air in the room was restless, too bright so that it pricked at you, too dark so that it tossed you about. Like the other two, Ann spent most of her time those days away from their room.

She studied with Eloise in the library. She lunched with Ruth at the Student Center. She walked about the campus with Bess. She ran errands downtown with Sarah. She returned late to the room and greeted whoever might be there (usually Hildy) before putting out her light and resolutely closing her eyes. She felt isolated, abandoned.

Finally, on Friday afternoon, she decided to answer Eloise's persistent query.

"Something's very wrong. It's Niki. And Hildy."

"Does that have anything to do with why Niki has excused herself from practices?"

"It does, indeed it does," Ann said. "The trouble is Niki's long paper. It's all one of my ideas. I was talking one day and what I said is what Niki wrote. Hildy saw it. Then I read it, to be sure. Hildy didn't read it."

"What does Niki say?" Eloise asked. "You needn't quote her precisely."

"She says she hasn't broken any rules."

"What does Hildy say?"

"Nothing. But you know what she is thinking."

Eloise nodded and studied Ann with pale, quiet eyes. "What about you? What do you say?"

"I don't know. I didn't write it, there's that. On the other hand, it *is* my thinking. But, I mean—if a professor gives a lecture and you think he's right, and you understand something as he has explained it—and then you write an exam based on that understanding—what about that?"

"You're not a professor," Eloise said.

"That's not the point, is it?"

"Not exactly," Eloise said. "So you feel that it's not plagiarism, exactly."

"Not the lie outright," Ann agreed.

"How do you *feel* about it?"

"Honestly? I don't care. Except for them. And my peace of mind. I don't know if they're as—unhappy—as I am, but. . . ."

They sat at a long oak table amidst stacks of books. Behind long windows, snow hurried down in flurries. Eloise dabbled with her pencil on a sheet of paper, making intricate little boxes in a geometrical design.

"I'd advise you to consult Miss Dennis," Eloise said, finally. "Why don't you talk to her?"

"About what? Behind their backs?" Ann believed there was no solution.

"Alternately, you could just wait until enough time passes and everyone has forgotten. Everything dies down, in time."

"It wouldn't be fair. I'd be telling on Niki."

"Often, if you give problems time enough, they straighten themselves out."

"Wait. If we all talked to the Munchkin, all three of us. That might work. Do you think it might, Eloise? If we all agreed to accept her decision. Eloise, you've done it. You've figured out what to do."

Eloise glanced over at Ann. "That wasn't what I had in mind, but it's more expedient than what I had thought of."

"If I can get Hildy and Niki to agree. How can I do that?"

"You can do it. It's the kind of thing you can do."

"I hope so. Niki won't like it. Lord, I feel better."

"A weight has been lifted from your shoulders?" Eloise suggested, smiling.

"And—with luck—placed on somebody else's," Ann agreed.

Miss Dennis, her voice puzzled on the telephone, was sorry she could not see them sooner, but the first free time she had was Sunday afternoon. She would be out of town but could return for a late afternoon meeting. She would be happier if Miss Gardner would divulge the nature of the problem? But, if she could not do that, then Miss Dennis would expect them at four. Unless, with a lift of hopefulness to the thin voice, things worked themselves out before then. Well, if Miss Gardner felt that was unlikely. . . .

Ann's next step was to speak with her roommates, individually. Hildy went up to the room after dinner. Ann followed her and accosted her as she sat reading an astronomy textbook.

"Hildy?" Blue eyes, magnified by thick glasses, looked up at her. Ann had planned a tidy little speech, defining the problem, justifying her decision to contact the Munchkin, explaining her motives. She did not use it. "I've made an appointment with Miss Dennis. Sunday at four. For all of us."

Hildy waited.

"I think she will have to judge for us. I haven't told her what the problem is. I think we can all agree to go along with what she decides."

"No," Hildy said. "I cannot agree to believe what I do not believe."

"But, Hildy," Ann protested.

"Can I?" Hildy asked. "Mustn't I rather know for myself?"

"I trust Miss Dennis," Ann said.

Hildy studied her. "You do not know, for yourself, what is the right in this?"

Ann shook her head.

"And you are unhappy. Yes, I can see that you are. You would want me to do this?"

"Please."

"Then I will go to the meeting."

"And abide by her decision?"

"What does that mean?"

"I don't know. I don't know what she'll say. I guess it means we can be finished with this quarrel. We can go back to normal."

"It is Niki who has the quarrel. And you, also, have the quarrel."

"And you don't?"

Hildy shook her head. "But even so, yes, I will meet and will abide. This—division—it is not good."

Niki, to Ann's surprise, agreed immediately. "Sure, that will settle things, one way or the other. I should have guessed you'd cook up some plan, Annie. Sure, I'll go along with whatever the Munchkin says." She grinned. "It'll screw up my plans if she has me thrown out for plagiarism though."

"Could that happen?"

"Don't act so innocent. This is the East, as you so often remind me."

"But I don't want that to happen. Niki? Really I don't. That's not what I had in mind."

"Ann. Annie. I know that. But if you're going to be a mover you've got to accept results. Don't worry, it's OK with me. That's the way things happen. Screwups. Unless, of course, the Munchkin sees it my way. I thought about that, I did. So don't worry, Annie. I'm not worried."

"So you think she'll say that the paper is all right?"

"Who knows? I think it is. What do you think?"

"I don't know," Ann said. "And I don't care. Frankly, I don't. I just want this thing finished."

"Me, too," Niki agreed. "Will Hildy go along with this?"

"She said she would abide. That was the word she used. But she didn't say abide by the decision. I don't know, Niki. I don't know anything. I don't know what Hildy will do. Or why she'll do it. I don't know what you'll do, or why. But—we need somebody else's opinion."

"It's not opinion you've contracted for. You know that, don't you?"

"I guess so."

"And I will go along with whatever the Munchkin decides. You have my word on that. I don't have any choice in the matter."

"I could call off the meeting. Should I?"

"I don't know, Annie. Should you?"

"No."

* * *

Sunday morning it snowed. Flakes fell from low gray clouds. It was the first, light, snow of the long winter. Snow, only an inch deep, that would not stay long on the ground. At most it would make the roads slick for a couple of nights. During the day the sun would melt the snow, while the cold at night would freeze it. However, this snowfall was a herald for heavier snows to follow, storms that would block roads and blanket mountains, snows to leave the world more beautiful than it had been, beautiful especially the long-branched evergreens. This light snow was a vague reminder, an absent-minded promise.

By late afternoon, it died down to flurries that drifted idly. The three girls did not walk together to their meeting. Hildy remained in the library until it was time. Ann was with Eloise, who accompanied her most of the way to the little house and left her with wishes for good fortune and an acknowledgment that she did not see how that was possible. Niki was already in the house when Ann arrived. Her bike was parked in the snow. Hildy arrived shortly thereafter.

Miss Dennis, silent, led them into the study, poured them tea, and sat in her leather chair. Ann once again sat facing the little woman. Hildy was cross-legged on an oriental rug, before the fire. Niki put her cup on the mantelpiece and stood behind Ann, restless, chewing on her finger.

"So it is serious." The Munchkin was the first to speak. "Can it be this serious, I wonder. Miss Gardner?"

Ann looked at Hildy and then at Niki. They both waited. She collected her thoughts. "We, all of us, want you to decide a question we can't decide for ourselves. Except Hildy."

"If it is within my province, I will do so."

"I don't know why I'm the one to talk," Ann said, "but maybe I am. I'm not so involved. Niki's freshman paper presents a thesis of mine." She considered this. It was fair enough, bare enough.

"The question is a point of plagiarism, I think. Niki believes that she has not plagiarised, because she wrote it all herself, following ideas as I had stated them. Hildy believes—" Ann realized that she did not know what Hildy believed, although she understood it. "Hildy believes not," she concluded.

Miss Dennis studied them from behind gray eyes. "You ask me then to sit in judgment?"

"Yes," Ann said.

"You are prepared to accept the terms and consequences of judgment? Miss Jones?"

"Why not?" Niki shrugged.

"Miss Keonig?"

"No."

"Hildy!" Ann cried.

Miss Dennis raised a hand to silence Ann. "I think I understand Miss Keonig. I sound pompous, but it is a most disquieting position you put me in. However, I think Miss Koenig"— She gazed at Hildy. "And we have read Plato together."

"Yes," Hildy said.

The fire crackled. Its lights glinted off Hildy's glasses. Behind her, Ann felt Niki's dark presence, her impatience.

"Let us begin then," Miss Dennis said. "Can you tell me, Miss Gardner, how this occurred?"

"I'll try. You see, we often help one another with our work. For example, Niki and Eloise Golding showed me what I was doing wrong when I studied for the Coordinated Sciences course. Because I had a D at midterm. And once I helped Hildy revise an English paper."

"What did that entail?"

"I read the paper and tried to figure out what she had done wrong."

"Did you advise her on content?"

"I don't think so. Did I, Hildy?"

"You didn't." Niki spoke.

"Anyway we help one another in that way. Niki asked me to give her advice about English. She wasn't satisfied with her grades."

"They were poor? I don't remember that," Miss Dennis interrupted.

"Not bad. But she wants a B in English. She needed an A on her long paper to bring up her cumulative average. But I'm trying to show how we were in the habit of talking about the courses and helping one another if we could."

"There is nothing wrong with that. There is much right with it."

"That's what I think. So the long papers came due. Hildy—I asked her what she was writing about. I think that's how it happened. She told me, and it was *King Lear* and I talked about a pet idea of mine. Because I studied *Lear* in English last year."

Miss Dennis asked, "Are you apologizing?"

"I sort of lectured," Ann said.

"It is a temptation. But that is not the source of the present problem, is it?"

"No it isn't. Niki's long paper says what I said. It's my ideas."

"I see. In how much detail did you speak?"

"I was thorough, but I didn't quote extensively. I showed how the idea related to major aspects and possible major themes. I was fairly general."

Miss Dennis turned to Niki. "Miss Jones?"

"It's just that simple. I want an A and I figured Ann's ideas would be of high quality. Impeccable quality." Niki grinned. "I remembered what she had said, pretty much. I went over the play with that in mind and worked out textual proof. I wrote the paper."

"How did it happen that you two read this paper? I think I am correct in saying they have not been returned."

Niki answered for them. "That was all up-and-up. These two—they're not in question. I had it on my desk and Hildy saw the title. She hasn't actually read it. Ann's read it, but she asked me first. They're clean."

"And you?"

"A little sullied, I think. No more."

Miss Dennis slid down from the chair and poured more tea. She stirred sugar into hers. Ann watched her hands, deft and tiny, without rings, the nails cut square. Hildy sat cross-legged watching the flames.

"What do you feel about this, Miss Koenig?"

"To take somebody else's idea is not right. A paper must be your own, your own ideas and your own writing. Otherwise you must acknowledge the person from whom you have taken. That is so?"

"That is so. Let me ask you this: when Socrates refers to just judges, what does he mean?"

"He means that a few among those who sat in judgment dealt with the facts of his case. The others, the unjust judges, made their decisions because of their own emotions, or for presumption about where this habit of questioning would lead. Some perhaps even for revenge. But the just judges understood that under the law and under the gods Socrates had acted and taught rightly. His purpose was to bring out the truth."

Miss Dennis asked, "How is it that you know that?"

"You taught me," Hildy answered. Her eyes regarded Miss Dennis steadily. "I understand. You think it is not so simple."

"I think it is not simple," Miss Dennis agreed.

"Can you show me the rightness of it?" Hildy leaned forward. "If you could. I can see how it is not simple. I can think of that and understand it. But in myself I cannot make it right. In myself I know it is wrong. There is a lie in that paper. Can you show me that there is not?"

"That is Miss Jones's job," the Munchkin said.

"Oh no," Niki's voice grated. "I won't do that. I don't have to."

"Yes," Hildy said. "You do."

Miss Dennis agreed.

Niki shook her head again, denying it.

Ann gave way to exasperation. "What are you after, Niki?" She twisted her head to look behind her. Niki's eyes were closed and her fingers clutched the fragile handle of the teacup. "You agreed. Remember? You said you would."

Niki opened bleak eyes. "Yeah. OK. Look, Hildy," she began. "There is a convention about ideas in print, and when you are plagiarising them and when you are not. If you take somebody else's words and present them as your own, that's cheating. We're agreed about that. No question. I didn't do that.

"But what about ideas without print? What about conversations, where people exchange ideas? Ann talked about this, and she made good sense to me. I agreed with her ideas. Are they still just hers then? Or, if I am convinced by them, do they become mine? I think they are mine also, from that point on. So, when I write them out, it is my own work. And there is no plagiarism involved."

They all watched Niki as she spoke. A silence followed, where only the fire chattered. Niki waited.

"No," Hildy said. "That is not the truth of it."

"I am not lying." Niki loomed forward.

"You are not telling the truth," Hildy said quietly.

"You don't want to hear the truth. You don't want to see what really is the truth." Niki came out from behind Ann's chair and paced the room as she spoke. "You and your categorical negatives and affirmatives. Things aren't that simple. Yes or no, that's not enough."

"It is the very beginning," Hildy said.

"There is no very beginning," Niki answered. "You live in a dream world, where God is a daddy who keeps things orderly. Where right is different from wrong. That's all illusion, and you don't admit it. I'll tell you what's right. Winners are right, by definition. They have the power to make themselves right. In this world you have to know what you want, and go after it. Whether it's good or bad, you have to fight for it, hard and sometimes dirty. If you can't, well tough luck on you. If you're not willing to kick in a few teeth, you won't get what you want, if you're not willing to lose a few of your own teeth."

She paced back and forth, too large for that room. She looked at nobody as she spoke. Her eyes had an inward focus. "We're not free agents. I'm not. You're not. I never made a free choice in my life. So I'm out for myself—where's the crime in that? So is everybody else. Even you Hildy. I can show you. I want to go to Berkeley and I need B's for that. To get a B in English I need an A on a paper. Annie gave me an A paper idea and I took it. Simple as that. That's what's simple. And what about you? You're going back to marry a man your father has selected for you, to raise chickens and darn socks. You've turned your back on Stanton too. On what it stands for. On your friends here. And you've already done that, always done that, from the first. But you're not thinking about that, or them, or the money the College has invested in you. The volleyball team, what about them? You're so concerned with being right. But you've used Stanton, the same way I have. You've lied, by implication. You may say it's different because you put it on your application, but that difference doesn't mean anything." Niki crouched between Hildy and the fire. She thrust her face into Hildy's. "Do you hear? That difference doesn't mean anything. Nothing. Because we're the same, you and me. Call it what you like, we're the same thing. That's all we can be because we're human beings and there's nothing simple about that. Only our rhetorics differ. And it doesn't matter what we do with our lives, or why we do it. Because we just die in the end and it's over. The great accident, the joke. People are frightened so they convince themselves there is meaning to it. History, progress, knowledge: none of it works. None of it makes any difference whatsoever to anythng. The world isn't going to be saved. It isn't even lost. It just is. We scrabble around on its surface. Like bugs. The biggest bugs grab what they can. That's it."

Hildy shook her head, mute.

"You can fool yourself. You can fool Annie here and all the rest, and even her," Niki's head jabbed toward Miss Dennis. "You can't fool me. I wish you could, but you can't.

"The truth is that it doesn't matter how you get what you want as long as you're safe from society and the law. What I want is a chance to get even for some of the things society does, and the law does. Before they blow us all up. Nobody will care how I got it, once I've got it. And I did not break the rules."

Niki stood up again, above Hildy, and she spread her hands apart. "That's the way it is, Hildy. I'm sorry, because that's not the way you want it to be. I'm sorry because you're—I like you. I admire you. But that's the way it is. You can't beat me on this one."

It was Niki who had tears in her eyes.

"If we can return to the particular event," Miss Dennis said, "and I think we should . . ." Ann and Hildy nodded their heads. Niki's face was immobile. "Let me tell you what I see as justice in this matter. The paper, Miss Jones's paper, is safe."

Ann understood that and her heart flooded with relief.

"Miss Jones," the Munchkin went on, "is not."

Ann's sense of security vanished. She waited for Miss Dennis to say more.

But the woman had no more to say.

"What should she do?" Hildy asked.

"Should isn't in question. You heard her," Niki said. "What I will do is—nothing. That's it. It's over."

Hildy stood up, taller than Niki. "You do not care about being right. You think to win is to be right."

"That's not fair, Hildy. It's not even true," Ann protested.

"I see that now," Hildy continued, as if Ann had not spoken. "Miss Dennis?"

"I cannot argue it with you, Miss Koenig."

"Why not? You must make me see."

"I can't. I have made my decision, under the rules. It is a correct decision and I will stand by it."

"Hildy," Ann asked, "if I don't mind, why should you?"

"It is not for you and me to mind," Hildy said. "It does not matter for us, or for Miss Dennis. For Niki to be right, that is what matters."

"There's nothing wrong with what I did. Miss Dennis— albeit reluctantly—just said so."

"Do you believe that? Niki?"

Niki looked straight at Hildy, hard and straight. "Yes."

Hildy shook her head. "No, you do not." She gathered her coat and left the room, unhurried.

Ann sat crumpled in her chair.

"I'm off too," Niki said briskly. She thrust her hand out to Miss Dennis. "Thank you."

Miss Dennis took her hand, but did not shake it. She held it within both of her small palms. "Don't thank me, Miss Jones. I have done you no favor. Illusions are of more than one kind."

Niki swallowed. "But we cherish our own," she said. Then she, too, left.

Miss Dennis turned to Ann. "You had hoped for more, I think." Ann nodded. "But you will have to find your own way," Miss Dennis said. "I can't do that for you."

"I guess I should have known," Ann answered. "Anyway, I do thank you, for your time and trouble. I won't bother you like this again. I'd already thought of everything that you said." She carried the tea tray into the tiny kitchen.

Miss Dennis walked with her to the door. "We have to find our own compromises," she said. "People like us. I have been inadequate here. I wish I could have been more."

"I can't imagine what else you might have done," Ann consoled her.

"Neither can I," Miss Dennis said. "But Miss Koenig can imagine. And Miss Jones can."

Ann walked slowly back to the dormitory. Leaden skies hung low and sullen. In the gathering darkness, the air was piercingly cold. She jammed her hands into the pockets of her coat and scuffed her feet. She slipped frequently. Films of water had begun to freeze on the sidewalk. She approached the dormitory through disheartened pines. Windows glowed with yellow light, warm and welcoming, but she did not want to be welcomed or warmed. Her own room was dark. She dropped her coat on the bed and sat on it.

The room had been abandoned. She had been abandoned. Hildy's glasses were folded on Hildy's dresser in a line with the comb and brush. Niki and her typewriter were gone. Ann sat and waited. Nothing happened. The usual noises occupied the rest of the hall, the other rooms. Her own room held barren silence. She turned on the bedside light and lay back, studying the ceiling, until supper.

Sunday supper was always sparsely attended, and the most dismal dishes from the deepest dark corners of the iceboxes were brought to the tables. Niki and Hildy did not appear.

Ann returned to the empty room after the meal. She hung up her coat and undressed. She put on her nightgown. She got into bed and pulled the covers up over her head.

She could not sleep. It was only seven o'clock, she thought to herself, and besides, if she could sleep she would only wake up terribly early.

It wasn't the failure, her own failure, that distressed her. She decided that. It was the hopelessness.

And it was being in the middle. Wishy-washy. Niki knew what she wanted. Niki was certain and sure. Hildy too. But she, Ann, what was she supposed to do? How was she supposed to figure out which side she was on? She'd chosen Hildy's, but she couldn't *be* Hildy. She suspected that Niki was—not right, that was Hildy's word—correct. Safe was the word the Munchkin used.

Miss Dennis had not solved anything. Ann had only made things worse. For everyone.

Hildy was right. Hildy was always right. That didn't help Ann at all.

Ann discovered that she didn't understand either of her roommates. She had thought she knew instinctively about Hildy. She had thought she could intellectualize Niki and know her. She hadn't understood either one of them. And now she had a feeling of sympathy for Niki and a kind of fear of Hildy, to add to her inadequate understandings.

She got out of bed, took a dime from her wallet, tied her bathrobe tight, and slipped her feet into loafers. The slippers were under the bed and she was too tired to bend over. She went out to the pay phone and dialed an operator who placed the collect call. Home.

Mrs. Gardner accepted charges and made bright inquiry into Ann's health and classes and social life.

Ann brushed those aside. "I think I'll come home this weekend. Is that all right with you?"

"You know it is, dear. But with Thanksgiving the following week, don't you want to save your weekends?"

"I want to come home."

"Then by all means do so. You know we're always happiest when you children are home. Shall I tell your father? Or would you like to surprise him?"

"I hadn't thought of that. Let me surprise him."

"He'll enjoy that. I hope I can remember—"

"Mother! It's your own idea."

"That should help, shouldn't it? What do you think, a leg of lamb, or a steak? Which sounds better to you for Friday?"

"Steak, by all means, steak. It's been a long time since I've had steak. And really rare, and with mushrooms? Could you do that?"

"It sounds good. Shall I meet the five o'clock bus?"

"No, I'll get a cab. If you're not home, Dad will suspect something."

"That's right. He is suspicious, isn't he, by nature. I've never given him cause—it must have to do with the law, don't you think?"

"Maybe he just knows human nature better than we do."

"Maybe so. It'll be good to see you, Ann. I had my mind set on not seeing you until next week, so this is a special treat. What a good idea this is."

"Thanks, Mom," Ann said.

"For what? This is your home."

Ann returned to the room. She studied the family picture (all of them, strung out in a long line, six strong) for a few minutes before she sat at her desk and opened her history textbook.

At eleven she went back to bed and slept. When she awoke to the alarm the next morning, Hildy's bed was rumpled and empty. Niki's had not been disturbed.

Ann shrugged, half-glad to be alone. They had a practice that afternoon, but she would not worry about that. Hildy's glasses were still on the bureau. Ann considered taking them down to breakfast, but decided not to.

She had also decided, she dicovered as she sat down beside Hildy in the bare morning light, that she was not going to be drawn into the quarrel any further.

"Morning," she said, her voice expressionless.

Hildy turned her face to Ann's voice. "You were sleeping so well. I did not think you would wake."

"I set the alarm. You abandoned the glasses?"

"Yes, I think so. Don't you?"

"I would," Ann agreed. But she wouldn't, she admitted that to herelf, even though she understood that it was what should be done. Even though she admired Hildy for the uncompromising decision. "No, I wouldn't," she said, to be truthful; but even if Hildy asked her what she meant, she wasn't going to explain. Her self-consciousness made her awkward. She hit her egg too hard with the knife, and yolk oozed down over her fingers. "Where's Niki?"

Hildy shook her head. "I don't know."

Ann broke a piece of toast into the egg cup. "Do you care?" (One did not raise such questions over breakfast, she knew that. The hell with it, she thought.)

Hildy did not take offense. "Yes," she said.

"I know," Ann apologized. "I needed reassurance. We have a practice today, so she'll be there. That's what I figure."

"I too am hoping that," Hildy said. "It wasn't your fault, Ann."

"I figured that out for myself," Ann said. "Still—"

Ann ate hastily. She gulped the last of her coffee. "See you."

Hildy gazed at her. Not uneasy, curious.

"Oh," Ann said. "By the way, I'm going to Philadelphia this weelend, home. I thought I ought to tell you."

"We play Wednesday and then not until after Thanksgiving. There is no worry."

"I wasn't worried. I just thought I should tell you."

"I thank you," Hildy continued to stare. "You have slept very deeply, yes?"

"What is that supposed to mean?" Ann demanded, but her defenses crumbled and she sat down again. "Hildy? When you see me, what do you see? Without glasses, I mean."

"I cannot explain." Hildy looked away.

Ann wanted to protest, but found she couldn't. She was embarrassed. "I'm sorry," she said. Then, "No, I'm not, not really. Thank you. See you at practice, OK?"

Niki was not at practice. Nobody had seen her all day. Ann, walking back from the gym with Hildy, walking close so as to be able to support one another on the unexpected icy patches, allowed her worry to surface. Hildy shared it.

"What she would think," Hildy said, "I cannot guess at it. What she would do."

"She could have left school," Ann said. "She has a charge card."

"When she fears and what she fears and how she acts. She cannot be predicted."

"Or gone to another dorm?"

"You, you go home, that is so, isn't it? You go to something you know can be trusted. But Niki has no such place, inside herself or outside."

"She can't just disappear," Ann said. "Can she? Did she take her clothes? Her typewriter's gone."

"This is my fault," Hildy said. "I should not have seen. Or seeing, I should not have spoken."

"No more than mine," Ann said.

"That is not true. Don't think that. I can see further into Niki than you can. I am more responsible."

Ann started to argue then remembered what she had seen in the Munchkin's eyes and through Hildy's glasses. "I really thought she would be at practice."

"I also. Should we do something?" Hildy asked.

"Not me," Ann said quickly. "I'm finished *doing something*. I've retired."

Hildy looked hard at her. Ann hid her eyes, studying the sidewalk before them.

After supper, instead of accompanying Hildy to the lab, Ann made a systematic search for Niki. The signout book revealed nothing. Niki's clothes were still in her drawers and the photograph of her father stood on the dresser top. Ann went downstairs, to the living room. "Where's Niki? Do any of you know?"

One of the bridge players looked up. "Wasn't she in the smoker? That's where she was this afternoon."

Relief melted Ann's bones. She hurried down the hallway to the smoker. She didn't want to talk to Niki, just see her, see that she was all right.

The smoker was empty, an empty ugly room, like the diner of a bus terminal.

Ann went back upstairs, slowly, making a list of people Niki might be visiting. If Niki had been in the smoker this afternoon she hadn't disappeared and she hadn't moved out.

Ann found Niki in the room. She sat at her typewriter, turned around to face Ann, her face gray with fatigue but her eyes alight. "Annie. I was wondering where you were."

"You were wondering." Ann said. "Where have you been?"

"In the smoker."

"All this time? Since yesterday?"

"Yeah. Why?"

Ann didn't answer. She stood in the doorway, a little angry. Everything was all right again, the world was in order. Ann realized, reluctantly, that she cared as much about Niki as about Hildy.

"Can you help me?" Niki asked. "Come in here. I wanted to ask you—" She looked guilty and then, with a deep breath and jabbing forefinger announced, "Don't gloat. I wrote another paper. OK? I need a letter for the professor, to explain as little as possible. But I don't know how to say it. So, I told her to call the Munchkin if she doubts its propriety. Do you think that's all right?"

"It's terrific," Ann said.

"Of course, the lady might not accept this paper at all. But that's not my problem."

"Is that what you were doing? Writing another paper?"

"Yeah."

"Why? I mean I'm glad—you don't know how glad—but I thought—"

"You want the truth?"

"That would be nice," Ann said.

"For Hildy. That's the only reason. For her sake."

"Because . . . why?"

"Because of yesterday. I didn't need to lay all that stuff on her yesterday."

"This paper will more than make up for that," Ann said.

"You think so? I'm not so sure. You don't know Hildy as well as you think you do, Annie. I don't think this paper will make any difference to her at all. But I wanted to do it, so I did."

She won't give an inch, Ann thought, then she grinned. "Uh-uh. You're not going to get through to me that way. Is it good, the paper?"

"Better than my usual, more thoughtful. Maybe a B-plus. So, I've made some progress. I'll admit that to you, Annie. I'm pretty pleased with it. Want to read it?"

Ann declined the offer. They waited for the slow hours to pass before Hildy's return. Ann held in her excitement. Just when you least expected it, she thought, something wonderful happened, to make everything different. Better. She tried to concentrate. Niki interrupted her. "How come you didn't go to the lab?"

"I was looking for you."

"You were worried about me? That's sweet, real sweet. You really were, weren't you. What did you think?"

"I don't know. That you'd bolted or something. Hildy was worried too," she excused herself.

"Can't you get it through your head that I don't care what happens here?" Niki said, her voice gentled by an unuttered laugh. "This place, and its rules and standards and systems—it doesn't mean anything to me. You should have known better than to worry. I keep a good perspective on things."

"Except winning," Ann quarreled.

"You've got to let steam out somewhere. Basic psychology, Annie."

At nine-fifteen (Ann had just glanced at her watch, which showed a slow progress of ten minutes since she had last looked) an unaccountable silence seeped in through the walls. Niki, at the window, said, "There's a cop car outside, but no lights flashing. What's going on?" Ann joined her, to look down at the darkened road. They watched Miss Dennis step cautiously from the car and walk heavily up to the porch. The car drove away.

"I don't know," Ann said. "Something's happened."

"Do tell." Niki grinned. "I'll go you one better: it's something nasty. Is the real world going to come and get somebody, even here in the East, do you think? Even here in our ivory tower?"

"This is the real world too," Ann said. "As real as any other."

"Annie, I wish it were."

"I wonder, I really do wonder. I mean, you have your experience and I have mine, but you don't admit mine." Ann thought. "And I don't admit yours. But I can see yours and you can't see mine."

"Incoherent," Niki chided, "imprecise; but I am following you."

"And Hildy on the other hand—but how am I supposed to know, or choose?"

"Why bother? It all comes to the same thing at the end. We all die."

Ann turned on Niki, searching. "So what? No, I'm serious and I don't care if it sounds simple-minded. You say, *We all die*, as if that explained everything. I don't see that it explains anything. For that matter, we all live, which is the same thing backwards. And that's the important thing, isn't it? To live well?"

"That's just semantics, Annie. Look, if we could live forever, or if we could make any difference, then it might matter how we live. But to glorify life just for its mindless self—holy crap, Annie, toads live, and slugs, and think of those Romans who watched lions eat human beings and cheered. Toads, slugs, adders, cows—they all do a better job of it than people do."

"Why is that supposed to define me to myself?" Ann demanded.

"Because it's what you are, beneath the good manners and circle pins and topsiders and do-unto-others morality. Ruthless. Self-seeking. If you want to know yourself, you have to know that. When you try to ignore it—you are lying or deceiving yourself, however you want to name it. What you are, and I am, and even our precious Hildy is—vile."

"But even if I am, do I have to wallow in it?" Ann snapped. Niki grinned again.

"Moreover, I'm not sure I am," Ann continued. "I'm pretty

sure Hildy isn't. And"—she matched the gaiety in Niki's eyes—"I'm willing to leave open the option that you aren't."

"So Hildy wins."

"This has nothing to do with winning!" Ann cried. "Can't you see anything except winning and losing?"

"Nope. There's nothing more to be seen. Little imbecile victories and the game is rigged against us, from the inside and the out."

Ann turned back to her desk, angry and dismayed.

"But it's nice to see you angry." Niki patted Ann on the head and returned to the window. "Good and angry. It gives me hope for you."

"And you're contradicting yourself," Ann said.

From the window Niki reported, "Now the Munchkin's leaving. The path must be icy as hell: she's practically crawling. None of the usual Munchkin bounciness."

"Hear how quiet it is?" Ann said.

"Is that a hint?"

There was a quick knock at the door and Niki called "Come in." The housemother stepped in, pulling the door closed behind her, turning to be sure the latch caught, and holding her pose there unaccountably, her back to them.

Ann stood up, one hand on the back of her chair. "Mrs. Smythe," she said, as something, the silence that had been mounting, choked in her throat.

"Girls," the housemother said, turning to face them. "I'm afraid I have some very bad news for you. Very bad news indeed, shocking—I can't believe it myself."

Ann felt her eyes ballooning as the other parts of her body receded. She looked at Niki, because she could not find her own voice to speak.

"I don't know how to tell you—"

"Just do it," Niki urged.

"Sit down, please, first. Please sit down."

"Something's happened to Hildy," Niki said, without moving. She explained to Ann, "Otherwise she'd ask one of us to leave. So tell. Tell, goddammit."

"There has been an accident," Mrs. Smythe said. "Miss Dennis came to tell me—and I think she is the one who should speak with you but she said she had others to speak to and would be by later—so I—"

"What about Hildy?" Niki demanded. "I don't care about the accident, what about Hildy?"

Mrs. Smythe backed away. "I don't want to be the one—"

"Is she hurt?" Niki moved forward. "Is she dead? Is she all right?"

"She's dead."

Niki nodded. A sharp, brief chop of the head, and the event recognized, accepted.

Ann did not move, but she drew away from the dialogue, except for her eyes. There was nothing of her in the room. From deep within her, from some atom at the storm center of her being, a voice called out firm denial of this event.

"It happened as she was going up to the observatory," Mrs. Smythe reported. "She was riding her bike. I don't understand, because there's shoulder on both sides—but a car somehow hit her. There was a woman driving and she had been drinking, Miss Dennis told me that. But still, I don't know how except that the road is so icy. Miss Dennis said the car ran her down. Sometimes people have heart attacks. Maybe it skidded—and hit her."

"The car," Niki said.

"Yes. She was killed instantly, of course."

"Of course."

From the dense blackness of deep space, where the stars lay scattered in their unfathomable harmony, came an assurance to Ann that this was not so. Her head moved from side to side.

"Is there anything I can do for you? Until Miss Dennis returns? Is there anything I can get you?"

"A nice cup of tea," Niki suggested. "Or maybe a fifth of scotch and we can have a real old-fashioned wake. I think that's it, scotch and a side of beef, a couple of coffeecakes and we'll have the neighbors in. Whadda you think, Annie?"

"That's a terrible thing to say—even for you, Miss Jones."

"Yes. Well then, no, no thank you, very kind I'm sure," Niki muttered. "There's nothing. I think we would be best alone for now."

"As you wish. I am terribly sorry," Miss Smythe said.

Niki did not answer, just waited for her to leave.

"Where were her glasses?" Niki demanded of the closed door.

"No," Ann said. "No."

Niki picked the glasses up off the dresser top and looked at them. She slammed them down again.

"I don't believe it," Ann said.

"You better believe it, Annie. It's the kind of news that's always true."

Ann's throat was swollen.

"The old crap about too good for this world—don't try that on me. Ann? Annie? I should have thought of it. It's the same world, isn't it? The same rotting world and this is the kind of thing that happens. I don't know why I should be surprised."

Tears filled Ann's eyes. Wiping at her nose, she rubbed mucus all over her face and did not care.

"Well." Niki stood stiff in the center of the room. "That's finished. Write it off. Win some, lose some. And none of it matters. Go ahead and cry, Annie, don't mind me. You'll feel better. And in time—"

Niki's body stiffened, her back arched, she gagged and threw up onto the floor. She bent over, heaving, vomiting.

Ann fetched a towel and placed it over the vomit on the rug. "Sit down," she said, snuffling.

Niki looked at her with wild eyes, gagged, and threw up again. "I'm OK," she said, vomiting.

The laundry service supplied each girl with three towels a week, Ann, stone-faced now, noted when she pulled out the last of Hildy's towels. By that time Niki was only retching. Still, they would need more towels and Ann did not want to leave the room. She thought perhaps pillow cases would do as well, and sheets. Niki sat stiff on her bed.

When Miss Dennis entered, without knocking, she carried a bottle of brandy. Niki guzzled down a glass and threw it up.

A doctor came and gave Niki a shot. She passed out on the bed. Ann declined medication. She and Miss Dennis sat the night through in silence.

Early in the morning. Niki opened her eyes. Miss Dennis stood over her. "Can you stand up?" she said to Niki. Niki obeyed. "Can you walk downstairs?" Niki moved stiffly to the door.

"She will be with me," Miss Dennis said to Ann.

Ann nodded.

"You should go to classes today," Miss Dennis said.

Ann said she would not. She would be here today.

"I will come see you later," Miss Dennis said.

Ann made herself respond. When they had left, she lay down on her bed and seized sleep.

chapter

10

A late morning light, cold and distant, distinct, filled the room. Ann did not simply awake. She sat straight up and her spirit opened to grief. Weeping, she moved from absolute unconsciousness to absolute consciousness.

Weeping ceased and she undressed, dressed, went down the hall to the bathroom, returned emptied and cleaned and with the conviction that such commonplace business should cease. She made her bed, gathered up the mound of soiled towels, tossed them onto the floor of the closet, and shut the door on them.

She put on Hildy's glasses and stood looking out the window. Then she took them off. "OK," she said aloud, "Hildy's dead."

Ann sat at her desk to translate Greek. To approach a problem with clear limits, to manipulate and solve it. Her hand on the page, around the pen; her eyes on the words; her mind over syntax and definition: all moved cautiously, careful of bruised spirit. She worked mechanically.

A knock on the door elicited a mechanical response. "Come in." She was ready.

Eloise entered, carrying a tray covered with cloths. "Ann?"

"Hi. Thanks." Ann willed Eloise away, back out the door. She could endure no imbalance in her fragile calm.

"I'm going to sit with you," Eloise said. She set the tray on Hildy's desk and lifted the cloths from it. She hung her coat over the back of the chair. "However, you don't have to talk to me." She stood beside Ann. "Miss Dennis has sent me. You should eat something but I'm afraid the eggs may be cold. We weren't sure so we made eggs and toast, and some sandwiches. Tea, milk, I can get you a Coke downstairs. Ann? Come and eat something."

Ann obeyed. She drank lukewarm tea and ate a slice of toast. Then, hungry, she finished the sandwiches. No longer hungry, she began the scrambled eggs, but Eloise stopped her.

"You don't have to eat everything. You look a little better. Did you sleep?" Eloise's eyes peered at her from behind her glasses.

"Yes, I slept," Ann said. "I'm OK, I think. It was the shock—I mean, it's not the kind of thing you plan on." She found herself once again slowly weeping.

"I'm sorry," she apologized. "I can't seem to—"

"Do you want to talk?" Eloise asked.

Ann shook her head. She gave herself over to sorrow.

"I'll just sit here then. If you want, I'll read something. Or talk, if that's what you want. What I won't do is go away."

Ann snuffled. Nodded. Accepted a Kleenex and blew her nose again. "What about you?" she asked Eloise. "How are you?" She wished she could stop crying.

"I grieve," Eloise answered. Her face, her whole body, was passive.

Then Ann wanted to talk. "Rember when Odysseus went to the Hall of Hades? Junior year, remember? To talk to the seer about his fate, but he saw Achilles too. And we all said that Achilles taught Odysseus the value of life."

Eloise quoted: "I would rather follow the plow as thrall to another man, one with no land allotted him and not much to live on, than be a king over all the perished dead." She nodded her head. "I remember."

"But that isn't true," Ann said. She spoke through her tears, ignoring them. "Because he asks about his son, and when Odysseus tells him the boy is growing famous in battle, Achilles walks away happy."

Eloise stared at her, frightened. Ann thought probably she shouldn't continue; but if knowledge didn't help you see things, now, then knowledge wasn't ever any use. Wasn't ever true.

"If Achilles thinks it's so bad to be dead, then why is he glad when his son is pursuing the path that he chose? The way that killed him. I never understood that," she sobbed.

"But you didn't say anything, I don't remember you said anything," Eloise protested.

"And I don't understand that now," Ann said, blowing her nose again, wiping at her eyes.

"I'll tell you what I think," Eloise offered. Ann nodded. "I think that—once you've noticed it—you have to follow it through. On the one hand, Achilles rejects Odysseus's praise of the glory, the immortal fame. On the other hand, he rejoices that his son is acquiring glory. It's a paradox."

"Do you understand it?" Ann demanded. Eloise shook her head. "Unless," Ann went on, "a man must go for glory, or excellence, even though it is meaningless. Must," she repeated, on a rising sob. "So it isn't meaningless, to a living man. And maybe then it isn't meaningless at all. If we could only see—"

"See what?"

Ann shook her head, she didn't know. They were silent then, waiting.

Later Miss Dennis arrived. She sat at Niki's desk. It was afternoon by then. The little woman looked as gray as her clothing. She had not slept. "May I speak with you? Both of you?"

They nodded. Ann reached for her self-possession.

"I have talked to Mr. Koenig. He does not see a need to send his daughter home for burial. We will hold services here, in O'Rourke Hall, tomorrow morning. Wednesday. Miss Koenig will be buried in the College cemetery. Her possessions—he said we may dispose of them. He wishes only that whatever money remains in her account after expenses are met be sent to him. So. We will do that." She looked at Eloise who nodded her head.

"Do you have any requests for the service, Miss Gardner?"

Ann did not. And her tears had started again. Again and again.

"Then I will manage it. Somehow. But you will have to help me with choosing the clothing."

Ann didn't understand.

"The clothing for Hildy to be buried in," Eloise explained.

"Oh, of course. I didn't think," Ann said. She went to the closet and opened the door. A stench flowed out. "Oh." She bent over, picked up the fouled towels, and stood, holding them in her arms. Eloise took them from her and went out of the room.

Ann pushed back dresses, one by one, as if she were shopping. What kind of clothing was appropriate? "Does it matter?" she asked Miss Dennis. "What are the conventions for this?"

"Whatever you think is right," the Munchkin said. "The coffin will be closed."

Ann's mind swerved violently around that information. She pulled out her own dress, the dress Hildy had worn to the tea. "This one."

If it meant anything to Hildy, it was what she wanted to do. To be with her. To stay with her, or to go with her as far as possible.

"Underclothing?" Miss Dennis asked.

Ann pulled out a drawer and selected pants, bra, and a slip. "Stockings?" she asked and then answered herself. "No. It's so stupid. Do they want shoes?" She picked Hildy's one pair of pumps off the closet floor and handed the small pile of clothing to Miss Dennis.

Eloise returned.

Ann didn't know which was worse, the unhealthy quietude or ordinary noises. She felt a need to be thrust into the middle of life. And a need to be left silently with death.

"Where is Hildy now?" she asked.

"In the hospital mortuary," Miss Dennis answered. "She will be moved to the funeral home early this evening."

"Do you want to view her?" Eloise suggested. "Sometimes that helps."

"I'm afraid that is not possible," the Munchkin said.

Eloise turned on her: "What do you mean?"

"The body," Miss Dennis covered her forehead with one of her small hands. "I'm sorry—I had to identify her. The body is disfigured. So. I was not going to tell you that."

Ann doubted everything then and had to know. "Did she die right away? They said she did. Was that the truth?"

The Munchkin nodded. "Yes. I made sure of that. I too wanted to know that."

Eloise turned to Ann: "They do it for your own good sometimes. They don't tell you what really happened. Then later you find out—you always find out, there's always someone who tells you what really happened—and that's worse. But she doesn't lie, does she?"

"I have asked Miss Golding to stay with you," Miss Dennis said.

Ann nodded.

"I have asked her to come and stay. To sleep."

Ann's mind was on another track. "Then why do you want those clothes?" she wondered. "And underclothes too." And Hildy was so beautiful.

"Convention," Miss Dennis said. "I do not know what should be done about Niki. I will call her father. Is there anything I can do for you?"

"No." Ann was swept with pity for this woman, who, childless, must still be caught in the position of bereaved parent. "Can we help you in any way? Can we see Niki?" She was being swept by too many emotions, she was at some vortex; but Eloise stood with her there, wherever, showing her how to endure.

"Perhaps this evening. She will stay with me, I think. If she elects to remain at the College."

"But she has to," Ann said. "She wrote another paper." Her eyes flowed and she ignored them. "If you could hand it in, there's a letter on top. If it matters anymore."

Miss Dennis picked up the paper. She looked through it. She spoke slowly. "We go on in the hope that it does matter. Yes, I will do this." She put the paper on the clothes and picked up the mound.

"Will you bring a suitcase for Niki with you, tonight?"

"Of course," Ann said. "Thank you. I'm sorry for the trouble we've given you. Again."

Miss Dennis put the pile of clothes down again. She placed both hands on Ann's shoulders and looked into her face. "You must not apologize, not for this. You must not feel responsible. There is no responsibility, not even the wretched woman who drove the car. You cannot console yourself that way. Miss Gardner? The sorrow will abate, in time. That is all."

Ann nodded, wept.

Sarah and Ruth and Bess came by, grim and depressed. Eloise left Ann with them while she went to pack a suitcase for herself and gather together her books. Ann chattered, her voice high. Sarah and Ruth and Bess chattered back. Together they

managed to fill the room with bright chips of sound. But Ruth
came to sit beside Ann on the bed and their forearms touched
until all four girls fell silent. For a minute then, Ann felt
swathed, swaddled, by unspoken understanding, a deep female
belonging, a feeling she had sensed seeing cows huddled
together on the ground awaiting rain. A sisterhood.

"This game tomorrow. After," Ruth said. She looked at
Ann.

"Carol came to see me and said she could play. Since we
were a player short," Sarah said.

"No," Bess spoke vehemently. "I mean, we aren't going to
play, are we?"

"Do you want to?" Ruth asked.

Ann hadn't thought about it. She rubbed her arms against the
cold.

"What's the point?" Sarah asked. She stood up and moved
around the room. "We wouldn't be any good anymore. Would
we?" she asked Ann.

"I don't know," Ann said. "I don't know about Niki,
either." There were tears on her face again. Bess made
murmuring, comforting noises.

"Anyway, it doesn't matter anymore. It wouldn't be the
same," Bess said heavily.

"You see," Ruth tried to explain, "if I got out on the court,
I'd feel—" Ann passed her the box of tissues. The sense of
physical absence, that was it, the terrible glimpse out of the
corner of your eye. When you turned your head there was
nothing there. You knew before you turned your head. It would
be worse on the volleyball court.

"Why bother, without Hildy," Bess said.

What Niki would say to that, Ann thought wearily. "But,"
she said.

"But what?" Sarah asked, watching her.

"But if it doesn't matter now . . . I don't know . . . we
were wrong to think it mattered then. Before," Ann said.

Nobody answered her.

"I *couldn't*," Bess said.

"What are you saying?" Sarah asked Ann. "That Hildy
would want us to?"

"No," Ann answered. "That's so stupid. But, I think *I* want
us to."

"Why?" asked Ruth.

"Because—I don't think it'll be easy, but—we should, because we were good. Even when Hildy went out. It was being excellent that was important, wasn't it?"

"So you think we could—win," Sarah said.

"I don't know. I don't even care," Ann answered. "I care about not quitting. Everybody would understand, but it wouldn't be right. Would it? Would it?" she insisted.

"What about Niki?" Ruth asked. "Miss Dennis told us—I suppose Carol—"

"No," Sarah said. "I don't know how the rest of you feel. I don't care how you feel—I don't want anybody else."

"Just not to let it go by default," Ann finished her thought. "I'll talk to Niki. OK?" Nobody answered, so she guessed they were agreed.

That evening, Ann and Eloise took Niki a suitcase, while everybody else in the dormitory was sitting down to supper at the accustomed tables with the usual company. Ann realized her distance from the ordinary world. That she would have to return to it irritated her. The intrusive world.

Eloise stayed downstairs while Ann went up to see Niki. "I don't know what she'll say, or do. I don't—"

"That's OK," Ann said, understanding how far Eloise had come to risk refusal of the offer to share Ann's room.

Niki sat up in a narrow four-posted bed in Miss Dennis's tiny guest room. Tranquilized, wearing a high-necked white nightgown, she was a listless stranger. Ann sat on the bed, not beside Niki but with her. The Munchkin brought in a plate of sandwiches. Niki would not eat. "Nothing stays down," she explained. "You remember."

"Try some tea," Ann urged. Niki cooperatively took a cup and sipped from it.

"And how are you holding up, Annie?" she asked.

Ann thought to make a brave reply, but decided on the truth. "Better than you, but not much."

"Another advantage to having background?" Niki asked. "It goes with the circle pins and round collars, the stiff upper lip."

It was a blunted needle, but a needle all the same, and Ann welcomed it. She returned the gift. "Miss Dennis handed in your paper," she said.

Niki's face convulsed, and then her body convulsed and she retched. Ann left her to the nurse's care.

"What did I say that for?" Ann asked.

Eloise consoled her. "You didn't mean to upset her."

"I don't understand why it's so hard for her. She *believes* in a world where this kind of accident happens, and worse things, like rapes of little girls and the elderly eating cat food because it's the best they can afford. She believes in a terrible world. In destruction."

Eloise answered thoughtfully. "What Niki believes in may not be what she wants to be true. What about you?"

"I don't know!" Ann cried. If Eloise was right—how would Niki live?

"I believe in God," Eloise said, although Ann had not asked her. "I believe not passionately, but hopefully. That's how I make my peace with Hildy's death. How I will make my peace, in time."

"Hildy didn't believe, not in that way. She knew," Ann said. "Maybe she was right. Niki believes the opposite."

They walked on without talking. Ann was thinking, about Homer, and Hildy, and Niki. If she just kept on reading and thinking, studying, learning— Not only in school but all her life—then would she begin to understand? Understand what? she asked herself bitterly: Why Hildy had to die? How Hildy came to die, she had seen. How Hildy lived: that was a good place to begin. Where it would end—there was no way of knowing where things would end. But if you could chart direction, that would be something. There didn't have to be a purpose, but there might be. And if you were careful about the truth, you might glimpse it.

Ann remembered to call her parents. "I'm sorry," she told her mother, "I've changed my mind. I won't be there this weekend after all. Is that OK?"

Mrs. Gardner's voice was surprised, cautious, alert. "Don't worry about it, Ann. Has something come up? You sound odd."

"Yes, something came up." She moved her mouth to find the words. "I'm all right."

"What has happened?"

"My roommate, Hildy—"

Mrs. Gardner waited, then suggested, "I remember. The one you're particularly fond of, the volleyball player. What about her?"

"They're both volleyball players."

"Oh. I see."

"Hildy died."

"Ann?"

"There was an accident, a car hit her."

"Were you there?"

"No, no. It's all right. I mean I'm all right. She wasn't wearing her glasses is what happened. I'll tell you about it."

"When was this?"

"Yesterday. Monday. Last night. Evening, actually. But we didn't know then."

"My dear child. Would you like us to come up?"

"No, that's too much trouble. I just thought I'd call and tell you."

"Yes. Well—that's right. Do you need anything?"

"Don't worry. Eloise is with me. Eloise Golding from the Hall? Did you ever meet her?"

"I don't remember."

"Anyway . . ."

Three hours later, Mrs. Gardner knocked on the door of Ann's room. Mr. Gardner was downstairs, she said, because he wasn't allowed upstairs, not at this hour, she said, speaking into Ann's hair. She soothed Ann and introduced herself to Eloise. She led Ann down through the dimly lit hall. Mrs. Gardner said they were staying at the Inn and had thought to have Ann with them, but now she saw that was not necessary and thought that Eloise should have company. Ann did not argue, because perhaps they were right. They had been right to come to her.

Mrs. Gardner sat Ann on the stiff living room sofa, and Mr. Gardner sat on her other side. They probed gently at Ann with questions, listened to her, passed her handkerchiefs, and kept their arms about her. Mrs. Gardner said she would call Miss Dennis, to see if there was anything to be done. She said she couldn't understand Hildy's parents, their behavior was inhuman. Ann said, things were different, people were different.

Not that different, they couldn't be, Mrs. Gardner said, holding her daughter close.

When Ann returned to the room, Eloise was lying in Niki's bed, her face bare under the light. Ann spoke naturally, which she had thought never to do again. "They're terrific. I know why they came. Listen. Eloise?"

"I'm listening."

Ann looked at Eloise, solid, comforting. "I'm glad you're here, Eloise, really glad." She should remember that Eloise needed to be told. "But my parents—they came for my sake, that of course. But also to reassure themselves. Do you know? When something happens—and you want to be sure everyone you love is all right, because you've been forced to remember how vulnerable we all are. You need to touch. You know?" Eloise nodded. "They want us to have breakfast at the Inn tomorrow, you and me. Will you?"

"I would enjoy that. You're fortunate in your parents."

Ann knew it, as she turned out her light and lay back in darkness, holding close that sense of the strength and the mystery of human love. What Niki would say— It didn't help, really. It couldn't change anything. The ties of need and responsibility and affection, and of blood: she had her first glimpse of how they would always bind her. She was immensely grateful.

She could think now. Some definition was needed. She needed some definition, an armor that would contain and defend her. She could construct it out of cruel facts, and she knew them. It was Niki's vision of the world, chaotic and accidental—brutish. She could accept that. She recognized its reality. She could put words to it and make it her own. She could try to face fear and outface it.

Or Hildy's vision, if what Ann saw through the glasses was anything like what Hildy could see without them. Beyond externals. An armor of faith, the purpose accepted though not known, within which the Christian knight moved, certain of the answers to questions that are better not asked, wise in his unquestioning surrender, sure of direction if not destination.

Then, she would have to fit Hildy's death into the plates of armor, either design: she turned and buried her face in the pillow, to muffle her weeping.

* * *

The funeral services at O'Rourke Hall were conducted by the College chaplain. The stage where they had first seen the Munchkin now held the flower-decked coffin, two chairs, and a podium. The long curtain had been pulled in from both sides to combat the emptiness of the stage. The air smelled dusty.

The auditorium was not filled. Ann, sitting at the front between Eloise and her father (her mother sat on the far side of Eloise) saw many of the freshmen, and other faces, some of which she recognized, faculty, volleyball opponents, staff, and some adults who must have known Hildy from her church because a minister sat in the midst of them.

Niki sat nearby, pale, holding hard onto the hand of a handsome man Ann recognized as her father.

They stared at the stage, at the young chaplain sitting with his hands folded, at Miss Dennis wearing a mouse-gray suit, at the coffin dressed out in bright floral displays. Somewhere among them were the flowers Eloise and Ann had ordered with Mrs. Gardner that morning. Ann had insisted on white. "For the soul," Eloise had explained, but "For Hildy," Ann answered. Two long candles burned beside the podium, creamy white in tall bronze holders, as big as your arms, Ann thought. Their flames gleamed.

Mrs. Gardner leaned over and put a gray-gloved hand on Ann's hands, which she held clasped tightly together on her lap. Ann nodded at her mother, reassuring, and the hand withdrew. Ann put one of her hands into the pocket of her coat and wrapped her fingers around Hildy's glasses.

The chaplain came forward. He prayed. He spoke the words. Ann did not listen. Her eyes flicked about. Pallid and square, Eloise sat stoically beside her, her arms lying along her thighs, hands still. Niki hunched forward in her seat, Ann saw, listening to the mellifluous voice that flowed over their heads. Niki's eye met hers and the dark girl cocked an eyebrow toward the speaker. Ann raised her chin imperceptibly in agreement. Niki perceived it.

Miss Dennis stepped up to the podium to deliver the eulogy. She looked over the audience as she opened a piece of paper before her. "We are here to speak of Miss Koenig," she began in her nasal voice. Then she stopped. She cleared her throat. Her Munchkin face, with its expression of wisdom and worry, mapped with tiny wrinkles, seemed to swell. She stood, patient in her silence, holding the paper with her small hands.

"When Socrates came to die," she spoke into the microphone, "he had already declared his understanding of death. Either, he said, it is a long, unbroken sleep, or it is the commencement of a just judgment. Words of great comfort: words of great courage. Yet his old friend Crito, no less aged than Socrates himself, urges Socrates to escape from prison, to avoid death. Socrates refuses and cites his responsibility to the laws. The laws of Athens, that is, the laws of men. He does not directly speak of that law which has required him to keep faith with these other laws, but its presence governs his words and choices, as it has all his life. And it is that one law which most concerns us."

She stepped back to her chair. Mrs. Gardner turned her face to her husband and raised her eyebrows over the girls' hands. But Ann thought she almost understood.

A murmur filled the huge room and rose gently to the domed ceiling. The chaplain led the closing prayers. Unknown men, that minister among them, bore the coffin on their shoulders to the broad doors at the back of the Hall, and the oaken doors swung open. *Ave atque vale.* Hail and farewell.

The Gardners drove Ann and Eloise to the cemetery. Ann stood among the mourners. A light snow was falling. Cloth bands held the coffin suspended over the hole in the ground. Ann reached into her pocket and put on Hildy's glasses. By herself, she could not bear to see this.

The chaplain, looming darkness at the head of the grave, uttered the final prayers. Ann forced her eyes to the coffin: indistinguishable from the earth except for the soft hues of flowers it bore. The empty place beneath it was warm as breath. Fitness, continuity, necessity, and the merry bouquet of color. Ann's eyes filled with tears and they flowed down over her cheeks, where snowflakes stung at them. Tears did not alter what she saw through the glasses, and she knew what it was: the death of a friend; the placing into the earth of Hildy's golden lightness and sure vitality.

Ann removed the glasses, put them tenderly into her pocket, wiped at her eyes with the back of her hand, and turned away with the others. They huddled around the cars. Ann introduced her parent to Miss Dennis and left them there while she introduced herelf to Niki's father. He stood with sadness in his handsome eyes and his arm around Niki.

"Niki," Ann said. "Niki? We've got a match this afternoon. Can you play?"

Niki's face lifted.

"We've got a match to win," Ann insisted.

"Annie. *You* talk about winning?" Niki studied Ann.

"Can you play? Will you? Because now you really are essential. I'll give you that now. We all are essential now."

"Yeah. I'll play."

"I don't think you should," Mr. Jones protested. "You've had a rough time of it."

Niki stood away from her father. "It's OK. I won't blow lunch all over the court. It's OK to do. I just won't eat lunch. How's that?"

He shrugged. "If you say so. You know best."

"Yeah," Niki agreed, her face as wan as her eyes.

It was then that Ann saw a young man standing alone, one of the pall bearers. He hadn't left the graveside. He had straight white-blond hair and a high pink color in his cheeks. His hands hung out of a worn overcoat. He wore heavy mittens, but no hat. Ann went over to him. "You must be Hildy's brother," she said.

He looked at her with untroubled blue eyes.

"What are you doing here? I didn't think anybody was coming. I'm her roommate, Ann."

The young man removed a mitten to shake Ann's hand. Tears welled in her eyes again.

"I came to see her gone," he told Ann. "I had some money saved, so my father, he said if I wanted to spend it this way I could."

"I'm so sorry," Ann said, "we all are. Tell your family, how sorry we are."

"Yes, ma'am," he said. "I guess we'll miss her. She was some worker, Hildy was."

Ann was shocked, a little angry, and immensely sad. "Some volleyball player too," she said quickly.

He smiled at that. "She sure was."

Ann smiled back at him. "Do you want to get her things, books and clothes?"

He shook his head. "No, thank you, I just—it didn't seem

right for her to stay so far away and nobody come to say goodbye. I guess she had a lot of friends here.'' He surveyed the small crowd now moving into cars.

Ann gulped, nodded, blinked against the increasing snow. She tried to think of how to tell this young man how much she had admired his sister, knowing her and playing volleyball with her and working with her. Something that would show him that they, too, had appreciated Hildy's rare qualities.

"She taught me a lot," Ann said.

This utterly confused him. "But—she said you were smart. How could Hildy teach you?"

"By example," Ann said, which didn't answer him but answered her.

He nodded his head again. There wasn't anything more to say. "Do you have a ride back?" Ann asked.

"I came with her minister. He's waiting for me." They shook hands in farewell.

Ann went slowly over to join her parents. Mr. and Mrs. Gardner suggested that she come back to the Inn with them, but Ann declined. "There's a game this afternoon," she explained.

"You aren't going to play volleyball?" her mother said wonderingly.

"It's a match," Ann said.

"But surely," her mother said, raising her voice over Mr. Gardner's murmured "If Ann thinks—"

"How can you?" her mother demanded. "Why should you?" she asked.

"Because we're a good team," Ann said. "You could stay and watch if you wanted."

Mr. Gardner said they probably shouldn't, if they wanted to get home ahead of the snow. They drove Ann back to the dormitory. Ann thanked them for coming to be with her. Mrs. Gardner hugged her and her father gave her a thoughtful look. "You're sure it's what you want to do?" he asked.

Ann nodded. "I think I really needed to have you here," she blurted out.

"Of course," her mother said. "Good luck to you—if you really are going to play."

"We really are going to," Ann told her. "It's the right thing to do."

* * *

So they played the match and won it. (The team never lost a match, in all the four years they played together.) They played as if there were more at stake than the game. In time, the team (always these same six girls) took on some of Niki's fierceness to win. As if, having lost grace, they must acquire a human substitute. They played well, too, better each season than before, each of them and together, as if having once had grace they could never be entirely lost.

At the end of the four years they had four tin trophies, this team, gilded statuettes of a young woman stretching up with hands outthrust. When the time came to graduate, Ruth took one and Sarah another, Bess and Eloise the others. Niki said she didn't need any reminders, she wasn't in danger of forgetting. Besides, she said, she was going to law school and the only acceptable trophies for a lawyer were tennis or sailing. And Ann, Ann kept Hildy's glasses.

When Niki returned to the room (after Christmas, after her father's wedding), Eloise remained. It came about this way:

Ann arrived first from the vacation. Then Eloise came to put two tentative suitcases down by the door. She asked if Niki was back yet and absented herself. "There are some source books on reserve at the library and if I don't get to them now, they are liable to be gone. I should be—an hour?"

Ann nodded and suggested to Niki when her roommate appeared that Eloise move in permanently.

"She's a bitch," Niki said, tossing underwear into a drawer.

"Oh, come on, Niki, even you can't think that of Eloise."

"No, I can't. Not even me." Niki's smile flashed. "Ah, Annie, I'll tell you, but only you, it's good to be back. Nobody out there makes jokes in Greek." Ann sputtered. "And I'm not old enough for eternal youth. I'm glad to be here."

"Even—considering?"

"Even with Hildy dead?" A space of silence. "Yes—curse it."

"I still—" Ann began. Niki came and stood before her. She placed one of her hands on Ann's shoulder.

"Still and always, I'm afraid."

"What about you? Are you OK?"

"Weeping and gnashing of teeth," Niki said. "I lost, after all."

"Yeah, well, you're alive," Ann said harshly.

Niki said nothing to this. Instead, she said. "Which reminds me of the bitch. My stepmother."

"I got your card. My mother was puzzled by it."

"She read it?"

"Postcards are meant to be read by anyone who sees them. That's the tradition."

"Sorry, Annie," Niki said. She didn't sound sorry. She called up over her shoulder, "Sorry, Mrs. Gardner. Dad's pretty happy though, which is what counts, seeing as it's his marriage." She continued unpacking. "I think I'll go to law school. I was thinking about it, over the vacation."

"Why?"

"I was talking to some people, mostly at Berkeley—"

"Did you apply?"

"No. I don't know, Ann. I've been thinking, I might stick it out here. It'll be good for you." She grinned. "And maybe me too," she added. "Do you want to hear about law school?" Ann nodded. "They were saying—you don't want to hear it all, but the upshot is that the establishment has to go. The economy, the state, the church." She waved a hand up into the air, describing the direction of exploding institutions.

"Your kind of people," Ann murmured.

"I thought so too," Niki said. "But," she added, "listen. She was drunk, the woman who killed Hildy. She's an alcoholic, or something—poor bitch. But there was some bartender who kept pouring booze into her and he must have known. I'd like to get that guy. Because he's responsible— maybe even more than she is. And the law can't touch him. It can barely do anything, even to help her. I'm not wild about that kind of law, Annie, and piss-all if I'll let it go."

Ann started to ask how Niki had found all that out, but Niki interrupted her.

"Annie?" Niki turned to face her again, thrusting a finger at her. "Are we going to be friends after all? I mean, friends—not hello-how-are-you people. I'd like that, Annie, and I'll tell you why. Might as well now I've started. Because you've got a good eye for the true thing, for excellence. Hildy said. So, see, if we were friends—if you were my friend it might mean I was the true thing. See what I mean?"

Ann laughed. Then she stopped. "Hildy said that?"

"Yup."

"And you think so too?"

"Yup."

"We probably will," Ann said. "Be friends."

"You could sound a little more cheerful."

"And you really think I've got an eye for excellence?"

"A natural affinity. It must be the Northeast, something in the rarified air. You attract it. Trust me, Annie."

"Then listen to what I think. I think Eloise should come live with us."

Niki stood open-mouthed, briefly. Then she laughed, her head thrown back. "Serves me right," she said, laughing. She returned to her unpacking. "It's OK by me. But you'll have to be careful not to pick on me, you two preppies."

When Eloise returned, Niki greeted her. "It's fine with me as long as you don't cower. I can't stand people who cower."

Eloise hesitated in the doorway.

"Come on in, dammit. You live here."

"I don't know," Eloise muttered.

"You heard me! See? You're cowering already and you don't even have the balls to come in and cower to my face. Look at Annie—she's survived a season with me."

The same response crossed over all of their minds and hovered in the center of the room. They stared unseeing at it. It was Eloise who eventually gave it quiet voice: "And Hildy?"

Nicki said: "Hildy survived me. I'm the one who maybe didn't."

Eloise answered her levelly. "Whom do you think you are deceiving?"

"If it's not you, then we'll all be all right together," Niki said. She went back to her unpacking, then whirled around and faced them:

"What do you mean, *whom*. Are you picking on me? Annie? Wasn't I right? You two are going to gang up on me, with your whoms and your round collars and your Topsiders. Especially those Topsiders. But you're gonna have to accept my sneakers, they're permanent. Hear that? Both of you."

Ann wished she had thought of sending Niki a circle pin for

Christmas. She would find out when Niki's birthday was. A circle pin engraved inside, *to Nicole from Annie*.

Niki got an A on her long paper. She showed it to Ann and Eloise before she threw it out. "It's a lie," she remarked. "It's an A-for-pity." She looked at them. "Hildy would have said so too," she said.

"And she'd have been right," Ann said.

"Are you going to accept it?" Eloise asked.

"What else can I do? There's no machinery for protesting a grade that's too high."

"You haven't answered my question though, have you?" Eloise asked quietly.

Then Niki smiled. "Now that you mention it, there must be something I can do." She fetched the paper out of the wastebasket. "The machinery for protest is there. It would be a pity not to use it. I'll tell you, Eloise, I'm beginning to think you're as smart as our Annie says you are."

"I am," Eloise said.

They gave Hildy's clothes to the Good Will and her books to the bookstore. They threw out her notebooks and papers.

Ann always kept Hildy's glasses and sometimes wore them, as she had before. Grief remained in her, intractable. Memory also remained and grew golden. In time. She had Hildy's glasses and could see through them. She knew better than to forget, or want to. After Hildy's life, her death, no blind peace.

About the Author

CYNTHIA VOIGT was raised in Connecticut and was graduated from Dana Hall School and Smith College in Massachusetts. For a number of years she was a teacher of English and classics and before that she worked at "various jobs in various states."

She lives in Annapolis, Maryland, with her husband, their two children, and the family dog. In addition to writing and teaching (to which she has recently returned), she enjoys cooking, eating, crabbing, and family summers on an island in Chesapeake Bay.

Her first novel, *Homecoming*, was nominated in 1982 for the American Book Award. *Dicey's Song* is a sequel to that book, and the winner of The 1983 Newbery Award.